TEMPTING

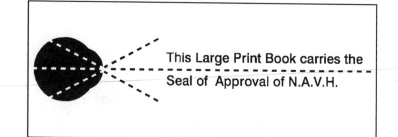

This Large Print Book carries the
Seal of Approval of N.A.V.H.

TEMPTING

SUSAN MALLERY

WHEELER PUBLISHING

An imprint of Thomson Gale, a part of The Thomson Corporation

THOMSON
™
GALE

Detroit • New York • San Francisco • New Haven, Conn. • Waterville, Maine • London

THOMSON
★ ™
GALE

LIBRARY OF CONGRESS CATALOGING-IN-PUBLICATION DATA

Mallery, Susan.
    Tempting / by Susan Mallery.
        p. cm.
    ISBN-13: 978-1-59722-651-6 (alk. paper)
    ISBN-10: 1-59722-651-3 (alk. paper)
    1. Politicians — Fiction. 2. Large type books. I. Title.
PS3613.A453T46 2008
813'.6—dc22   2007036583

Published in 2008 by arrangement with Harlequin Books S.A.

Printed in the United States of America on permanent paper
10 9 8 7 6 5 4 3 2 1

TEMPTING

CHAPTER ONE

"Let me make this easy for you," the man in the expensively tailored suit told Dani Buchanan. "You don't get to speak to the senator until you tell me why you're here."

"Amazingly enough, that information doesn't make things easier," Dani Buchanan murmured, feeling equally scared and excited which made for a very queasy stomach. She'd already talked her way through a receptionist and two assistants. She could actually see Mark Canfield's door at the end of the corridor. But standing between her and a long warehouse hallway was a big, determined-looking guy.

She thought about pushing past him, but he was pretty tall and she wasn't. Not to mention the fact that she'd actually worn a dress and high heels — neither of which were normal for her. The dress was no big deal, but the heels were killing her. She could handle the pain in the balls of her feet and the slight pulling in her arches, but how did anyone stay balanced on these things? If she moved at anything faster than a stroll, she was in danger of snapping an ankle.

"You can trust me," the man said. "I'm a lawyer."

He actually made the statement with a straight face.

Dani laughed. "A profession designed to inspire trust? I don't think so."

His lips twitched, as if he were holding in a smile. A good sign, she thought. Maybe she could charm her way past this guy. Not that she'd ever been especially good at charming men, but she didn't have much of a choice. She was going to have to fake it.

She drew in a breath and tossed her head. Of course her hair was cut short, which meant there was no flip over her shoulder. Which left Dani completely out of charming-men-type tricks. Good thing she'd sworn off dating for the rest of her life.

"Think of me as the dragon at the gate," the man said. "You're not getting past me until I know your business."

"Didn't anyone ever tell you that dragons are extinct?"

Now he did smile. "I'm living proof they're

alive and well."

Fine, she thought absently. She would go all the way to fine for this guy. He had a nice face — handsome enough that you wouldn't turn to stone looking at him, but not so pretty that he wouldn't need to develop a personality. Killer blue eyes. A strong jaw, which meant stubborn.

"I'm here for personal reasons," she said, knowing that wasn't going to be enough, but feeling the need to try. What else was she supposed to say? That she'd recently discovered she might not be who she'd thought she was and answers to her questions were in this building?

Dragon-man's face tightened as he crossed his arms over his chest. Dani had the instant sensation of being shut out and judged, all at the same time.

"I don't think so," the man said sharply. "The senator doesn't play those kind of games. You're wasting your time. Get the hell out of here."

Dani stared at him. "Huh?" What was he . . . Oh. "You think I'm implying the senator and I —" She grimaced. "Yuck. No! Never. Eww." She took a step back, a dangerous act, considering the shoes, but she had no choice. Distance was required. "That is too disgusting for words."

"Why?"

She sighed. "Because there's a chance I'm his daughter." Better than a chance, if her upset stomach were anything to go by.

Suit-guy didn't even blink. "You'd do better to imply you were sleeping with him. I'd be more inclined to believe you."

"Who are you to pass judgment on what Mark Canfield may or may not have been doing twenty-nine years ago?"

"I'm his son."

That got her attention. She knew all about the senator's large family. "Alex, I presume?"

Dragon-guy nodded.

Interesting. Not that she and the senator's oldest son were blood relations. Mark Canfield and his wife had adopted all their children, including Alex. But it was possible they were family.

Dani wasn't sure how she felt about that. Dealing with her known family was complicated enough. Did she want to take on another one?

Obviously, she thought. After all, she was here.

The sense of needing to belong by blood burned hot enough to give her the answer. If Mark Canfield really was her father, she wanted to get to know him, and no one was

10

going to get in her way. Not even his adopted son.

"I've been patient through one secretary and two assistants," she said firmly. "I've been polite and understanding. If nothing else, I'm a registered voter in this state and I have every right to see my senator. Now please step aside, before I'm forced to escalate the situation."

"Are you threatening me?" Alex asked, sounding almost amused.

"Would it work?" she asked.

He slowly looked her up and down. In the past six months she'd learned that male attention was not a positive thing in her life. It inevitably ended in disaster. But even though she'd sworn off men, she still felt a little quiver as his steady gaze drifted across her body.

"No, but it might be fun," he said.

"You are such a guy."

"Is that a bad thing?"

"You have no idea. Now step aside, dragon-boy. I'm going to see Mr. Canfield."

"Dragon-boy?"

The amused voice hadn't come from the person in *front* of her. Dani turned toward the sound and saw a familiar man standing by an open door.

She recognized Senator Mark Canfield

11

because she'd seen him on television. She'd even voted for him. But those acts had been from a distance. She'd never thought of him as more than a political figure. Now he was here and there was a very good chance he was her father.

She opened her mouth, then closed it. Words faded from her brain as if she'd just lost the power of speech.

The senator walked toward them. "Are you dragon-boy, Alex?" he asked the younger man.

Alex shrugged, looking faintly uncomfortable. "I told her I was the dragon at the gate."

The senator put a hand on Alex's shoulder. "You do a good job, too. So is this young lady causing trouble?" He turned to Dani and smiled. "You don't look especially threatening."

"I'm not," she managed.

"Don't be so sure," Alex told him.

Dani glared. "You're being a little judgmental here."

"You're going to make trouble with your ridiculous claims."

"Why are they ridiculous? You don't know for sure, yet."

"Do you?" Alex asked.

The senator looked at both of them.

"Should I come back at a better time?"

Dani ignored Alex and turned to the senator. "I'm sorry to barge in like this. I've been trying to make an appointment to see you but every time they ask me why, I can't give them the real reason. I . . ."

The enormity of what she was about to do crashed in on her. How could she just blurt out what she'd been told? That twenty-nine years ago he'd had an affair with her mother and she was the result? He would never believe her. Why would he?

Mark Canfield frowned at her. "You look familiar. Have we met before?"

"Don't even think about it," Alex told her. "You don't want to mess with me."

She ignored him. "We haven't, Senator, but you knew my mother. Marsha Buchanan. I look a little like her. I'm her daughter. And, I think, maybe yours."

Mark Canfield's face barely showed any reaction at all. Must be all that political training, she thought, not sure what she was feeling herself. Hope? Terror? A sense of standing on the edge of a cliff, not sure if she should jump?

She braced herself for rejection because it *was* crazy to think he would just accept what she said.

Then his expression softened as he smiled.

"I remember your mother very well. She was . . ." His voice trailed off. "We should talk. Come on in to my office."

Before Dani could take a step, Alex moved in front of her. "You can't do this," he told the senator. "You can't meet with her in private. How do you know she's not with the press? Or the opposition? This could be a setup."

Mark glanced from Alex to her. "Is it a setup?" he asked Dani.

"No. I have ID, if you'd like to run a background check on me." The last statement was aimed at Alex.

"I will," he said smoothly and held out his hand.

"You expect me to hand over personal information right now?" she asked, not sure if she should be impressed by his efficiency or nail him in the shin with the pointy toe of her shoe.

"You expect to speak with the senator. Think of this as a security deposit."

"I'm not sure this is necessary," Mark said calmly, but he didn't try to stop Alex.

Dani dug in her purse for her wallet and pulled out her driver's license.

"You wouldn't happen to have your passport on you?" Alex asked.

"No, but maybe you'd like to take my

fingerprints?"

"I'll do that later."

She had a feeling he wasn't kidding.

Mark glanced between them. "You two finished?"

Dani shrugged. "Ask dragon-boy."

Alex nodded. "I'll join you as soon as I get one of the IT people working on this." He waved Dani's license.

"IT people?" Dani asked as she followed the senator into his office.

"Information technology. You'd be amazed at what they can do with a computer." He smiled and closed the door behind her. "Or maybe not. You're probably very computer literate. I wish I were. I know as much as I need to so I can get by, but I still have to call Alex every now and then to get me out of a bind."

He motioned to a conversation area at the rear of the room. There were two worn sofas, a couple of chairs and a coffee table that looked as if it had served time in a frat house.

"Have a seat," he said.

She perched on the edge of one of the sofas and glanced around the room.

It was big and open, but lacking in windows. Not a surprise, what with the entire campaign office being in a warehouse. From what she'd seen so far, the senator didn't believe in spending a lot of money on appearances. The desk was old and scarred, and the only color on the wall came from large-scale maps of different parts of the country.

"Are you really running for president?" she asked. That someone she'd just met could be doing so now was beyond astonishing. It was just plain weird.

"We're exploring the possibility," he told her as he settled in a chair opposite the sofa. "This isn't a permanent arrangement. If my campaign looks like a go, we'll move to a more accessible location, but why spend the money now if we don't have to?"

"Good point."

He leaned forward and rested his forearms on his knees. "I can't believe you're Marsha's daughter. It's been what? Thirty years?"

"Twenty-eight," Dani said, then felt herself blush. "Although I suppose for you it's been closer to twenty-nine."

He nodded slowly. "I still remember the last time I saw her. We were having lunch downtown. I remember everything about how she looked. So beautiful."

There was a darkness in his eyes, as if he were lost in a past Dani couldn't begin to imagine. She had so many questions and wasn't comfortable asking any of them.

Mark hadn't been married then, but her mother had been. Dani barely remembered either of her parents. The man she'd always thought of as her father, at least until she'd found out otherwise a few months ago, was little more than a blur.

Still, she found herself thinking about him, wondering when her mother had stopped loving him and whether Mark Canfield had been a part of that decision.

"I never knew why she ended things," Mark said quietly. "A couple of days after that lunch, she called me and said she couldn't see me anymore. She wouldn't say why. I tried to get in touch with her, but she'd taken the boys and gone away. She wrote me and told me she was serious about us being over. That she wanted me to get on with my life, to find someone I could have a real relationship with."

"She left because she was pregnant with me," Dani said.

The moment was too surreal, she thought. She'd wondered what her first conversation with Mark would be like, but now that she was having it, she felt almost disconnected.

"That would be my guess," he said.

"So that means you really *are* my biological father."

Before Mark could answer, the door to his office opened and a woman entered. She gave Dani a quick glance, then looked at Mark.

"Senator, you have a call from Mr. Wilson. He says you know what it's about and that it's urgent."

Mark shook his head. "His definition of urgent and mine differ, Heidi. Tell him I'll call him back later."

Heidi, an attractive woman in her early forties, nodded and left the office.

Mark turned back to Dani. "I think it's very possible I'm your biological father."

The interruption had thrown Dani. It took her a second to mentally recreate the emotional storm that had been swirling inside of her. But the senator seemed very calm about the whole thing.

"You didn't know about me before?" she asked.

"Your mother never said anything and I never considered she could be pregnant."

And if you had? But before she could ask that, the door opened again and Alex entered.

"I've run a preliminary background check on her," he said as he crossed the room. He stopped in front of Dani and looked down

18

at her. "No felonies."

"You mean that bank robbery conviction from last week hasn't posted yet? The federal government is just so busy these days."

"This isn't a situation I find amusing," Alex told her.

Dani stood. Despite the dangerous heels, she was still a good six inches shorter than him. "You think I do? I spent my whole life thinking I was one person and suddenly I may be someone else. Do you have any idea what it's like to question your very existence? I'm sorry if my search for my father gets in the way of your daily schedule."

She was mad. Alex could see the fire in her eyes. She was also scared. She tried to hide the latter, but it was visible, at least to him. When he'd been very young, he'd learned what it was like to live in constant terror and the ability to recognize it in others had never left him.

But was she who she claimed? Her timing made him more suspicious than normal and he was, by nature and training, a cautious man. With him, trust had to be earned and once broken, was never given again. He doubted there was anything Dani Buchanan could do to make him trust her.

Alex studied her, searching for similarities

to the senator. It was there, in her smile, the shape of her chin. But how many random strangers had a passing resemblance to each other? She could have stumbled across some information about the senator's affair with Marsha Buchanan and decided to use that to her advantage.

"We'll need to do a DNA test," he said flatly.

"I agree," Dani said, meeting his gaze with a steady look of her own. "I want to be sure."

"I'm sure," Mark said as he stood. "But testing will confirm everything. In the meantime, Dani, I'd like us to get to know each other."

Dani's smile was both hopeful and apprehensive. "Me, too. We could go to lunch or something."

"No public meetings," Alex said.

Mark nodded. "He's right. I'm a public figure. Having lunch with a pretty young woman would get people talking. We don't want that." He thought for a second. "Why don't you come over to the house for dinner tonight? You can meet the family."

Dani physically took a step back. "I don't think so," she murmured. "I'm not ready for that. Your wife doesn't know about me and —"

"Nonsense. Katherine is an amazing woman. She'll understand and want to welcome you into the family. Alex and Julie don't live at home but there are still six Canfield children for you to meet." He frowned. "Not blood relations, of course. Katherine and I adopted all our children, but then you probably know that."

"I did some research on the family," Dani admitted.

And found out there was plenty of money, Alex thought cynically.

"You could have a few meetings here," he said. "Before you take Dani home."

But the senator had made up his mind and he was rarely convinced to change it. "No, dinner will work. Dani, you might as well find out the chaos you're getting yourself into right away. Besides, Katherine will adore you." He glanced at his watch. "I have a meeting I can't be late for. Alex, give Dani the address. Say six tonight?"

Alex nodded. "Are you going to tell Mom or should I?"

Mark considered the question. "I'll do it. I'll leave a little early." He smiled at Dani. "See you tonight, then."

"I, ah, all right," Dani said, sounding a little shaken.

Mark left the office.

Dani clutched her handbag so tightly her knuckles turned white. "The family. I didn't expect that."

No, she'd probably thought she could weasel her way into Mark's good graces without having to face his children.

She turned to him. "What about your mother? Is this going to bother her?" She briefly closed her eyes, then opened them. "Stupid question. Of course it will. I know they weren't together when he had his relationship with my mother, but still. A kid from his past can't be easy to accept. I don't want to make trouble."

"Too late for that."

She tilted her head. "You don't approve of me."

"You don't want to know what I think of you."

Surprisingly, she smiled. "Oh, I can imagine."

"I don't think so."

He didn't frighten her, which annoyed him. He was used to intimidating people.

"So when's the DNA test?" she asked. "I assume you'll be hiring a lab?"

"Someone will be at the house tonight."

"Will they be using a cheek swab or would you prefer dismemberment?"

"I don't want you hurt," he told her.

"No. You just want me gone." She sighed. "I wish I could make you believe that I'm just looking for my father. I need that connection. I don't want anything from him other than to get to know him. I'm not the enemy."

"That's only one person's opinion." He moved closer to her, hoping to crowd her into stepping back again. She didn't. "You have no idea what you've gotten yourself into, Dani Buchanan," he said coldly. "This isn't a game. My father is a United States Senator who is considering a run for the presidency. There is more on the line than you can imagine. You will not be allowed to compromise him in any way. I'm not the only dragon at that particular gate, but I'm the one you're going to have to worry about most."

She leaned toward him. "You don't scare me."

"I will."

"No, you won't. You assume there's something I want, which means you have leverage over me. But you're wrong." She shifted her handbag onto her shoulder. "It's okay. I respect what you're doing. In your position, I'd do the same thing. Protecting family is a big deal. But be careful about how far you take things. You don't seem like the kind of man who enjoys apologizing. I'd hate to see you have to come crawling back to me when you discover how wrong you are about me."

She had guts. He had to respect that. "You'd love me to come crawling with an apology."

She smiled. "I know, but I was trying to be polite."

CHAPTER TWO

Dani walked through the main dining room of Bella Roma. The tables were set for lunch with the white linens in place and fresh flowers on the tables. She paused to randomly pick up a couple of glasses and held them to the light. They sparkled the way they were supposed to.

She'd only been working at the restaurant a couple of weeks, which meant she was still on the steep side of the learning curve. The good news was Bella Roma was a well-run restaurant with an excellent staff and a great menu. The better news was that her boss, Bernie, was a terrific guy to work for.

After setting down the glasses, she walked into the kitchen where low-key chaos reined. The real activity wouldn't begin before they opened for lunch in twenty minutes. For now there was the prep work. Penny — her sister-in-law and possibly the best chef in Seattle, not that she would ever mention that to Nick, the head chef here — always said that a kitchen lived or died by its prep work.

Three huge stockpots simmered on back burners. The scent of garlic and sausage filled the air. One cook chopped vegetables for salads while another sliced meat for the sandwiches and antipasto platters.

"Hey, Dani," one of the cooks called. "Come taste my sauce."

"That's not what he wants you to taste," another cook yelled. "She's too pretty for you, Rico. She wants a real man like me."

"You're not a real man. The last time I had your wife, she told me."

"If my wife saw you naked, she'd laugh so hard, she'd hurt herself."

Dani smiled at the familiar insults. Restaurant kitchens were usually loud, crazy places where the constant pressure meant everyone had to work as a team. The fact that the majority of workers were men meant a challenging situation for the average woman. Dani had grown up hovering around the kitchens at the various Buchanan restaurants, so she was immune to any attempts to shock her. She waved at the guys, then checked the list of specials Nick had posted against the menu inserts for that day.

"The panini sounds delicious," she told

the head chef. "I can't wait to try it."

"I have something better for you, sweet cheeks," one of the guys said.

Dani didn't bother turning around to find out who was speaking. Instead she picked up one of the large carving knives. "I have a set of these myself."

A couple of the guys groaned.

Nick grinned. "As long as you know how to use them."

"I do."

That would back the cooks off for a while. She knew that as long as she did her job and they learned they could depend on her to respect them and not do anything to make their work more difficult, they would come to respect her. It took time to build a good relationship with a kitchen staff and she was more than willing to put in the effort to make that happen.

"You want to make any changes to the specials?" Nick asked casually.

Dani wanted to laugh at the ridiculous question, but kept her expression carefully neutral. Nick didn't really want her opinion. If she tried to give one, he would rip her head off . . . probably just verbally. The division of labor was very clear. The head chef ran the kitchen, the general manager ran everything else. Dani's position of authority stopped the second she stepped through the swinging doors.

"No," she said sweetly. "They look great. Have a good lunch."

She pushed through the doors, back onto her turf. She and Nick had to work together. Either of them could make the other's life a living nightmare. As the new kid, it was up to her to prove herself, which she was happy to do.

One of the advantages of her new job was how it helped her focus. After her meeting with Mark Canfield, she'd found herself unable to concentrate, until she'd come to work. Alex Canfield had gotten to her, invading her brain on a regular basis. She tried to tell herself that he was completely uninteresting, not the least bit attractive and not someone she would waste her time on but she knew she was lying. There was something about him that compelled her. The fact that he was her biological father's adoptive son added a level of confusion that told her she needed to run in the opposite direction. Considering the past year in her romantic life, it was advice she should listen to.

She walked through the dining room to her office. On the way she passed the wine cellar, where she did a quick spot inventory on two different wines. The number of bottles in the bin matched the number on the list from her computer.

"Excellent," she murmured as she stepped back into the hall. So far working at Bella Roma was a dream. There was nothing she wanted to —

"Dani?"

She turned and saw her brother Walker. She grinned. "Here to figure out how to do things right?" she asked as he pulled her close and kissed the top of her head.

"You wish."

Walker, a former Marine, had recently taken over the Buchanan empire, such as it was. He ran the corporation that owned the four family restaurants. He'd been pushed into the leadership role when Gloria, the Buchanan matriarch and grandmother to Dani's three brothers, had suffered a heart attack and broken hip. Weeks into the job, he discovered it was his calling.

Dani was happy for him. Walker was a hell of a guy and he was doing a great job. She never actually wanted to run the business, she'd just wanted to have a chance to prove herself running one of the restaurants. While Gloria had put her in charge of Burger Heaven, she hadn't let her move up at all. After years of trying to please a woman who actually seemed to hate her, Dani had been told the truth. In blunt terms, Gloria had explained that Dani wasn't a real Buchanan. That her mother had had an affair and Dani was the result.

With Gloria as the matriarch of the family, Dani wasn't related to her at all. As Gloria had only ever been critical and distant, Dani should have been relieved.

But she wasn't. Despite their lack of blood connection, Dani knew Gloria would always be her grandmother — at least in Dani's heart. Gloria's past behavior meant being close was unlikely.

Dani told herself she didn't care. At least there was a bright side.

Now that she knew Mark Canfield could be her real father, she had a whole new family to bond with. The downside was she'd spent her whole life as a Buchanan and she didn't want to be anyone else.

Walker released her. "How are things going?"

"Great. I love it. Bernie's the best and the kitchen staff is only terrorizing me a little. That means I'm starting to win them over. Of course if they weren't terrorizing me at all it would mean that they hate me, so it's a delicate balance. What are you doing here? Looking for a decent meal for a change?"

The slam made him grin. "You think pasta with red sauce can compete with anything Penny can come up with?"

Penny had married their oldest brother, Cal. She was an extraordinary chef and worked at The Waterfront, the seafood restaurant in the Buchanan stable.

"If you're going to put it like that," Dani grumbled, knowing Penny was a genius. "But we have a lot of great stuff you don't offer. Now that I think about it, we need to open an Italian place. It's very popular and the profit margin is fantastic."

Walker stared at her. "I'm not here to talk business."

"But an Italian restaurant is a great idea."

"An excellent one, if you want to ignore the fact that you're trying to talk me into competing with your current boss."

Oops. Dani glanced around to see if anyone had overheard her. Damn. When was she going to remember that she wasn't a Buchanan anymore? That she didn't owe them any loyalty and that she should be putting all her energies into Bella Roma?

"Okay," she muttered. "Point taken. So if you're not here for the garlic bread, what's up?"

"It's Elissa," he said.

Dani grabbed his arm. "Is she okay? Did

31

something happen?"

"She's fine. We're moving forward with the wedding plans. She wants to have a fairy-tale wedding with lots of flowers and twinkle lights. I want her to be happy."

Until this minute, Dani would have had a hard time imagining her big, tough brother talking about twinkle lights with a straight face. She would have bet he didn't even know what they were. But since falling for Elissa, he was a different man. More open, more connected, more aware of twinkle lights.

"I'm sure the wedding will be beautiful," she said.

"She wants you to be in it. She's not going to have a maid of honor. Apparently it's too complicated. So she'll have a lot of attendants and she would like you to be one. But she didn't want to pressure you, so she asked me to ask you so you'd be more comfortable saying no."

Dani smiled. "Really? She wants me in the wedding?"

"Of course she does. She likes you. Plus, you're family, and don't say you're not. I'm tired of that conversation. You're as much a Buchanan as any of us. You're my sister. You could be an alien dropped off by the mother ship and you'd still be my sister."

His fierceness might have worried someone who didn't know him, but Dani recognized it as his way of saying he really, really cared. She might not be sure of her place in the universe or her last name, but she was clear on how much she mattered to her brothers.

"You're not getting rid of me," she said. "Don't worry."

"I have to worry. I'm older. It's in the job description. So do you want to be in the wedding or not?"

"So smooth," she told him. "So persuasive. So elegant in your communication."

He scowled. "Was that a yes?"

"It was a yes. I would love to be one of Elissa's attendants."

"Good. How was your meeting with the senator?"

She led him to a table and sat down. "It was interesting. Strange. I didn't feel a connection or anything."

She told him about how Mark had been willing to accept her story.

"Alex is insisting on a DNA test, which I think is a good idea. Then we'll both be sure."

"Alex is his son?"

"Adopted, but yes."

"Is he a problem?"

His fierceness might have worried some-one who didn't know him, but Dani recog-nized it as his way of saying he really, really cared. She might not be sure of her place in the universe or her last name, but she was clear on how much she mattered to her brothers.

"You're not getting rid of me," she said. "Don't worry."

"I have to worry. I'm older. It's in the job description. So do you want to be in the wedding or not?"

"So smooth," she told him. "So persua-sive. So elegant in your communication."

He scowled. "Was that a yes?"

"It was a yes. I would love to be one of Elissa's attendants."

"Good. How was your meeting with the senator?"

She led him to a table and sat down. "It was interesting. Strange. I didn't feel a con-nection or anything."

She told him about how Mark had been willing to accept her story.

"Alex is insisting on a DNA test, which I think is a good idea. Then we'll both be sure."

"Alex is his son?"

"Adopted, but yes."

"Is he a problem?"

Fiona was beautifully dressed in a suit that flattered her slender figure and perfect red hair. Katherine glanced down at her own designer suit. Despite an aggressive exercise routine and constantly watching what she ate, her body had begun to change. She'd never minded the thought of getting old, but when faced with the reality of a thickening waist and the unpleasant realization that gravity was not her friend, she thought longingly of the easy resilience of youth.

"I have the guest list prepared," Fiona said efficiently. "All but three of the designers have confirmed and I'm going to keep pressuring the last three until they cave. I'm determined we top last year's proceeds by at least twenty-five percent."

"Both the hospital and I appreciate your enthusiasm," Katherine said as she stepped out of her shoes. She'd been presenting their plans for the fashion show fund-raiser, then had worked the subsequent late-afternoon tea. She'd been on her feet for hours and they were letting her know about it — another sign of getting older. When she'd been Fiona's age, she would have been able to do that and then go dancing all night.

"We should just send a check," Katherine said as she poured herself a glass of water, then offered one to Fiona. "Much less work."

Fiona smiled. "You always say that, but you don't mean it."

"You're right." While Katherine's charity work filled much of her days, she loved knowing the money raised would make a difference.

The sound of someone running caused her to turn. Anticipating the greeting, Katherine set her glass on the counter, crouched down and held out her arms.

Seconds later Sasha burst into the room and flew across the hardwood floors.

"Mommy, Mommy, you're back. I missed you so much. Yvette read to me and Bailey and I watched princess videos and I had mac and cheese for lunch, then Ian read us a story and did the voices."

Katherine straightened, hugging the little girl close. "You had a good day."

"I did." Sasha smiled.

She was just five, with café au lait skin and dark eyes. Her hair hung in a tangle of curls. Katherine suspected her mixed heritage and classic bone structure meant the little girl was going to grow into a real beauty. She and Mark were going to have trouble with boys far sooner than they wanted. But for the next few years, they only had to worry about their baby growing up strong.

"Do you want to say hello to Fiona?" Katherine asked.

Sasha wrinkled her nose slightly, then dutifully said, "Hello, Fiona. How are you?"

"I'm fine." Fiona smiled at the girl. "You're getting so big."

Sasha didn't answer. For some reason, she'd never gotten along with Alex's ex-wife, which was odd. The child was exceptionally loving.

Yvette walked into the kitchen. "I knew your mama had to be home, the way you went tearing off. Tell me I did not hear you running down the stairs."

Sasha grinned. "You did not."

"Good. How was the presentation?" Yvette asked Katherine.

"Exhausting, but successful. And here?"

"Wild, crazy, loud."

"So normal?"

"You know how your children are," Yvette told her with a grin. "They're going to make me old before my time."

"You're younger than me," Katherine teased. "I get to be old first."

"We'll have to see."

Yvette held out her arms and Sasha went willingly. The petite dark-haired woman carried her out of the kitchen.

"She's so good with the children," Fiona said. "You were lucky to find her."

"I know. She's the reason Mark and I could adopt so many children."

Without help, they would have been forced to stop at three or four children. Katherine didn't even want to think about that. She loved all eight of her children and couldn't imagine her world without even one of them.

"You have a perfect life," Fiona murmured.

Katherine thought about her aching feet and the hot flash that had kept her awake for two hours the previous night. "Not perfect, but it makes me happy."

"Your children are such a blessing."

Katherine glanced at Fiona and saw the pain flash in her eyes. Her chest tightened in sympathy. By now Fiona should have a child of her own. Maybe two. If all had gone well . . . But it hadn't. Everything had changed when Alex had announced he wanted a divorce. He'd never told Katherine why and Fiona claimed to be equally confused by his unexpected change of heart.

Katherine knew there had to be a reason. Alex was her oldest and the child of her heart. They had been through so much together. He wasn't the sort of man to simply walk away without a reason. He was far from heartless or cruel. So why had he left his wife?

Katherine wanted to say something to comfort her friend, but she couldn't think of what that would be. Fiona smiled bravely.

"Sorry. I didn't mean to get emotional. I know you're already in an awkward position and I don't want to make things worse. I just want you to know that I so appreciate you allowing me to help out with the charity work. It means everything to me. You could have easily cut me out of your life."

"Never," Katherine told her. "Whatever happens between you and Alex has nothing to do with our friendship." She continued to hold out hope that her son would realize what he'd done and go back to Fiona.

Fiona drew in a breath. "I'm going to slip into your office for an hour or so, if that's all right. I want to download fashion show menus for the past ten years. The last thing we want to worry about is a repeat entrée."

"Thanks for doing that. I'll go up and check on the kids. Come find me before you leave."

"I will."

Fiona left. Katherine turned toward the staircase, but before she took a step, she heard the garage door. That could only mean one thing — Mark was home.

She knew it was completely foolish, but even after twenty-seven years, her heart still beat faster whenever she thought about seeing her husband. So many of her friends talked about the spark going out of their marriage — how nothing was ever exciting or fresh. It wasn't like that for Katherine — it never had been. Her love for Mark had only grown. In the cliché of movies and TV, he was her handsome prince. While she loved her children, he was the one who truly claimed her heart.

She ran a hand over her hair, then smoothed the front of her jacket. There wasn't time to freshen her makeup, so she bit her lips to make them redder and drew in a breath. Being pretty for Mark mattered. Seconds later the utility room door opened and he stepped into the kitchen.

He looked exactly as he had the first time she'd seen him. Tall and handsome with dark blond hair and deep blue eyes. Those eyes always crinkled slightly, as if he knew a really funny secret. He still took her breath away every time she saw him.

"Hi, sweetheart," he said as he moved toward her. "How are you?"

"Good. You're home early."

"I wanted to see you."

Her heart quickened at his words.

He leaned in and kissed her. The second his mouth touched hers, the familiar wanting flared to life. She hid her reaction to the casual kiss — a trick she'd learned in the first few months of her marriage. But that didn't make the need go away.

Years ago she'd read an article about relationships. The author claimed that in most marriages there was the one who adored and the one who was adored. She knew that was true for them. Mark loved her, but he didn't worship her. He didn't understand how deeply her feelings ran. She'd learned to control the wild, romantic and sexual feelings swirling inside of her whenever he was close, but she'd never been able to make them go away. He was the only man for her. At least she'd been lucky enough to marry him.

He took her hand in his and smiled. "Come on. Let's go talk."

"Don't you want to say hi to the kids?"

"Later. I want to talk to you first."

Mark was a typical guy. Despite his ability to chat with contributors for hours and never break a sweat, anytime *she* suggested they talk, he had a thousand other things he needed to be doing. So why the sudden change? What was there to talk about? She shivered slightly.

They went into his book-lined study. He shut the door behind them, then led her to the leather sofa. His expression was unfamiliar. Was he upset? No, that wasn't right. More resigned. About what? Cold, hard fear knotted in her belly.

Was he leaving her?

Her brain pointed out that even if he was desperate to get away, leaving his wife while exploring the possibility of running for president wasn't a good idea. Her heart whispered that of course he loved her. He'd been busier than usual lately, but that was to be expected. She should stop worrying about nothing. Still, her hands trembled slightly as she folded them in her lap and looked at him.

"What is it?" she asked.

She would guess that from the outside, she appeared totally calm and in control. That's what Mark would see. What she wanted him to see.

"A young woman came to meet me today," Mark told her. "Or maybe not so young. She's twenty-eight. I guess that means I'm getting old. Are you still interested in being married to an old guy? After all, you're the hot one in our relationship."

He spoke easily, smiling, holding her gaze. She should have been relaxed. But she wasn't. She was terrified and she couldn't say why.

"You're not an old guy," she said, doing her best not to visibly tremble.

"Fifty-four."

"I'm fifty-six," she pointed out. "Are you going to trade me in for a younger model?"

"You're the most beautiful woman in the world," he told her. "You're my wife."

Soothing words that should have made her feel better. But they didn't.

"So who is this young woman?"

"Her name is Dani Buchanan. Dani for Danielle, Alex told me later."

"Alex? What does he have to do with this?"

"Not anything, really. He was there and he met her. Tried to run her off. Your son is quite the watchdog."

"He cares about his family."

"I know." Mark touched her cheek. "Katherine, do you remember when we were engaged the first time? How you ended things with me?"

She nodded slowly. She'd been an only child from an old money East Coast family. Her parents hadn't approved of her relationship with a brash young man from Seattle. Mark had charm and energy but no family to speak of and certainly no pedigree. Still, Katherine had loved him and had won her family over to her way of thinking. Mark had proposed and she had accepted. But six weeks after the engagement, she'd broken things off. She'd been unable to tell Mark the truth about herself. Rather than have him pity her, then leave her, she'd ended their engagement and he'd gone back to Seattle.

"I came home to figure out what to do with my life," he said. "While I was here, I met someone. I didn't mean for anything to happen, but it did."

The fear turned sharp, cutting her from the inside. She felt both cold and hot. Her whole body ached and still she sat there unmoving, determined to show nothing.

"You had a relationship with this woman?" she asked calmly.

"Yes. She was married. Neither of us meant for it to happen. No one knew, because of her husband. I didn't want to hurt anyone. One day it ended. I never thought much about it again, until today. Dani is her daughter. My daughter."

Katherine stood. Maybe if she moved, the pain wouldn't be so bad. Maybe then she could breathe. But the white-hot pokers pricked her everywhere and the spacious study offered nowhere to hide.

"Obviously I didn't know," he said, as if unaware that anything was wrong. "Alex suggested a DNA test so we can all be sure. It's a good idea. She seems like a great girl. She looks like Marsha mostly, but I see a little of me in her. With the campaign, we'll have to be discreet, of course."

Mark kept talking, but Katherine couldn't hear him. He had a child. A child of his own. A child he'd met.

"I invited her to dinner," Mark said. "I want you to meet her. We don't have to tell the kids who she is right away. But eventually we will."

She turned to him. Her face felt frozen. She wasn't sure she could speak. "She's coming here?"

"Tonight." He stood and crossed to her, then took her hands in his. "I know you'll like her. Didn't you say you wanted another daughter?"

He couldn't mean that. He couldn't not know what he was doing to her. And yet he kept talking as if he thought everything was fine. As if she wasn't devastated that some other woman had been able to give him something she, Katherine, never could.

Alex arrived early for dinner at his parents'

house. He'd thought about calling his mother, but had then decided it would be better to speak with her in person. His father might think she would take the news of Dani Buchanan in stride; Alex wasn't so sure.

Before he could head up the stairs, Fiona stepped out of his mother's study.

"Hello, Alex."

He remembered a Discovery Channel special on spiders. Fiona reminded him of a black widow, just biding her time until she could eat her mate.

"I didn't know you'd be here," he said.

"Meaning you wouldn't have come home if you'd known?" Her green eyes widened with emotion. "Do you hate me so much?"

"I don't hate you at all." Hate would mean having strong emotions about her. He didn't. He could look at her and acknowledge her physical beauty, yet feel nothing. In a perfect world, she would have disappeared from his life after the divorce. Unfortunately, he had a feeling she was never going away.

"The ice queen cometh."

Alex turned and saw his brother Ian rolling toward them. Alex grinned and stepped toward him. He bent slightly so he and Ian could perform their complicated ritualistic

46

greeting. Alex did most of the hand slapping and turning. It was easier for him. Ian's CP limited his mobility. But what his younger brother lacked in physical prowess he more than made up for in brains and creativity.

"She's always hanging around," Ian told Alex. "I think she has a thing for me."

Fiona shuddered visibly. She looked over Ian's thin, twisted body as he sat in his wheelchair.

"That's disgusting," she snapped.

Ian raised his eyebrows. "But after last night . . . What do you think, Alex? You're the expert on what turns Fiona on."

Alex stared at his ex-wife. "Not as much as you'd think."

Fiona seemed torn between fury and pleading. "Alex, you can't let him talk to me like that."

"Why not? Ian has a great sense of humor."

"Something you wouldn't understand, babe," Ian said. "Humor is not your thing." He turned and rolled out of the room. "Love ya," he called over his shoulder.

Fiona drew in a breath. "I've never understood that boy."

"You've never tried." It had taken Alex a long time to figure out how Fiona felt about

Ian, but he'd finally understood that she couldn't stand to look at the kid. It was as if the variation on normal had disgusted her. That truth was only one thing on a long list of reasons he'd walked away from her and their marriage.

"Alex, I don't want to fight."

He crossed to the wet bar and opened a cabinet. After pouring himself some scotch, he faced her. "I'm not fighting."

"You know what I mean." She glided close to him and put her hand on his chest. "I miss you so much. There has to be something I can say or do to help you forgive me. It was only one mistake. Can you really be so cold and unforgiving?"

"I'm the bastard king," he said, then took a sip. "Literally. Well, the bastard part anyway."

She drew in a breath, as if determined to ignore his baiting of her. "Alex, I'm being serious. I'm your wife."

"You were my wife."

"I want to be again."

He looked her up and down. On the surface, she was everything a man could want — beautiful, intelligent, an excellent dinner companion. She could talk to anyone, anywhere. Nearly all his friends had wondered how he had let her get away.

"Not happening," he told her flatly.

"But I love you. Doesn't that mean anything?"

He thought about that night nearly two years ago. When he'd come home unexpectedly.

"No," he said. "It doesn't mean a damn thing."

CHAPTER THREE

Dani stood on the porch of a large, impressive house in Bellevue and told herself that the world wouldn't end when she rang the doorbell. It might feel as if it would, but that wasn't real. Besides, just standing out here, lurking, would upset the neighbors. What if they called and told Mark's wife about a potential thief hovering? Katherine Canfield would open the front door and find her there. It was not how Dani wanted them to meet.

"I'm babbling in my head," Dani muttered to herself. "This is bad. Seriously bad. I think I need therapy. Or at least a frontal lobe transplant."

She forced herself to push the bell. As the soft ringing sound echoed inside the house, she felt her heart speed up until it was in danger of bursting into warp eight and zipping off to the nearby non-earth galaxy.

The door opened. Dani tried to brace

herself, but there wasn't enough time. Then all the air flowed out of her lungs when she recognized the man standing there.

"Thank God," she said before she could stop herself. "It's just you."

Alex raised his eyebrows. "Just me? So I wasn't intimidating enough at our last meeting? None of the threats worked?"

Oops. "No, no. Of course not. You were terrifying. I won't sleep for weeks. Dragons. I'm going to have nightmares about them. Seriously. It's just compared with meeting your mother . . . no offense, but you're a snap."

He didn't even crack a smile. Was it that the man didn't have a sense of humor or was it her specifically that he didn't find funny? She thought about pointing out this was actually pretty good material, but decided not to. There was a better than even chance she would be barfing from nerves shortly. Why push her luck now?

He stared at her for several seconds. She smiled tightly. "It's the whole visitor, front door thing. You're supposed to invite me in."

"I don't want to."

"You'll warm up to me."

"I doubt it."

"I'm a very nice person."

He looked unconvinced but still he took a step back and allowed her to ease past him into the foyer.

The interior of the house was large, but homey. It was the kind of place designed to make someone feel at ease — too bad it wasn't having that effect on her at the moment.

She turned to Alex, but before she could speak a teenage boy rolled into the room. He was pale and thin, with dark hair and eyes. His right hand worked a control on his motorized wheelchair while his left hand lay bent and curled in his lap.

"Are you the stripper I ordered?" he asked as he eyed her. "I've been waiting over an hour. I was expecting better service from your company."

Dani tilted her head slightly as she tried to figure out how to handle the outrageous question. Finally she settled on the truth.

"I'm not exactly stripper material," she said with a grin. "I'm too short. I always picture them really tall and with those big headpieces like the Las Vegas showgirls wear."

"They couldn't drive in one of those feather things," he told her.

"They could if they had a sunroof and kept it open."

52

"Don't encourage him," Alex muttered. "Dani Buchanan, Ian Canfield. My brother. He can be obnoxious."

"An ugly accusation and totally untrue."

"Nice to meet you," Dani said and held out her hand to Ian.

He moved his wheelchair close and shook her hand. "You could be stripper material if you wanted," he said.

"What a lovely thing to say. It's a compliment I'll treasure always. My mother would be so proud."

Ian laughed. "Okay, I like you. That doesn't happen often. You *should* treasure the moment."

Dani laughed. "I will. You'll be prominently mentioned in my diary tonight."

He sighed. "It's a problem I have all the time. Chicks dig me. It's the supersized battery. They go crazy for power."

With that, he spun his chair and wheeled away.

When he was gone, she turned to Alex. "See. People like me."

"He's young and he doesn't know who you are."

"Meaning he won't like me when he finds out I'm inherently evil?"

Alex stared at her. His dark eyes gave nothing away. "Ian doesn't usually warm up to people."

"He's a perceptive young man. I like him, too."

"You think I'm going to be swayed by some pity banter with my crippled brother?"

Her brief good mood faded and she suddenly wished she were big and muscular so she could hit him and do some damage.

"Don't insult me and don't you dare insult him." She moved closer and poked him in the chest. "I'll accept that I'm a complication no one expected. You can be protective of your family all you want, you can even think the worst of me. But don't you dare take what was a charming moment in an otherwise insane day and make it something disgusting."

"Are you going to take me on?" he asked, obviously unimpressed by her temper.

"In a heartbeat."

"Think you'll win?"

"Absolutely."

One corner of his mouth twitched slightly. "We'll see."

Great. She was furious and he found the situation, or possibly her, amusing. Good-looking or not, she was thinking she could seriously grow to hate this man.

He motioned for her to walk into the large living room. As she passed him, she waved her purse in front of him. "I brought a small bag so there won't be that awkward moment of you asking to search it before I leave. This will make it so much harder for me to steal the family silver, though."

"It wouldn't have been awkward."

"You really are a lawyer."

"What does that mean?" he asked.

"You're not afraid to say what you think, you don't worry about insulting me and you're determined to see me as nothing more significant than lint. That takes a lot of training."

"Or the right motivation."

The room was done in earth tones. The comfortable furnishings had an air of grace. The paintings looked original, the carpets thick enough to sleep on, yet there were a few toys scattered around. This was not a room for show. People lived here and she liked that.

Dani turned to take it all in, then noticed a woman in a white coat perched on the edge of a sofa. She rose and walked over to them.

"Whenever you're ready," the woman said.

Ready for what?

Oh, right. "DNA test?" Dani asked. "You're not wasting any time."

"Do you want me to?" Alex asked.

Instead of answering, Dani turned to the woman. "Swab away."

She opened her mouth and the lab tech stroked the inside of her cheek with a cotton swab. Seconds later she was done and on her way. Dani stared after her.

"Let me guess. You're paying extra for a speedy result?"

"It seemed the smart thing to do."

She felt exhausted by the roller coaster of emotion she'd been through that day. There was enough stress in the situation without fighting with Alex, too.

"I want to know the truth," she told him. "Nothing more. If Mark Canfield isn't my father, then I'll disappear and we can all pretend this didn't happen."

Alex didn't look convinced. "You could have stayed away in the first place."

"I want to know my father. Even you must be human enough to understand that."

"I've already told you, I find your timing a little too convenient."

"I just got the information recently. All I want is to figure out where I belong."

He didn't actually say "not here," but the words echoed in the quiet room.

Despite them, Alex motioned for her to sit on the sofa. "Do you want something to drink?"

"No, thanks." Her stomach was too un-settled from nerves.

"They aren't telling the children. Not until the test results are back. You're going to have to go another few days before you can claim your glory."

She'd been about to sit. Now she straightened. "Dammit, Alex, that's enough. You're pushing me for no reason. I've committed no crime. I've been totally honest and upfront. The fact that you choose not to believe me doesn't change the truth. You're going to have to back off or we're going to have a problem."

He folded his arms across his chest. "We already do. I don't trust you. There's nothing you can say to make me want to try."

She narrowed her gaze. Part of her respected his stubborn determination to protect what was his. Part of her wanted to back the car over him.

"Then let's try this another way. How about you let me get close to screwing up before you bite my head off?"

She had no idea if he would accept her offer. She found herself hoping he would and not just because she might be related to his father. Something inside of her wanted Alex to like her. A dangerous possibility, she thought, given her history in the romance department and her potential, nonbiological family link with Alex.

"How close?" he asked finally.

"Within sight of, but not actually touching."

"I'll think about it."

Considering how he'd been acting, it was a major concession. Maybe he wasn't the Terminator. Maybe he could be bargained with or reasoned with. Although she had a feeling if she got in his way, he would rip out her heart without a second thought. Verbally, if not physically.

Silence descended. Awkward silence that made her squirm. She knew she was being tested, that whoever spoke first lost the game, but she couldn't stand to just sit there.

"The house is great," she said. "I like how it feels lived-in and not showy."

"My mother has excellent taste." He glanced at his watch. "The senator will be down shortly."

She tucked her hair behind her ear. "You did that before. At campaign headquarters. You call him the senator rather than Mark or my dad."

"It makes things easier for everyone. We're in a working environment there."

"But you're not at work right now."

His dark gaze settled on her face. "It makes things easier," he repeated.

How? "Are you showing respect or trying to make sure no one thinks of you as Daddy's little boy?"

One eyebrow rose, which seemed to be all the answer she was going to get.

"Did the question annoy you?" she asked. "I think it's both. The man *is* running for president." A concept Dani doubted she would ever be able to get her mind around. "But on a personal note, you'd hate people to think you were here because of your relationship with your father rather than on your own merit."

"You know this how?" he asked.

"I'm a good guesser. Am I wrong?"

"Would you like something to drink?"

She smiled. "You don't like questions, do you? It's that lawyer thing. You want to be doing the asking, not the answering. That's okay. So if you're working on the campaign, you're on leave or something from your law office?"

"Something like that," he said reluctantly. "If the senator decides to run for president, I'll work for the campaign."

"The whole political thing is new to me. I vote, but that's about it. Sometimes I watch the debates. It's not really my thing."

"The democratic process is not for the timid," Alex told her. "Running for president is not a decision to be made lightly. One good scandal can destroy an honest man's chance forever."

Which meant her. "I'm not here to hurt anyone."

"That doesn't mean it's not going to happen."

Dani was used to being liked and disliked on her own merits. She wasn't perfect, but she wasn't channeling the devil, either.

Before she could point that out, a slim, well-dressed woman in her fifties walked into the room. Dani rose automatically as she took in the woman's classically beautiful features and sleek upswept hair.

Alex stood, as well, crossed to her and kissed her on the cheek. "This is Dani Buchanan," he said. "Dani, my mother, Katherine Canfield."

Katherine's dark blue eyes crinkled slightly as she smiled in welcome. "Dani. How lovely to meet you. We're delighted you could join us for dinner tonight."

Her tone was as gracious as her words. Dani knew this had to be awkward for all of them, but Katherine's smile never wavered.

The older woman turned to her son. "No drinks? Nothing to eat? Are you planning to starve her into submission?"

"I asked," he said, sounding slightly defensive. "She said she didn't want anything."

Dani stared at him. Was this a crack in dragon-boy's armor? Was his need to protect his family by harassing her about to conflict with his mother's sense of good manners?

Katherine's smile widened. "I can only imagine how graciously you inquired." She turned to Dani. "I always enjoy a glass of white wine. Would you join me?"

"I'd love to," Dani said and had to fight the urge to stick out her tongue at Alex.

He muttered something under his breath as he crossed to the small bar in the corner.

Katherine sat down and motioned for Dani to do the same. "Mark mentioned you only recently discovered your connection to him."

"That's right. It's complicated, but my grandmother told me a couple of weeks ago. I've been working up the courage to go see him."

"We have both samples for the DNA testing," Alex said as he handed first his mother, then Dani, a glass of wine. "We'll have the results in a couple of days."

Katherine smiled. "There's certainly room for one more at our table. Mark and I have

61

always wanted a large family. We made the decision to adopt all our children long before we got married. But my husband is a typical man and should you turn out to be his biological child, I know he'll be thrilled to know he's passed on the family gene pool."

Everything about Katherine screamed grace and acceptance. Dani was stunned — but in the best way possible. If their situations were reversed, Dani wasn't sure she could be so open and friendly toward her husband's unexpected child, even after all these years.

"You're being very kind," she murmured.

"Too kind," Alex said.

Katherine glanced at her son, then turned back to Dani. "You'll meet our other children tonight."

"I already met Ian."

"Oh, dear." Katherine shook her head. "Should I brace myself?"

Dani laughed. "I think he's terrific."

"And?"

"He wanted to know if I was a stripper."

"I swear, that boy. I apologize for any offense."

"Please don't," Dani told her. "He's funny and charming. I really liked him." Unlike Alex, Ian had been genuine.

"Ian deals with life in his own way. He's brilliant. Stanford has offered him a four-year scholarship, as have several Ivy League schools. He'll get a technical degree and advance to a level where we'll have nothing to talk about."

She sounded proud as she spoke.

Alex sipped his drink. "You can always ask him about the latest stripper."

Katherine sighed. "I should have adopted only girls."

Dani laughed. "You love him. I can hear it in your voice."

"Of course I do," Katherine said. "He's my son."

There was such acceptance in her tone. The Canfield children were very lucky to have her in their lives. Mark was, too.

"We are telling them you're a friend of the family," Katherine continued. "Until we have confirmation on your relationship with Mark."

"Of course," Dani said quickly. "Even if I am Mark's daughter, there's no rush on letting anyone know. I don't want to make any trouble."

Something flickered in Katherine's eyes, but before Dani could figure out what it was, she heard the sound of running footsteps. Dani looked toward the door as several children rushed inside.

It was common knowledge that the Canfields had deliberately chosen special needs children when they'd decided to adopt. Two, a teenage girl and a younger boy, had Down's syndrome. The other children's issues were less visible. She glanced at Alex. All she knew about his past was that he'd been adopted when he was eight or nine. So what was his story and why had Katherine picked him?

Katherine held out her arms. The children hurried close, all talking at once. She touched and greeted each one, moving her hands as she spoke to a pretty girl of eleven or twelve.

Alex was next. The group enveloped him in hugs, then bombarded him with dozens of questions.

"You didn't tell me you'd be here for dinner. Why not?"

"Did you bring me anything?"

"Did you see the Mariners game last night? They kicked butt."

Finally he pulled two young boys onto his lap and pointed at Dani. "We have company."

"That's right," Katherine said. "Dani, these are my children. You've already met Alex, of course. Julie is away at college, so

64

she won't be joining us. Next is Bailey."

"Hi."

Bailey was the older girl with Down's. She had beautiful wavy red hair and a huge smile.

"I like your hair," Dani told her.

"I like yours. I'd like it cut short, like you have it." Bailey swayed slightly as she spoke, her voice was soft.

Dani shook her head. "Trust me. Of the two of us, you have the great hair. Don't change a thing."

Bailey blushed and dropped her chin to her chest.

Katherine looked at Dani for a second, then continued with the introductions. There was Trisha, who was deaf, Quinn, who looked normal but didn't speak, then Oliver, the other child with Down's.

"Last is Sasha," Katherine said, lifting the little girl onto the sofa.

Sasha sighed heavily. "I'm always last. I hate being last. I want to go first."

"You're the baby," Bailey told her. "Everybody likes the baby."

"I want to be the oldest."

Dani crouched down in front of Sasha. "I'm the baby of my family. I have three big brothers. Sometimes it's okay, but sometimes they don't tell me anything. I hate that."

Sasha bobbed her head up and down. "Me, too."

Alex didn't realize he was tense until he started to relax. Whatever Dani's intentions, she was doing okay with the kids. Unlike his ex-wife, who had never known how to deal with them. At least she'd left. Having Fiona at the table would have added a whole new level of awkward.

As he watched his siblings, he was reminded that the world wasn't always kind. In some ways, Ian had it the easiest. Everyone knew there was a problem the second they saw him. He was either accepted or rejected in an instant. But for kids like Trisha or Sasha, who was HIV positive, things could be more tricky.

He watched as Bailey studied Dani. His sister seemed enchanted by their guest. He shouldn't be surprised. Bailey was nearly fifteen — she was growing up.

Oliver pulled an action figure out of his pocket and showed it to Dani. She bent over the plastic toy and listened to his slow explanation of the figure's powers. She glanced at Katherine, who signed with Trisha.

What did she think of all this? Was it what

she expected? She was either genuine or putting on a hell of a show. He couldn't decide which.

His father's study door opened and Mark walked into the room. The other kids immediately rushed over to him and began battling for his attention. He gave Alex and Katherine an absent smile, then looked at Dani. For a moment, he seemed to forget who she was. Then he smiled.

"You're here, Dani."

Katherine rose. "Why don't we all go in to dinner? Alex, will you escort our guest?"

"Of course."

He moved next to Dani and offered his arm.

"That formal?" she asked quietly. "Or is this your way of making sure I don't go exploring?"

She had plenty of spirit, he thought. She wasn't afraid of him. As she stared up at him, he noticed her eyes were hazel, with long lashes. She smiled easily and she had the kind of mouth that made a man —

He mentally came to a stop. What the hell was he thinking? That she was attractive? Sexy? That he liked her?

Not possible, he told himself. She was the enemy, even if she didn't mean to be. She was nothing but trouble and he wasn't getting involved with her. He wasn't getting involved with anyone. What was that old saying? Fool me once, shame on you. Fool me twice, shame on me. He wasn't about to be fooled again.

After dinner, Mark led Dani into his study. She went willingly. While she'd enjoyed the meal and the lively conversation, it had been impossible for her to keep the children straight. She'd also been aware of Alex's unfriendly attention and Katherine's subtle study. She was emotionally exhausted by the energy of the family and doing her best not to screw up.

"What did you think?" Mark asked, after he settled into a black leather chair she suspected was his favorite, and she'd picked a place on the sofa opposite.

"You have a wonderful family."

"They're loud," he said cheerfully. "Katherine is brilliant with them. Adopting was her idea, you know. I wouldn't have thought of it. At first I wasn't sure. I didn't think I could love someone else's child as much as I could love my own. But I was wrong. They're all special to me."

"I could tell." He'd interacted with all the children. They obviously adored him.

"Katherine insists on being involved in

every aspect of their lives. We have Yvette, who helps out, but that's only so Katherine can pursue her charity work. If she didn't have that, she would be handling everything on her own. I travel a lot, back and forth to D.C. She's practically a single parent, but she never complains. It's just who she is."

As Dani had been impressed by Katherine, she agreed with the praise. But despite the words, she couldn't figure out what Mark really thought about anything.

She was being crazy, she told herself. Obviously Mark adored his wife and family. Who wouldn't? Yet she had no sense of emotion coming from him.

She reminded herself she didn't know the man. That until that morning, they'd never met. Maybe she could give him a break.

"I, ah, took the DNA test," she said. "The results should only take a couple of days."

"Good. I already know the outcome, but being sure is a good idea."

She nodded, feeling awkward. How could he be sure? And if he was, shouldn't the moment be more . . . something? She told herself not every situation could be scripted, like a TV sitcom, yet something felt missing.

"I want us to get to know each other," Mark said. "Why don't you come by the office for lunch? It will be more quiet than here."

"I'd like that," Dani said.

He probably felt as weird about all this as she did. Lunch was a great idea. After a few low-key meetings, she was sure they would start to connect. All this strangeness would fade and they would understand each other. They would be family.

Alex picked up his car keys. Dani had left a few minutes ago, so he could go home now. He'd been unwilling to leave before her, as if without him watching over her something bad would happen.

"You're frowning," Ian said as he rolled up. "You were frowning all during dinner."

"I'm cautious."

"I like her. She thinks I'm funny."

"She was being polite."

Ian grinned. Most people wouldn't know what the twisted expression meant, but Alex saw the humor Ian's uncooperative muscles tried to hide.

"You don't want anyone to know, but I think you like her, too," Ian said.

"I don't have any feelings about her." Which was almost true.

"She's pretty."

Alex shook his head. "You're seventeen.

70

You think every female is pretty."

"They're my hormones and I can use them if I want to." His grin faded. "Seriously. You should lay off her. She was cool."

Dani had reacted well to Ian, Alex thought. He would guess her past was the reason.

An afternoon on the Internet had turned up a lot of information on Danielle Buchanan, the youngest of the four Buchanan siblings. In college, her fiancé had been injured playing football. Despite the fact that he was a paraplegic and confined to a wheelchair, Dani had stayed with him through his intensive therapy and then had married him. She knew what it was like to live with someone who didn't fit in.

"I don't trust her," Alex said.

"Because she's Dad's real kid?"

Alex stared at his brother. "Why would you say that?"

Ian rolled his eyes. "I'm stealthy, remember? I heard Mom and Dad talking earlier. I know who she is."

There was worry and fear in his voice. Alex dropped to a crouch and took Ian's twisted hand in his own. "We don't know for sure yet. The DNA tests will take a couple of days. But even if she is Dad's daughter, you're still his son. This is your family and you're not getting away from us."

"She's normal."

"All the more reason not to like her."

Ian grinned again. "I saw you looking at her during dinner. You thought she was hot."

Alex straightened. "She's okay."

"You need to get laid."

"I'm not having this conversation with my seventeen-year-old brother."

"You don't have my good looks and charm," Ian told him. "But you could still go for it. Unless I get there first. We're adopted. It's not like she's a biological sister. Think she'd want to go to prom with me?"

"She's too old for you."

"You know what they say about older women."

Alex squeezed Ian's shoulder. "Go torture someone else. I'll see you in a couple of days."

"So you're going for it with her? Because if you're not, I want to know."

"Say good-night, Ian."

"Good night, Ian."

CHAPTER FOUR

Dani pulled up in front of Gloria's house. Climbing out of her car, she stared at the elegant, three-story building that had been constructed nearly a hundred years ago.

When she'd been little, the house had terrified her. As a teenager, it had represented a way of life she couldn't understand. In her early twenties, she'd seen the structure as something to be conquered. Later, it was like her grandmother — unapproachable and solitary. Now it was just Gloria's house. Not good, not bad, just a place where someone lived. Someone who wasn't the person she'd first imagined.

She'd both loved and hated Gloria for so long, it was hard to let go of either feeling. She'd resented the other woman's harshness in declaring that Dani wasn't a real Buchanan. But in the past few weeks, Gloria had apologized several times for what she'd done. She'd claimed to have changed and from Dani's perspective, she actually had.

Oddly, Dani found herself missing Gloria as her grandmother. Not the meanness or the impossible standards, but the connection. Gloria had been a part of her world since her birth and now they weren't related at all. Perhaps the smartest decision would be to walk away but Dani couldn't bring herself to let go.

She climbed the steps to the front door and rang the bell. Reid, the middle of her three brothers, opened it and grinned at her.

"We're not interested, but thanks for coming by."

She pushed past him before he could close the door. "Very funny."

"Hey, kid." Reid wrapped an arm around her. "How are you doing?"

"Good. Dealing with a lot of stuff."

Reid led her into the living room, where Cal, her oldest brother, and Walker, her youngest, waited. Both men greeted her. Cal handed her a latte from The Daily Grind, which he owned, then hugged her.

"Gloria will be out in a minute," Walker said as he pulled Dani close. "How are you holding up?"

She looked at her three brothers, the men who had been there for her any time she'd needed them and a lot of times when she hadn't. "I'm okay. I feel weird — sort of disconnected from my life."

They settled on the sofas in the huge living room. Dani ignored the city view in favor of her brothers.

"I met Mark Canfield yesterday," she said.

"And?" Walker asked.

"And, I don't know. He was very open to the possibility of me being his daughter. He admitted to the affair with Mom and said he never knew why she broke things off. He was nice and friendly. . . ."

"But?" Cal prompted.

"I don't know. I didn't feel any connection. I guess I had this fantasy that we'd run into each other's arms and instantly bond. I'm still trying to deal." She sipped her coffee. "Adding to the excitement is Alex Canfield, his oldest son. Alex sees himself as the protector of all things Canfield and me as a threat to his family in general and his father's presidential campaign in particular."

"Want Walker to take care of him?" Reid asked cheerfully. "He will. I'm guessing there won't even be a stain where Alex once stood. It will be like he never existed at all."

"I'm not sure we need to go that far," Dani said, remembering how Alex had annoyed her, but also how she'd kind of liked him. She respected his loyalty to his family, even if it drove her crazy.

"I went over to the house last night," she continued. "I met the whole clan. There are eight kids — okay, one of them was at college, and Katherine, Mark's wife. She's incredible. Beautiful and patient and all the kids have issues, but that doesn't matter. She's like a saint. I think I want to be her when I grow up."

"That all sounds good," Cal said. "So what's the problem?"

"I don't know. I keep feeling like I'm living someone else's life. That none of this is about me. I wanted to know who my father was, but I never expected this. Why can't he just be a plumber or sales executive? Why did he have to be a senator?"

Reid glared at her. "You're not going to choose them over us. Just so you're clear. You're one of us and we're not letting you go."

She smiled. "I know. You'll always be my big brothers, which is both good and bad."

"You're damn lucky to have us," Cal reminded her.

"Of course I am, and you reminding me over and over really helps." She looked at Walker. "I just want to know where I belong."

"Why not here?" he asked.

"Because there's more. I don't have your history. Not anymore."

She could see he wanted to disagree. They all did. While she appreciated how much they loved her, she wasn't sure they could understand what it had been like to find out she wasn't really a Buchanan. That her father was someone she'd never known.

"Just don't get any big ideas about turning your back on us," Reid muttered.

"I won't," she promised. "So that's my life. New father, new siblings and I'm loving my job at Bella Roma. What about with you three?"

Walker cleared his throat. "I'm hiring on permanently. Taking over the company." He looked at Dani. "I know it's what you wanted, but you said you'd changed your mind."

It was so like him to worry about her, she thought happily, feeling the love and support from all three of them. "I never wanted the company," she corrected. "I wanted to run one of the restaurants. Now I have something close to that. Sure it's not Buchanan's or The Waterfront, but it's still good. I'm glad you're part of the business, and a little surprised that Gloria would be so willing to leave you in charge."

"She's getting older," Walker said. "She knows she can't handle it all now."

"I'm not *that* old."

The strong voice came from the woman standing in the doorway. Dani looked at Gloria Buchanan, well dressed as always, as straight-backed as ever, barely leaning on the cane she now used to get around.

"I can handle it if I want to," Gloria continued. "I simply choose not to."

Dani's brothers rose as Gloria walked into the living room. Reid ushered his grandmother to a chair and everyone sat.

Dani eyed the woman who had been such a large part of her childhood. Doing well to impress Gloria had once meant everything to her. The praise had been hard-won and more meaningful because of it . . . until Dani had entered her teens and there hadn't been any more praise.

The old woman had been difficult and cruel, yet Dani still found herself missing Gloria. Which probably meant she, Dani, needed some serious time in therapy.

"Thank you all for coming," Gloria said, smiling at them, then leaning forward and touching Dani's hand. "I know you're all busy."

The touch was familiar and made Dani's chest tighten. A few years ago, a hint of kindness would have meant the world. After years of rejection Dani had done her best not to care what the old woman thought of her. Now Gloria was trying to reconnect and Dani wasn't sure what to do about that. Did she trust again or not?

"I want to talk about my estate," Gloria continued.

"Why?" Walker asked bluntly. "What aren't you telling us?"

"Nothing. Don't get too excited. I'm not dying anytime soon. I'm simply getting things in order. I'm unlikely to live forever."

Dani wondered if Gloria's recent medical trouble had made mortality seem more real. She wasn't sure how she felt about that.

"I'm worth a lot," Gloria said. "My shares in the family business alone are worth several million. I have investments, this house, some real estate, that sort of thing. I'm dividing it up for all of you."

Dani wanted to run. She didn't want to hear about all this. She was happy for her brothers, but as she wasn't actually Gloria's grandchild, there was no reason for her to —

"I'm dividing my estate into fourths," Gloria added.

None of her brothers reacted, but Dani felt as if she'd been struck by lightning. She couldn't hear, couldn't speak and sure as hell couldn't understand what was happening.

"Why?" Dani asked without thinking. "I'm not a Buchanan."

Gloria turned to her. "Of course you are, child. I'm sorry about what I said before. How cruel I was to you. There aren't any excuses. Not really. I wish I could have been different for you. I can't change the past, but I can make sure you know that you matter to me. That you all matter. The estate will be divided equally in value. Reid and Lori will get the house in a few years, when they're done with that ridiculous houseboat of his and are ready to start their family. Walker is taking over the business, so he'll get more shares. Dani will get my jewelry, along with a stake in the company. Cal, I happen to be a major stockholder in the Daily Grind. I'll turn that over to you."

Cal frowned. "I know the major stockholders. You're not one of them."

"You don't know the name of my holding company."

He swore under his breath. "You're good."

"No, but I should have been. Now don't expect to get anything right away. I haven't changed that much. But I wanted you to know it was there for you."

Reid stood and pulled Gloria to her feet. Then he hugged her. Dani rose and found herself pulled into the embrace. Soon they were all hugging and for Dani, it felt long overdue.

A few minutes later, the party broke up. Her brothers headed out, but Dani lingered. Gloria settled back on the sofa.

"Tell me about your meeting with your father."

Dani gave her a brief outline of what had happened. "I thought there would be more," she admitted. "I guess that's not fair."

"Sometimes we don't know our expectations until we're in the situation," Gloria told her. "Alex sounds interesting."

Dani laughed. "Are you matchmaking? Don't bother. My luck with men is hideous. Besides, he's so the wrong guy for me. We're practically related."

"You're not blood relatives at all. How was Katherine?"

"Elegant. Gracious." Dani sighed as she remembered the other woman's patience with her children. "Their family is like something out of a movie. All those kids and the household runs smoothly. Ian's in a wheelchair and a couple of the kids have Down's syndrome. Trisha's deaf. I know the others are special-needs kids, as well, but I don't know the reasons."

"Why that woman would burden herself and her husband that way is beyond me," Gloria said. "Who needs eight children with problems? It's ridiculous. She's practically a martyr. Does she want to be on a stamp?"

The mini outburst was vintage Gloria. Dani couldn't help smiling. "So you haven't changed totally."

Gloria sighed. "Apparently not. But I'm working on it. I've met Katherine a few times. She's lovely and gracious — reasons why we were never close."

"She was so nice to me. I don't think I would have been able to act that way if I'd been her."

"Perhaps not. Still, watch yourself. The situation is complicated." Gloria shook her head. "You'll do what you want to do. You've always been stubborn."

"I get that from you," Dani said, then pressed her lips together. "I mean —"

Gloria grabbed her hand. "Stop! Stop backtracking. You do get that from me. Maybe it's just from watching me be stubborn all your life. Dani, I still want to be your grandmother. We have a history. I want you to think about forgiving me for all I did. Is that possible?"

Dani wasn't sure. Did forgiveness imply

trust? Because she wasn't totally ready to believe Gloria wouldn't turn on her again. Still, under the circumstances, saying "Of course it's possible," seemed the right thing to do.

Dani flipped through the receipts for the night. Not bad for a Wednesday, she thought as she did a quick mental tally. Nick's pasta special had been a huge hit and they'd sold a fair number of her wine pairings, as well.

It had taken Dani the better part of a week to convince Bernie to offer wine pairing suggestions. He kept telling her that guests found it insulting to be told what wine went with what foods. As if the management assumed they were too stupid to figure it out themselves.

Dani argued that people liked being given ideas that allowed them to try a wine they might not have taken a chance on otherwise.

Their compromise had been to add a wine pairing to half the specials and see if they sold. She had a feeling Bernie would want to add more pairings to other items on the menu.

Her minor success pleased her. She wanted to do well in her work. This was her first real job outside the Buchanan empire, so in her mind, it was a make-it or break-it situation.

"Dani, one of our guests wants to talk to you. He didn't say why."

Dani smiled at the server. "Thanks, Eddie. Which table?"

"Fifteen."

"I'll head right over."

A request to see a manager could mean anything from a tirade to praise for exceptional service. Things ran smoothly enough at Bella Roma that Dani wasn't worried.

She rounded the corner and was halfway through her "Hi, I'm Dani Buchanan. How may I help you?" when she recognized the lone diner. The power suit was familiar as were the dark eyes and stubborn jaw.

"This is a surprise," she told Alex Canfield.

"I heard the food was good."

She glanced at the menu in his hand. "I take it you haven't ordered. Would you like a few suggestions?"

"Are you going to spit on my food before they bring it to me?"

She grinned. "It depends on why you're really here."

"Maybe I just want to get to know you."

"Oh, please. I may not have gone to law school and lost my humanity, but I'm not an idiot."

"You went to Cornell, which is tough to get into, and I never said you were an idiot."

As she stared down at him, it occurred to her she wasn't disappointed he'd shown up at the restaurant. Interesting. She also noticed she sort of enjoyed bantering with him. They were both verbal and quick.

But he hadn't answered the question — why was he here?

"Being an idiot was implied," she said.

He motioned to the chair across from his. "You could join me."

"Or I could not."

He glanced around at the dining room. "It's after nine. Your dinner crowd has left. Have dinner with me. We'll get to know each other. I'll even let you pick the topics we discuss."

Somehow she doubted that. He'd been less than friendly the last time they'd been together. She was ambivalent — understanding his need to protect his family and hating that she was considered the enemy. Still, she pulled out a chair and sat down. "I want to order the food," she told him.

"Why am I not surprised?"

"And the wine."

"Will you cut my food into tiny pieces and feed me, as well?"

"Only if you have bad table manners."

Eddie walked over and looked at her.

"Mr. Canfield and I will be having dinner together, Eddie." Dani placed the order, picking her favorites, then chose a bottle of Leonetti Cellar Sangiovese.

"Nice," Alex said when Eddie left. "The wine's a little pricey."

"It's worth it. Besides, you're rich. You can afford it."

He raised his eyebrows. "You're assuming I'm buying."

"You did the inviting."

"This is your place."

"Fine. You can take advantage of my employee discount."

He nodded. "I appreciate that." He passed her the bread basket. "How are you enjoying your job here?"

The implication being it was a new job. She wasn't surprised he knew that — no doubt dragon-boy had investigated every aspect of her life.

"I like it a lot. Bernie and his mother are great. I know Mama Giuseppe makes everyone crazy, but I think she's very entertaining. The kitchen staff are terrified of her. I like the food, the staff and the regulars. I hope to be here a long time."

"Why the restaurant business?" he asked.

"I never thought about doing anything

else. I grew up as a Buchanan. I want to say it's in my blood, but I guess that isn't true. It's what I know. Why did you go to law school?"

"My soul was getting in the way of being a ruthless bastard. I knew they'd suck it out of me."

She glared at him. "I answered *your* question seriously."

"Fair enough. I wanted to do the right thing. Be on the right side of the law. For that, I needed to understand it."

That surprised her. "You consider yourself an idealist?"

"Why not?"

"You're in corporate law and you're working on a presidential campaign. Is there idealism left in either place?"

"Democracy is alive and well."

"So is the need to raise millions of dollars for nearly every kind of campaign."

"We can still make a difference, either on a local and individual basis, or nationally and globally."

He was serious. She hadn't expected that.

"I'm getting worried," she admitted. "I don't want to have to like you."

"I'm totally charming."

"Not to me."

"It's a subtle charm."

"Apparently."

Eddie appeared with the bottle of wine. After he opened it, she hesitated, as if not sure who would do the tasting. Alex gestured to Dani. "Please. It's your party."

She nodded at Eddie, who poured her a sample. Dani swirled, inhaled, then tasted. "Excellent," she said. "Thanks."

Eddie poured, then left.

Alex sipped the wine. "Nice," he said.

"I like it." She eyed him. She had a feeling she knew the reason for his visit. So did his friendliness mean she was Mark's daughter or not?

"You're being nice, in a twisted kind of way," she said, deciding there was no reason to be subtle. "It's been two days. You have the results. I'm trying to decide how your presence here and attempts to get to know me figure into things."

His humor faded. "It's a match. You're Mark Canfield's daughter."

Dani set down her wineglass and braced herself for a flood of emotion. There wasn't any. Not elation or happiness or even an internal "golly wow." There was nothing.

"Okay," she said slowly, wondering if the feelings were going to be delayed. "Good to know."

"Are you going to the press?"

The blunt, almost rude question didn't surprise her. This was the Alex Canfield she remembered.

"What do you think?" she asked. "You've had plenty of time to delve into my background, interview my friends and tap my phone. Am I going to the press?"

She couldn't read his dark eyes. His body language was relaxed as he took a sip of the wine. He could have been mulling over how his stock portfolio had performed that day, or developing a way to murder her and leave her body in the woods.

How did this impact him? He was Mark Canfield's oldest son . . . by adoption. She was Mark's biological child. Did Alex have any feelings about that? Did he resent her or wasn't she significant enough to generate emotion?

"You have money, or at least access to it," Alex said at last. "So that's not why you came looking for the senator. I don't think it was for publicity, either."

"Grudging, but there it is," she murmured as she took a slice of bread and spread on garlic butter. "Acceptance. I'm touched. Deeply. I might even tear up."

"I have reason to be suspicious," he told her. "Your timing, for one thing."

"I contacted the senator within days of

finding out he might be my father."

"So you say."

She sighed. "I like you better when you're not assuming the worst about me."

"Do you know what a scandal could do to the campaign?" he asked. "How you could destroy everything we've been working toward?"

She tilted her head. "If I'm just in it for notoriety, don't I have a built-in reason for wanting to keep the news to myself? Wouldn't I have more fun with Daddy as president?"

"Interesting logic."

"I'm an interesting person."

He shrugged. "So it seems."

Okay — *that* was unexpected. Was it possible that, despite everything, dragon-boy liked her? She found herself warming to the thought.

She leaned toward him. "Admit it. You might have been wrong about me. I just might be an okay person."

"Maybe."

"Probably."

"I'll accept that."

He shook his head and grinned. "You're not easy, are you?"

"Never," she said, but she wasn't really focused on her answer. Instead she found herself caught up in what Alex's smile had done to his expression. For a brief second, he'd seemed approachable and funny and sexy as hell.

Interest perked up and stretched. Anticipation sniffed the air. Heat rolled over and made her insides quiver.

Dani recognized the signs. Attraction to a man. Something she'd sworn off of. No way, no how, not ever. Or at least until she stopped picking the wrong guy.

Alex might not be a lying, cheating weasel or an until recently ordained-into-service-to-God kind of guy, but he was the adopted son of her newly discovered biological father and deeply involved in said man's campaign for president. Getting involved was not remotely logical or sensible or even sane.

Not that it mattered. He wasn't the least bit interested in her. He probably didn't actually realize she was female. She was simply an impediment with a name.

So she did what made sense — she ignored her hormones, pretended Alex was charming, but gay, and leaned in to enjoy a yummy dinner accompanied by a great side of dragon baiting.

"You can't really believe that," Alex said as Eddie cleared the dessert plates.

"Why not?" Dani asked, humor brightening her hazel eyes. "The rich can afford it. Having everyone who makes over five hundred thousand a year financially sponsor a poor child makes perfect sense."

She was bullshitting, he thought, both frustrated and amused. She was smart and quick, but determined to find every button he had and stomp on it.

"I'm changing the subject," he said. "You're not being serious."

"Is serious required?"

"It helps."

"You're a little stuffy. I think it's the lawyer thing. We should —" She glanced at her watch. "Yikes. I'm keeping staff here late. That's not good."

He checked the time and saw it was after eleven. How had that happened? He would have guessed they'd been there an hour at most.

Dani stood. "I hate to make you eat and run, but I've got to get everyone out of here or they'll hate me forever. Dinner's on me."

He rose. "I don't think so."

"Don't get all macho on me, Alex. Seriously. Bernie won't even let me pay for it, so we're good. I appreciate you stopping by. Now leave."

"Ever gracious. When do you go home?"

"In about fifteen minutes."

"I'll wait."

She frowned at him. "Why?"

"I'll walk you to your car. It's late. You shouldn't go to your car alone."

She rolled her eyes. "I do it every time I work dinner, yet I've managed to survive. I appreciate the offer, but I'm good."

He shrugged into his suit jacket. "I'll wait."

She sighed. "I recognize that stubborn tone of voice. Fine. You can sit by the door."

"I live to serve."

"If only that were true."

He used the time to check his cell phone. There was a call from his mother.

He called back on her private line, which only rang in her office. If she'd already gone to bed, it wouldn't disturb her.

"You're working late," he said when she answered.

"So are you."

"I just finished dinner."

"A campaign dinner," she said. "You're working too hard."

He hesitated, then decided not to tell her otherwise. "I could say the same about you."

"Then we both need to reform. You mentioned you might come by later?"

"It would be close to midnight."

"I'll be up another hour at least."

"Then I'll be by."

He hung up just as Dani walked toward him with her purse over her shoulder. She wore a fitted red dress that emphasized her curves but covered her completely. It was a combination designed to make a man crazy.

He'd done his best to be immune to her physical charms, but he'd noticed all of them. The curves, the big eyes, the easy smile.

"Are you armed?" she asked. "Are we going to fight our way to my car, do you think? What about snipers? We could scurry along the perimeter of the building. Of course you're so big and strong, I don't really have to worry."

She was making fun of him. It should have bugged the hell out of him. Instead he found himself wanting to lean in and kiss her.

Kiss her? Where had that come from? Sure she was pretty and sexy and funny, but so what? He wasn't interested. Not in *her*. She was the enemy, or at the very least, a big problem. Yet once the thought shot into his head, he couldn't seem to let it go.

"We'll risk the snipers," he said as he pulled open the door.

"Oooh, you're so brave," she cooed. "I'm

over there."

She pointed to a late year import. He followed her to the car and waited while she dug her keys out of her purse. When she waved them in front of her, he started to take a step back.

At least that had been the plan. But instead of moving away, he found himself moving forward. Until they were close. Very close.

"You're a pain in the ass," he said.

"Right back at you."

"You should be afraid of me."

She pretended to yawn. "I'm sorry. Were you talking? I couldn't hear anything just then."

She made him crazy. So he kissed her.

He put his hand on the back of her neck, bent down and pressed his mouth to hers.

She went totally still. For once she didn't have a snappy comeback. Instead she rested one of her hands on his chest and softened her mouth against his.

Heat exploded between them like a fireball. Long-forgotten need flared until every part of him was hard, hot and ready. The desire was as immediate as it was powerful. Suddenly the hood of her car looked plenty inviting.

He brushed his tongue against her lower

lip and she parted for him. He dived inside, wanting to claim her and arouse her until she was as desperate as he was.

He put his hand on her waist and pulled her close. She melted into him, her body supple and soft, touching him in all the right places.

She tasted of wine and whipped cream. Even better, she matched his urgency with quiet moans.

It was a kiss of desperate lovers, one that left him shaken with a passion he'd never experienced before. All that in less than a minute and with the one woman he should never be with.

Reality returned in the form of male laughter coming from behind the restaurant. He drew back just as Dani pulled away.

They stared at each other in the overhead lights of the parking lot. She looked stunned, which was exactly how he felt.

She swallowed. "That can't be good. Us kissing. Like that."

Her breathing was still ragged. Considering he was hard enough to rupture steel, he appreciated knowing it hadn't been a party for one.

"Agreed."

She exhaled slowly. "To quote Julia Roberts in *Pretty Woman* — big mistake. Huge."

"Epic."

"Epic's good."

Her eyes were dark, her mouth swollen. He wanted her again. He wanted her naked and he wanted to kiss her everywhere. He wanted to hear her scream and feel her come for him.

Damn.

"You are so the wrong man," she whispered. "I couldn't be a worse woman. Well, that doesn't sound right, but you know what I mean."

He nodded. "So it never happened," he told her.

She gave a strangled laugh. "Right. Like we're going to believe that."

CHAPTER FIVE

Alex let himself into his parents' house and made his way to his mother's study. He paused in the hallway, trying to shake off a feeling of guilt. It was like being seventeen and tiptoeing in after curfew. Except he wasn't a kid and he didn't live here anymore. Still, kissing Dani? What had he been thinking?

He hadn't, he reminded himself. That was the problem. He'd been reacting — to her, to circumstances. The kiss hadn't meant anything. How could it? She was a complication in all their lives.

Yet his sexual reaction to her hadn't faded. He still hungered for her with a powerful need that shocked him.

He ignored the desire and the memories, then lightly knocked on the closed study door.

"Come in."

He stepped into the small cozy room and

smiled at his mother. "You're still up."

She rose and stepped around her desk to kiss him on the cheek. "I said I would be." She took his hand and led him to the small sofa by the window. "I suddenly have reports due on all my charities. It always happens this time of year and I'm always surprised. I wish I were one of those organized women who go through life with a plan."

"You have eight children. You get slack."

She smiled as she angled toward him on the couch. "You and Julie are both living on your own. Ian is more independent by the day."

Alex smiled. "So you're only worrying about five children, then. You're right. You should do better."

She laughed. "I see your point. I can make excuses if I want and people will understand. Honestly, I'd prefer to be more together, but I'll take what I can get."

And she would do it all because duty came first. She believed that and she'd raised him to believe it, too.

Alex remembered the first time he'd seen Katherine Canfield. He remembered her eyes — how blue they'd been and how kind. She'd touched him as they'd spoken. Her hand on his, her fingers on his shoulder. No adults ever touched him, except to hit him.

99

The other boys had tried to beat him up, but he'd been tough.

She'd been pretty and gentle and when she'd smiled he'd known he would do anything for her if only she would take him home and adopt him.

She had. She'd loved him with a fierceness that had made him feel safe for the first time in his life. She had a heart that gave and gave. Sometimes, when he saw her with his father, he wondered if she gave too much . . . to all of them.

Now, he took her hand and gently squeezed her fingers.

"Mom," he began, only to have her shake her head.

"Don't worry about speeches," she said quietly, her gaze meeting his. "I already know. Dani is Mark's daughter."

"How did you guess?"

She shrugged. "I sensed it the moment I saw her. There's plenty of Mark in her appearance — the way she holds her head, the shape of her chin. Your father will be delighted."

"What about you?" he asked.

She leaned toward him. "That's my question for you. How are you handling all this?"

"Finding out he has a biological daughter?"

Katherine nodded. "It doesn't mean anything. You know that, right? It doesn't change how he feels about you."

That's what Alex had told Ian. Neither of them had believed it then and Alex didn't believe it now.

"Everything changes," he told his mother. "The family dynamic has fundamentally shifted. Am I questioning my place in the universe? No."

"I'm more concerned about your place in this family and how you think this will affect your relationship with your father."

Alex didn't know if it would. Mark wasn't like Katherine. He loved his children, but there was always a distance. Would that be there for Dani or not?

"You're his wife," he said. "Are you okay with this?"

Katherine leaned back in the sofa and sighed. "Do I get a choice?" she asked.

"He didn't cheat on you. You were back East when he met Marsha Buchanan."

His mother nodded slowly. "You're right. I've told myself that. It's just . . ." She looked at him. "We'd been engaged before he returned to Seattle. We had a big fight and I broke up with him. He left and came back here. That's when he met Marsha."

Alex swore silently. Why did life have to

get more and more complicated? So Mark's affair with Marsha Buchanan wasn't as disconnected from Katherine as Alex had first thought.

What had they fought about? Did his mother care that Mark had gotten involved with someone else so quickly?

Stupid question, he told himself. Katherine would have been devastated. Had she known about Marsha before Dani had shown up?

"I'm sorry," he said awkwardly, not knowing what he could say.

"It's fine," she told him. "Don't worry about it."

But he did worry. He'd always wondered why his parents hadn't had children of their own. He'd assumed it was a conscious decision. A choice. Katherine talked about wanting to make a difference in the world, one child at a time. But was there another reason? Mark was obviously capable of fathering a child. Did Katherine have a problem?

He felt disloyal for even thinking the question, so he pushed it away. What the hell did it matter why? She was an amazing woman.

"I'm glad you picked me," he said. "Grateful. You made me who I am."

She touched his face. "I loved you from the first moment I saw you, Alex. But I didn't make you anything. You are the man you were meant to be. I'm so proud of you, but I won't take any credit. Flowers, maybe, but not credit."

He laughed. "I'll send starburst lilies in the morning." They were her favorite.

He didn't know what other children felt about their parents. How much they loved them or why. He could only go by the little he remembered of his biological mother and what he knew Katherine had done for him — even if she wasn't willing to accept his thanks.

"I always wanted a big family," Katherine said lightly. "Now we have one more."

She said the right things, she even smiled as she spoke. But her pain was alive and tangible. He needed to help, but didn't know how. Katherine had given him everything and in her time of need, all he could do was stand by and watch her suffer.

Dani's second trip to Mark Canfield's campaign headquarters was only slightly less scary than her first one had been. While she wasn't in danger of being tossed out on her butt, she was about to have a private one-on-one lunch with her biological father for the first time in her life.

What if they didn't have anything to say to each other? What if he didn't like her? What if he thought she was boring and wished she'd never found him?

"Not going to happen," she murmured to herself. "I'm charming."

The attempt at humor did nothing for the nerves doing Pilates in her stomach.

Dani walked inside the warehouse and gave her name to the receptionist. The young woman smiled.

"The senator is expecting you," she said. "Just wait here and Heidi will be out to take you back."

"Thanks."

Heidi? Heidi who?

She searched her memory and finally recalled the assistant who served as Mark Canfield's right hand wherever he went.

Dani hovered by the sofa, but didn't sit down. She was too nervous. The whole "this is my father" thing was still a weird statement rather than an actual part of her life. She didn't know Mark Canfield and he didn't know her. So far their blood ties hadn't helped form an emotional connection.

She was hoping this lunch would change that. Some private time could make all the difference.

Heidi walked up and smiled. "Hi, Dani. Welcome. The senator just got off a call with Washington and is available now. If you'll follow me."

Heidi led the way down hallways to a conference room. She motioned for Dani to step inside, then left. Dani glanced around at the bare space — aside from the long table and ten chairs, there was no other furniture, no decorations. At least the campaign wasn't spending money on anything frivolous.

Seconds later the door opened and Mark walked into the room. He smiled at her.

"Dani. You're here. Good, good. Alex told you the happy news?"

He approached as he talked, then unexpectedly pulled her close for a quick hug. When he released her, he gazed into her eyes.

"I knew who you were from the moment we met. I'm not surprised. You're so much like your mother. She was a wonderful woman. Beautiful, just like you."

Dani was willing to go as far as pretty or attractive, but she liked being told she looked like her mother. She could barely remember the woman. She'd been so young when Marsha had died that she wondered if her memories were hers at all, or just recollections formed from the stories she'd been told by her brothers and Gloria.

Mark perched on the edge of the table. "I remember the first time I saw your mother. It was a cold rainy day." He grinned. "Winter in Seattle — it's always cold and rainy." He shrugged. "It was the downtown Bon Marche. Marsha had her three boys with her. The youngest two were in a stroller and the oldest was still only four or five. She was struggling with the door to get inside. There was something about the way she looked, so determined. I jumped in to help, her eyes met mine, she smiled, and I was lost."

Dani sank into one of the chairs. "Just like that?"

Mark nodded. "We talked for a few minutes. I was about to leave, even though I didn't want to, when your oldest brother . . ."

"Cal?" she offered.

"Right. Cal said he needed to go to the bathroom. He said he was too old to go into the ladies' room with his mother and she didn't want him to go into the men's room alone. So I took him. Not the most romantic beginning, I know, but there was something about her."

Mark was traditionally handsome, with clear blue eyes and a ready smile. Dani had seen his face on billboards and in the newspaper, not to mention on TV. But until this moment, she'd never really *seen* the man himself. As he talked about her mother and the past, he finally seemed real.

He shook his head. "I can't believe how clear that day is to me. I invited your mother to lunch. When the hostess seated us, she assumed we were a family. That should have shaken me, but I remember thinking how right I felt with Marsha and her boys. We talked for hours." He looked at Dani, his expression slightly chagrined. "That was it. I fell for her that day."

A thousand questions crowded into Dani's brain. She had just started to ask the first one when the door opened and several people stepped inside, including Heidi pushing a cart with sandwiches and drinks on it.

"Oh, good," Mark said as he stood. "Lunch. Dani, who do you know here?"

She started to say "No one" when Alex entered the room. She rose to her feet, almost as if she needed to get away from him . . . or what she remembered about him.

She hadn't seen him in a couple of days. Not since he'd shown up at Bella Roma, wined her, dined her and kissed her.

The meal she could justify, but there was no way that kiss made sense. Of course her romantic life had been a disaster of epic proportions for nearly a year, so why would she think it would get any better now?

She braced herself for the sexual impact, then bravely met his gaze. Despite his casual, "Hello," she felt heat spiral through her. It paused in the most interesting places before moving on.

"Alex," she said calmly, ignoring the sudden visual of him taking her right there on the big table. He nodded, apparently far more able to dismiss the past than she was.

Mark introduced the other three people. There were two men and a woman, all in their midthirties, all in suits, looking professional and energized as they took seats at the table. It was only when Alex pulled out a chair and stared at her pointedly that she realized this wasn't a private lunch with her father. She was one of a crowd.

Disappointment tightened her chest. Had she misunderstood the invitation? She replayed it in her mind and realized he'd said lunch, but hadn't said they would be alone. She'd assumed.

Okay, this wasn't what she'd expected, but it was still fine. A political working lunch could be interesting.

She sat next to Alex, across from her father. Sandwiches and bags of chips were distributed, then one of the two guys whose name she didn't catch leaned forward.

"We can run numbers," he said. "A simple poll about the governor of Kansas. Midwestern sensibilities are dead on for us."

"Numbers would help," the woman added.

"We don't need numbers," Mark said. "Not yet. Alex, what are your thoughts on the poll?"

"It's going to come out eventually."

Dani felt as if she'd been dropped in the middle of a secret meeting. When Mark turned his attention to the other two men, she leaned toward Alex.

"What are they talking about?"

"You."

She blinked at him. You, as in her? "What do I have to do with anything?"

His dark gaze was as impersonal as if they'd never met. As if he'd never pulled her into his arms and claimed her with a kiss that had left her breathless.

How did he do that? Should she be insulted or impressed by his ability to compartmentalize?

"When word gets out that you're the

senator's daughter, we're going to have a situation to deal with."

A situation? She was a situation? "I'm not going to tell anyone," she said, glaring at him. "Stop assuming the worst about me."

"No one's doing that," Mark told her. "Information gets leaked. It's a reality of the political climate today. No one wants it to happen, but it will. We need to be prepared."

"Who knows?" the woman asked.

Mark looked at Alex, who glanced around the room. "We do. Katherine, Dani's family."

"No one in my family is going to say anything," Dani said, making a mental note to tell them all not to. "We don't have a whole lot of press contact."

"Katherine will be telling the children," Mark told them.

"That's not a good idea," one of the suits said. "Kids blab."

"It's what Katherine wants," Mark said calmly. "Family is important to her."

And Katherine was obviously important to him. Dani liked that. She liked that Mark had made it so clear he'd fallen for her mother and that now he was standing up for his wife. That meant he was a good guy, right?

She wished they could have spent more time together, just the two of them. But with him running for president, his time was limited. So they would get to know each other slowly.

She glanced around the room. Nothing about the space spoke of a national campaign for the highest office in the country. But it was happening. Her biological father was running for president.

Just thinking the statement made her want to giggle. She was so normal she was practically boring. She didn't belong in a world like this. Yet here she was — an unexpected member of the Canfield clan.

The lunch meeting wrapped up in less than an hour. Before Dani could circle around the table to speak to her father again, Mark was ushered out of the room by the suit guys.

She stared after him, trying not to feel snubbed.

Alex picked up the pad of paper he'd brought in with him. "He has a couple of conference calls," he said. "It's not about you."

She was torn, appreciating the kind words and wondering if she looked like a lost and abandoned waif. "Thanks. This is different for me. It's going to take me a while to figure everything out."

"It'll get easier."

He motioned for her to lead the way out of the room. As she stepped past him, he put his hand on the small of her back.

The touch was polite at best, but her body wanted to read a whole lot more into it. She could feel each individual finger pressing against her. The need to step into the touch flooded her until she had to concentrate so hard on *not* stepping closer that she was afraid she was going to trip.

"You've, ah, got a head start on me," she said, hoping she didn't sound flustered or stupid. "And can we talk about how weird it is that we're not related but we can technically both call him Dad?"

Alex smiled at her. "I call him the senator."

"I probably should, too, huh?"

"You're not on his staff."

"Not unless he plans on getting into the restaurant business." She sighed. "Is there a book or something — *Dealing with Unexpected Biological Parents for Dummies*? I could really use that."

Alex grinned.

Her mouth smiled in return. It was an involuntary response to a sexy grin by a handsome man she liked. Their eyes locked, and suddenly she was reliving that kiss in real time.

It had been good. Better than good. It had been hot and exciting and really, really tempting.

Oh, God. Talk about a mistake. There were fifteen reasons why they could never get together. It was . . .

They rounded a corner and she saw Katherine walking toward them. Dani instantly stepped away from Alex, fighting a surge of guilt, which was so weird. She hadn't been doing anything wrong.

She was so caught up in acting normal and blameless that it took her a second to notice the tall, incredibly beautiful woman at Katherine's side.

The four of them came to a stop.

"Dani!" Katherine said, sounding delighted to see her. "How wonderful to run into you." She leaned close and kissed Dani's cheek. "I want to be the first to welcome you to the family."

Katherine's graciousness awed Dani. Was the woman real? "Thank you. You're more than kind."

"I am many things, but they're not all good," Katherine said with a laugh. "Dani, this is Fiona, my former daughter-in-law.

Fiona, Dani Buchanan, Mark's daughter."

"Hi," Dani said, as she processed the information.

"Nice to meet you," the slender redhead said absently. Her attention was totally focused on Alex.

Former daughter-in-law? Dani turned to Alex. His ex?

Fiona pushed past her and slipped her arm through Alex's. "I need to talk to you, darling. Do you have a minute?"

She pulled him away before he could answer.

Katherine stared after them. "We were all so sorry things didn't work out between them. But maybe with time . . ."

Dani glanced between Katherine and the retreating couple. Alex had been married to the redheaded goddess? Of course. He couldn't have been with someone average. Who was next on his to-date list? Halle Berry? Scarlett Johansson?

Katherine returned her attention to Dani. "How was your lunch with Mark?"

"Interesting. Political. They're worried word will get out about me. I'm not going to tell anyone, of course."

Katherine patted her arm. "Leaks are a way of life. You'll get used to it. Let them worry about strategy. Did Mark mention

I've told the children?"

She had? "He said you were going to."

"They're very excited to have another sister. Whatever you do, don't give out your cell number or they'll start hitting you up for rides." Katherine laughed. "I want to have you over for dinner again very soon. We can all get to know each other. You're one of us now, Dani. That's both a good and a bad thing, so brace yourself. Now that we've found you, we're not going to let you get away."

"I'm okay with that," she said, overwhelmed by all that was happening.

"I need to run. I'll be calling you soon."

"And then she left," Dani said as she sat on a chair in Penny's office at The Waterfront. It was still several hours before the restaurant opened for dinner and the building was quiet.

Her sister-in-law frowned. "Katherine sounds great. What's the problem?"

"It's not her. You're right. She's wonderful. It's just there's so much going on. A month ago I barely knew Mark Canfield existed. Now I'm his daughter and part of a huge family. It's weird. Everything's happening too fast. I don't know what to think."

Penny smiled. "But this is what you

wanted. To find out where you belong. Although I have to tell you, you're still a Buchanan. Don't think we're letting you get away, either."

"Everybody wants a piece of me," Dani joked. "I'm going to have an entourage."

"There are worse problems."

"I know." She grabbed the mug of coffee on the desk and took a sip. "Fiona was stunning. She's one of those really beautiful women. The kind that makes every other woman in the room feel like a two-dimensional, badly done drawing."

"So you hate her," Penny said cheerfully.

"Only in theory. She may be nice." Although she hadn't looked nice. She'd looked . . . predatory. "I can't believe Alex used to be married to her. He never said anything about it. I went online and looked — they're divorced. It's final and everything. That is one advantage to a family like the Canfields. A lot of stuff gets reported in the press."

She glanced up and saw Penny staring at her. "What?" Dani asked.

"You checked to see if his divorce was final? Why would you do that?"

Dani stared into her coffee. "I was, ah, just curious."

"Oh my God! You're attracted to him?

116

Seriously?"

"No. Of course not. He's just a guy."

"You're lying! I can tell because you're blushing."

Dani touched her cheek and felt the heat. Damn. "Look, it's not what you think. Alex is . . . interesting."

"You're related."

"Not by blood. Don't be gross. He was adopted. I think he's nice and okay, maybe good-looking and there's some mild interest on my part, but it doesn't mean anything."

Penny didn't look convinced. "It complicates things."

"There's nothing to complicate. I'm not getting involved with him." She couldn't — no matter how great he kissed.

"No relationships," she told both Penny and herself firmly. "Do I need to remind you about my past?"

"No," Penny told her. "But maybe your luck has changed."

"Not likely."

Alex checked his watch, then excused himself from the meeting. He'd promised to take Bailey to dinner and he didn't want to be late. The various interactions of what might or might not happen if the press ever discovered Mark Canfield had a grown

117

daughter could be handled by professionals who made their living working those kind of problems. Give him a good corporate lawsuit any day. Compared to politics, that was easy.

Dani wasn't prepared for the circus that was a national campaign, he thought as he walked toward the front of the building. Someone should talk to her about what to expect. Maybe later he could —

He pushed through the swinging door that led to the reception area. Fourteen-year-old Bailey was there, but so was a man Alex had never seen before. It only took him a second to figure out something was wrong.

Bailey sat on the floor, a yellow Lab puppy sprawled across her lap. The guy crouched next to her.

"Tell me more about your new sister," he said, a tape recorder in his hand.

Bailey smiled. "She's pretty and really nice. Ian likes her and he doesn't like anybody."

"She's your daddy's little girl."

Bailey wrinkled her nose. "She's not little. She's big."

Anger exploded into rage, but Alex was careful not to let it show. He stepped between Bailey and the reporter, then offered his sister a hand up.

118

"Bailey, would you please wait for me in my office?"

Bailey's eyes widened. "Is it okay I played with the puppy?" she asked.

He forced himself to smile. "Of course. Give me a second, then we'll go."

"Okay."

She kissed the puppy's head, then eased it off her lap and stood. When she'd waved goodbye and passed through the swinging door, Alex turned on the reporter.

"What the hell do you think you're doing?"

The man was in his late twenties, short and skinny. He stood and scooped up the dog in one arm. "Whatever gets the job done, man." He grinned. "I hear you have a new sister. Congrats."

Alex grabbed his arm. "Who the hell do you think you are, using a puppy to get secrets out of my sister?"

The reporter's grin broadened. "Kids love dogs. Specially kids like her. The stupid ones."

Alex's vision narrowed until there was only his anger and the other man. The insult to his sister fueled the need to lash out and before he could consider whether or not he should, he shot out his hand and punched the reporter in the face.

The guy yelped, as did the puppy. Blood poured from his nose. The tape recorder fell to the floor and cracked open.

Alex stepped on it, crushing the electronic guts of the small machine, but it was too late. The damage had been done . . . in more ways than one.

The newspapers were delivered shortly after four in the morning. Alex was waiting for his. He walked into his kitchen and laid the front page on the dark granite counter. The message couldn't be more clear.

There was a picture of the senator, a blurry shot of Dani and a headline that read: Senator Canfield's Love Child.

CHAPTER SIX

Dani was running late, which meant she wouldn't be able to stop for coffee. Penny would probably have a pot going, but she was more into food than liquids, which meant the chances of getting a double shot latte with extra foam were about zero.

"Drive-through," Dani murmured as she opened the front door and stepped onto the tiny porch of her rental. "Drive-through and —"

Her morning exploded into a blinding series of camera flashes and yelled questions.

"How long have you known the senator was your father?"

"Are any of your brothers his kid, too?"

"Are you asking the family for money?"

"Do you expect a cabinet position if the senator wins the election?"

Dani froze, stunned by the dozen or so people standing on her front lawn. Her inability to answer any of them didn't seem to stop the bombardment of questions.

They called out to her, took her picture and seemed to be waiting for something. A reaction, maybe? They were going to have to accept wide-eyed amazement, because that's all she had in her.

"Go away," she managed at last and started toward her car.

Reporters surrounded her, pushing tape recorders in her face and shouting out more questions.

"What does Mrs. Canfield think about you being her husband's daughter by another woman?"

"Are you going to change your name to Canfield?"

Dani made it to her car and managed to squeeze inside. She started the engine and shifted into Reverse, but the reporters continued to huddle around her car. Not knowing what else to do, she eased her foot off the brake and let the car start moving. At last the reporters withdrew.

Her relief was short-lived. As she backed onto the street, several of them ran to their cars. She blinked. There was no way they were going to follow her, were they?

It was like something out of a movie, only this was real and she didn't know how to deal with it.

Her first thought was that she couldn't go to Penny's. Not with a parade of reporters behind her. She grabbed her cell phone and used speed dial to call Walker. The former Marine would know what to do.

The call went through to voice mail.

Dani swore. She drove through her quiet neighborhood, a six-car escort right behind her. She managed to lose two at the first light and three more at the second. Encouraged by that, she headed for a congested intersection, faked going straight, turned left on the yellow light and zipped around another corner. When she was sure she'd lost everyone, she pulled to the side of the road and called her other two brothers.

And got no one. Apparently they were all busy with their own lives. She stared at her cell for a second, then called information.

"Campaign headquarters for Senator Mark Canfield, please."

Thirty minutes later, Dani was in a back booth at the Totem Lake Shari's. She barely had time to order coffee before Alex entered the restaurant. He looked good as he walked purposefully toward her. Despite the trauma of her morning, she could appreciate the broad shoulders and long legs. If nothing else, he was a distraction.

As he slid in across from her, he passed her the morning paper.

"You didn't see this?" he asked.

She scanned the headline and groaned. "No. I don't read the paper or listen to the news in the morning. It's too depressing. I guess I have to change that." She quickly read the article. "How did this happen? I didn't tell them. I swear."

"I know it wasn't you." He explained about Bailey and the reporter and the puppy.

She stiffened in outrage. "That's horrible. Who is the guy? I have a former Marine brother who would be happy to beat the crap out of him."

"I already did that," Alex told her.

The waitress arrived with Dani's coffee. He ordered a second cup for himself. Dani used those few seconds to try to gather her thoughts and return to the real and rational world.

She held up one hand. "What did you say? You hit a reporter?"

He shrugged. "Nobody screws with my family."

"Don't get me wrong — I'm not complaining. I would have done it if I could have, but it's still a surprise." She would have thought Alex would be one of those totally controlled guys who never let emotion get the best of him.

One corner of his mouth turned up. "Tell me about it."

"It's impressive." So there was a lot of passion lurking inside the tailored suit.

"I'm tough."

He was joking, but Dani thought there was plenty of truth in the statement. He was tough and basically a good guy. She couldn't complain about him defending his sister. Which meant he was good-looking *and* a good guy. That could be a problem, when it came to trying to resist her attraction to him.

"Can you do that?" she asked. "Hit a reporter? I mean I know you can. Obviously. You did it. But is it a good idea?"

Alex's expression tightened. "It depends on whether or not the guy files charges. If he does, I'm looking at an interesting change in my future."

Dani didn't know what to say. Alex was a lawyer. Weren't they supposed to uphold the law or something?

She leaned back in the booth. "Okay, this is all crazy and happening way too fast. Let's start at the beginning. Some sleaze-bucket coerced Bailey into telling him about me. So the press knows and the story is out. What now?"

"Now we deal. You're going to be hounded by the press, at least for a while."

She'd been afraid that was what he was going to say. "Can we define both 'hounded' and 'a while'? Are we talking days, weeks or do I need to move to Borneo?"

"Moving isn't required, but it could take a while for the story to die down. Do you live in a house?"

She nodded. "A rental. Nothing flashy."

"It's not going to offer enough protection. You might want to think about staying with a friend until all this is over. Preferably one who lives in a secure building."

She didn't know anyone who fit that description. "I hate the thought of being forced to leave my home because of a story in the paper."

His gaze was steady. "There's having principles and there's reality. The press can make your life hell, at least in the short term."

"And I'm not even Paris Hilton."

"Who?"

She laughed. "You're such a guy."

"Good thing. Otherwise, *I'd* be in the paper."

"An interesting headline. Senator's Oldest

Son Secretly a Woman. That would be a complication."

His gaze dropped to her mouth. "In more ways than one."

Was it her or had it just gotten hot in here? She shifted on her seat.

"I'm sorry," she said. "I never meant to make a mess of everything. I didn't want to hurt anyone. I just wanted to find my father."

He reached across the table and took her hand. "This isn't your fault. You didn't do anything wrong."

His fingers were warm. She was sure he meant his touch to be comforting, so she couldn't blame him if she wanted to stretch and purr and have him stroke her all over.

"So you don't hate me anymore?" she asked.

"I never hated you."

"You came really close. There was a little hate in your heart."

"I didn't trust you. There's a difference."

"And now?"

"Now I think you're who you say you are."

"What changed your mind? My sparkling personality?"

He released her hand. One corner of his mouth turned up. "What else could it be?"

Before she could answer, she caught sight

of her watch and groaned. "I'm late," she said. She tossed five dollars on the table as she slid out of the booth. "Thanks for coming to talk to me."

He picked up the money and tucked it into her jacket pocket. "I'm always up for a good rescue."

Dani opened Penny's front door without knocking and burst into the house.

"I'm late, I know," she said. "I'm sorry."

Penny stood and hugged her. "What happened? We were getting worried."

The "we" in question was Penny; Lori, Reid's significant other; and Elissa, Walker's fiancée.

"I have the best excuse ever," Dani said as she handed Penny the newspaper she'd brought with her. "I was chased by the press. I had to call Alex and tell him what was going on. Apparently I'm a story."

Penny scanned the headline, then held out the paper so Lori and Elissa could see what it said.

"It could be worse," Lori told her. "You could have been abducted by aliens."

"Good point," Elissa teased. "No one wants all that anal probing."

Dani laughed, then shrugged out of her coat and collapsed on the sofa next to

128

Elissa. "You've managed to put my life in perspective. Thank you."

Penny sank onto the floor and pulled out a notepad. "So what happened to get all this in the press? Who blabbed?"

Dani explained the situation. The three women were outraged that some jerk had taken advantage of Bailey.

"Tell Walker," Elissa said fiercely. "He'll make the guy pay."

Dani was intrigued by the seemingly gentle Elissa being so willing to attack. Although it made sense. Walker was a warrior at heart — he would need a woman who was emotionally strong and secure within herself.

"Apparently Alex already did that," Dani said. "The senator's eldest son, a card-carrying member of the Washington State bar, punched a reporter."

Lori winced. "That can't be good."

"He said he didn't know what was going to happen. It depends on whether or not the reporter presses charges." Dani had a bad feeling he would. All the more attention on the event. Although the downside for the reporter was that he would come off as a jerk. Would he care about that?

Penny eyed Dani. "So the cool, conservative lawyer has a passionate side."

Dani had thought the same thing, but she wasn't going to get into that with her sister-in-law. Not right now. "Enough about me," she said firmly. "We're here to plan a wedding." She turned to Elissa. "Where do we stand?"

Elissa drew in a breath. "It's going to be a big, splashy affair. I can't help it — that's what I've always wanted. A fairy-tale wedding with lots of flowers and twinkle lights. I want a dress with a big skirt and my hair up."

Dani felt a twinge of envy. Elissa was happy, in love and getting married. Not that Dani felt any burning need to be married this second, but she would like to fall in love with a great guy.

Not going to happen anytime soon, she reminded herself. In the past year she'd been left by her husband, who claimed she hadn't grown enough in their marriage — a total sham to cover up his cheating. She'd fallen for and been seduced by a seemingly perfect man who turned out to be married. Last but certainly not least, she'd met a kind, quiet guy who had only recently left the priesthood. It was a challenge she hadn't been willing to take on.

Her love life had become a cautionary tale.

"You should absolutely have the wedding

you want," Lori said firmly. "Fluffy dress and all."

"I agree," Penny said with a sniff. "Even if you're not concerned about the food."

Dani groaned. "Don't go there," she told Penny. "It's Elissa's choice."

Elissa shifted to the edge of the sofa and touched Penny's shoulder. "I'm sorry," she said quietly. "I should have talked to you about this before. I don't want you catering the wedding."

Penny's eyes darkened. "Yes, I know. That's been made very clear."

Elissa continued as if Penny hadn't said anything. "It was a tough decision for me. I know you're the best chef I could ever hope to find, but you're going to be my sister-in-law. What kind of sister would I be if I made you work on my wedding? I want you to enjoy yourself. I refuse to be selfish. Our guests will simply have to understand."

Penny shrugged. "It's your call."

"I would love for you to cater the rehearsal dinner, if that isn't too much trouble. I know it's still work for you, but we're talking maybe fifteen or twenty people. That's nothing for you."

"True," Penny said slowly. "I guess that would work. I could give you some names for the wedding. I know a few people who won't screw things up."

Elissa smiled. "I would really appreciate that."

Dani leaned toward Lori. "Impressive. Penny could have held a grudge for years."

Lori lowered her voice. "Penny and Reid already had this out a while ago. He's the one who first pointed out Elissa wanted her family having fun, not working in the kitchen."

Reid and Penny had always been friends — through her first marriage to Cal, their divorce and now that they were married again.

"What about your wedding plans?" Dani asked Lori.

Lori ducked her head and blushed. "Nothing's set," she said. "I wouldn't do this. A big wedding isn't my style. We've talked about flying off somewhere and eloping."

"Take pictures," Dani told her. "Otherwise, there'll be hell to pay."

"I will."

Elissa said something to Lori and talk returned to the wedding. Dani looked at the three women her brothers had fallen in love with. A year ago Cal, Walker and Reid had been drifting — now they were settled and happy. Maybe she would be next. All she needed was one good man.

Alex immediately popped into her brain and she pushed him out just as quickly. Not him. Their mutual, nonrelated father was running for president, the press was all over her, and he had an ex-wife beautiful enough to start a cult. Did she really want that kind of trouble in her life?

Absolutely not. Although the man sure could kiss . . .

"We need to find a way to spin this," John said.

John was Mark's media expert. He was single-minded, which Alex guessed was required for success in the position.

"Damage control," someone else said. "Something public. This has to be handled, and quickly."

The "this" in question was Dani Buchanan. Alex wondered what she would think about the meeting. He had a feeling she would hate being the cause and resent anyone using the word *handled* in a sentence about her.

"A charity event," John said. "Katherine does them all the time. She's on committees and crap like that, right?"

Alex raised his eyebrows. "It's her life's work," he said mildly. "That raises it up above the level of crap, don't you agree?"

John looked momentarily uncomfortable. "Sure. Whatever. My point is she's visible. What if she and Dani worked some charity together? If they were copresenters or co-hosts? Whatever they have. A luncheon, a benefit. Something good, though. Not obscure and not foreign. A happy, local, media-friendly charity."

Mark nodded slowly. "Katherine would agree to that."

She wouldn't like it, Alex thought. But she would do it because Mark asked.

"Will Dani?" John asked. "Can you make her?"

Mark looked at Alex. "Will she do it?"

Alex wondered when he'd become the resident expert on Dani Buchanan. Or had his father sensed the sexual tension between them? Alex had done his best not to let his interest show, but every now and then Mark surprised the hell out of him.

"Once she understands what's at stake, she will," Alex said.

"Good." John entered some information into his BlackBerry. "We need to work on spinning the story. Right now it's just out there and they're running with it. We need some control. They're going to find out Dani's mother was married when you slept with her. That's not good. Of course you weren't married, which helps, but still. I'll have to work on this."

The meeting continued for another ten minutes. When it ended, Mark asked Alex to stay behind.

When they were alone, Mark looked at him. "Anything else happen with the reporter?"

Alex wasn't surprised Mark already knew. "You mean did I really hit him? Yes."

"There's nothing in the paper yet, but I got a call. You're in deep shit on this."

Alex had been expecting a bad reaction. Even so, he felt a tightening in his gut. If he was convicted, he was screwed. Not that he would change anything about that moment. The bastard had deserved it.

Mark stood and glared at him. "What were you thinking?"

"I wasn't. Someone had used Bailey. I was defending my sister."

"You think Bailey appreciates what you did? Do you think she understood what was happening? You could get disbarred for this."

"I'll handle it."

"As long as no one pisses you off, right?" Mark paced the length of the conference room. "Dammit, Alex, you're going to ruin your career. Don't you care about that?"

Alex stood. "I know there will be consequences. I said I'll deal with it and I will."

"You have to learn to walk away."

The words shouldn't have surprised him. Mark was nothing if not a consummate politician. "I don't walk away where my family is concerned."

"Then I hope you're ready to give up the law, because it's about done with you."

Dani walked into the restaurant and wasn't surprised to find a crowd. The parking lot had been overflowing with cars. What she didn't expect was to be attacked by several reporters with flashing cameras and tiny, digital tape recorders.

"Have you met with your father today?"

"How long have you known you're related to Senator Canfield?"

"Did your mother's husband know about her affair?"

Dani drew in a deep breath, then held up both hands. "If you'll be quiet for a moment, I have a statement I'd like to make."

They were instantly silent.

Power, Dani thought humorously. *I must remember to use it for good.*

She cleared her throat. "This is a privately owned restaurant. It is not public property or in the public domain. You are more than welcome to order a very expensive dinner, complete with cocktails and dessert, and tip really well, or you can leave." She looked at her watch. "You have thirty seconds to decide. Then I'm calling the cops and having you arrested for loitering."

A couple of the reporters headed out. One moved toward her.

"You can't do this," he said. "You're a story."

She dug her cell phone out of her purse and flipped it open. "Twenty. Nineteen. Eighteen."

The man swore and left. Seconds later, the foyer of the restaurant was empty. Dani breathed in a sigh of relief, then headed for the tiny office she shared with Bernie. Her boss met her in the hallway.

"Impressive," he said. "I didn't know what to do with them. We've never had reporters here."

Dani shook her head. "I'm sorry. I never meant for any of this to be a problem for you."

"Hey, maybe they'll mention us in the paper. That could be good for business."

He was taking this far better than she could have hoped. Still, he couldn't be happy about reporters lurking around the restaurant.

She went to work. Business was good. Dani made several rounds, checking on guests and making sure there were no reporters getting in anyone's way. A little after nine, she saw a single man seated at a corner table.

She recognized him immediately and felt her entire body go on sex-alert. Hormones hummed something that sounded a lot like "Take me. Take me now."

She walked to the wine cellar and pulled out a favorite bottle, then returned to the table. Alex rose when she pulled out a chair.

"Unless you were expecting someone else," she said.

He smiled. "No. Just you."

Simple words that shouldn't have meant anything. But there was something about the way he said them that made her go weak at the knees. Good thing she was already sitting down.

"Are you eating or just visiting?" she asked.

"I'm hungry."

"The ravioli on special is excellent. I'd highly recommend it."

"Then that's what I want."

Was it her or had his voice gotten lower and sexier? It was all she could do to keep from fanning herself.

"How are you holding up?" he asked.

"I'm still taking it all in. The press was here earlier."

"Your boss told me. He said you handled them perfectly."

"I appreciate the praise, but I'm not taking credit. I told them to buy dinner or get out."

"What's wrong with that?"

"Nothing. It worked."

"Would you really have called the police?" he asked.

"In a heartbeat."

Dani ordered for them and asked the server to let her know if anything needed her attention. He poured the wine, then left.

Dani took a sip from her glass. "I'm making a mess everywhere I go. Should I quit my job?"

"No."

"But they'll be back. Until something more interesting comes along, they're going to mess with my life."

"If you quit, they win. You're not a quitter."

There was something in the way he made the statement. "You know this how?"

He shrugged. "I've heard."

"What, exactly?"

Alex looked uncomfortable, which she

hadn't expected.

"When you first showed up, I had you investigated," he said.

He waited for the burst of anger, but there was only resignation. "A thrilling by-product of being part of the Canfield family?"

"You claimed to be the senator's daughter. What else was I supposed to do?"

She wanted to say he could have believed her, but that was too naive. After what she'd been through today, she understood the need for caution.

"So what did you learn about me?"

"The basics. Date of birth, where you went to school, how much you have in the bank. That sort of thing."

She sipped her wine. "None of that says I'm not a quitter."

He hesitated for a second, then said, "I know about your first marriage. To Hugh. I know he was injured and you stood by him. You did whatever was necessary to get him up and functioning. You could have walked away, but you didn't. Even knowing he was going to be in a wheelchair for the rest of his life, you married him."

A polite way of saying even though they would never have a normal sex life, she'd married him. "I loved him," she said. "More fool me."

"Because you got a divorce? It happens."

It had happened to him, too, she thought. "Apparently your research isn't as thorough as you thought. Hugh left me about a year ago. He claimed I hadn't grown enough as a person in our marriage. I can't tell you how much that pissed me off. If I hadn't grown, it had been because I was busting my ass, taking care of him. Pushing him, as you said. But it turned out to be a bunch of lies. He was having an affair. Maybe several. That's why he wanted out of the marriage."

Alex's expression didn't change. "Then he's a fool."

"Good answer."

Two and a half hours later Alex walked her to her car. She knew he would and she knew what would happen when they got there. It was like being in high school again, and dating a guy she had a serious crush on. The evening was just a prelude to what they both wanted . . . the kissing.

Now that she was an adult, there were other, more interesting pleasures, pleasures she wasn't ready to think about yet. Not with Alex. But kissing seemed safe.

Although dinner had been good. Lots of getting-to-know-you conversation that had her liking Alex more than she should.

He pulled her into his arms. She went willingly, pressing her body against his, enjoying the hard planes of his chest and the way they fit together. Despite her brief affair with Ryan, she was still getting used to kissing a man while they were both standing. She liked it.

He brushed his mouth against hers, using just enough pressure to let her know he was serious, but not so much that she wanted to step back.

His urgency aroused her. She wrapped her arms around his neck, angled her head and parted her lips.

He swept inside, teasing her tongue with his. They circled and danced; he moved his hands up and down her back. She moved closer, wishing for more contact from him. But he didn't oblige. It was too soon and they were in public. They were taking enough of a risk, making out like this.

As he nipped her lower lip, she found she didn't really care if anyone was watching. Not when desire swept through her, making her lean in closer. He cupped her butt, causing her to surge against him. Her belly nestled his erection.

He was hard, she thought, delighted it had been so simple to arouse him. She liked that in a man.

She must have laughed, because he pulled back slightly and stared into her eyes.

"Want to share the joke?"

"I just . . . You're, um . . ." She glanced down then back at him. Thank God it was dark. Otherwise he would see her blushing.

"Dani?"

She dropped her hand to his crotch and lightly touched him.

"Are you offended?"

She grinned. "No. I'm impressed. There was one other guy after Hugh. A disaster. One before him, a million years ago. But mostly I've been dealing with a paraplegic. Our sex life was different. A lot of work for me. I didn't mind, at least not while things were good between us. We were in love and I wanted us both to be happy."

"But it wasn't easy?"

"No."

"I can be easy."

She laughed again, then kissed him. "And here I thought you'd be a stuffy lawyer."

"Me? Never."

CHAPTER SEVEN

Dani drove out of the Bella Roma parking lot and realized she didn't want to go home. The thought of the press lurking around her small house gave her the creeps. She pulled to the side of the road to figure out where she should go instead.

All of her brothers would welcome her, but she wasn't comfortable barging in. Her list of girlfriends was pitifully small. Between working and taking care of Hugh, she hadn't had time for much of a social life. Which left only one person.

She punched in the numbers on her cell. The call was answered on the first ring.

"Hi. Did you see the paper?"

"Of course. It could be worse. When Reid was in the paper, they said he was bad in bed."

"Okay, that helps with my perspective. I don't want to go home. There are reporters everywhere."

"Then come here. I have a perfectly good gate I'm willing to use on your behalf."

"Are you sure?"

"Where else would you go?"

An interesting question, Dani thought as she pulled into the open garage at her grandmother's house. When she stepped out of her car, she hit the button to close the garage door, then went inside. Gloria was waiting for her at the top of the stairs.

Dani climbed to the first floor. "I really appreciate this," she said. Or at least that's what she meant to say. Instead she burst into tears.

Gloria pulled her close and hugged her. "I know it's not all right at this minute, but we'll make it all right. I promise."

Katherine poked her fork into the small scoop of pasta salad on her dinner tray, but she didn't bother to eat any. She couldn't. Her stomach had been a mess all day. She knew the cause was an unfortunate combination of stress and pain, but knowing the reason didn't make it any better.

She felt as if she'd been run over and left for dead on the side of the road. Every part of her ached. Getting through the day, smiling at her children, pretending everything was fine had taken all she'd had and then some.

The newspapers lay where she'd left them, the headlines clearly visible on the leather ottoman. She'd known the news would come out — it always did. But so soon? And like this?

A few friends had called to check on her. They'd been kind. She'd heard the questions in their voices but no one had come right out and asked if she was the reason she and Mark had adopted. Perhaps they hadn't needed to ask. Perhaps they already knew.

It shouldn't matter, she told herself. Being unable to have children was no big deal. It happened to thousands of women. They went on to lead fulfilling lives. She had, as well. She loved her family. She wouldn't change anything about it . . . except possibly to have given Mark what that other woman had been able to provide.

She heard his footsteps on the hardwood floor. He came into her study and sank down at the end of the sofa.

"What a day," he began, after kissing her on the mouth and touching her cheek. "Talk about hell. We're caught up in damage control. The way the press got the story makes it more difficult to spin, but we're working on it. We haven't run any poll numbers, but the consensus is this won't hurt us too much. With the right slant, it could really work in our favor."

"That's something," she said calmly, when what she really wanted to do was scream at him. Couldn't he tell this was hurting her? Didn't he know that she was devastated?

If she had to guess, she would say he hadn't had time to think of it yet. He was too caught up in his campaign.

"Have you talked to Alex?" Mark asked. "He hit that damned reporter. He's going to be charged. There's a problem I don't want to deal with."

"He was defending Bailey. I'm sorry there are going to be consequences for him, but I can't regret what he did. It was the right thing."

Mark stared at her. "You're right. We can leak that to the press. No one likes anyone taking advantage of a child." He smiled. "You're brilliant. You should be on my payroll."

It was a familiar comment. She was supposed to follow it up by saying she would rather be in his bed. Tonight, she couldn't.

"People have been calling," she said. "Friends, acquaintances."

"You'll handle it," he said with a yawn.

"You always do."

Unexpected anger boiled up inside of her. "What if I don't want to handle it? I didn't ask for any of this, Mark."

He looked at her and frowned. "It's not like I knew and kept it from you. Dani was as much a surprise to me as she was to you."

Somehow Katherine doubted that. After all, Mark had known about his affair with Marsha Buchanan.

"You must have met her as soon as you moved back to Seattle," Katherine said. "Within a few weeks."

He was smart enough to look wary. "I did. I was angry about our breakup and I wasn't looking to get involved. It just happened."

"You loved her." She spoke calmly, not wanting him to know how important his answer was to her.

He shrugged. "Does that matter now? It was a long time ago. Katherine, this isn't going to help."

She pushed to the edge of the sofa, but didn't stand. "Nothing is going to help. Everyone will know I'm the reason we couldn't have children. Everyone will talk about me and pity me. Everyone will know I'm the one who's broken. All my work will mean nothing."

He slid across the sofa and pulled her

close. "Of course it means something. Do you think the people you help care if you can have children or not? For the record — you're not broken. You're the tough one."

She pushed him away. Perhaps for the first time in her life, she didn't want him touching her.

She stood. "You have what you've always wanted. A child of your own."

He rose. "That's not fair. I was fine adopting. I've never complained about the situation."

Her anger grew. "How big of you. Perhaps you should mention that during the campaign. 'My wife couldn't have children and I didn't complain. Won't that make me an excellent president?' Do you still love her?"

"What? No. It's been thirty years. I barely remember what she looks like."

Katherine desperately wanted to believe that. She wanted him to convince her that she was the only one who mattered.

"Were you still with her when I came back to you?" she asked.

"No. We'd broken things off."

"Did you end it or did she?"

He looked away. "Does it matter?"

Of course it mattered, but she already knew the truth. Marsha had ended the relationship.

"Why did you marry me?" she asked. "Was it for the money?"

He looked at her then, his blue eyes dark with an emotion she couldn't read. "Is that what you think of me?" he asked.

"Don't try to distract me, Mark. I want to know the truth."

"You're not going to believe anything I tell you tonight. You want me to be the bad guy. I'm sorry Dani has disrupted our lives, but I'm not sorry she's alive. I can't be. Thirty years ago, you ended our relationship. I came back to Seattle and yes, I fell in love with another woman. It's been over for years. I never think about her. You're my wife, Katherine. I love you. We have a life together. A family. Doesn't that mean anything?"

It meant so much more than she could ever explain. At least to her. But what about to him?

She loved him so much. Too much. What would have happened if Marsha hadn't ended things? What if she, Katherine, had asked him to choose? Who would he have wanted to be with?

He was right, she wouldn't believe him, whatever he said. Mostly because she already knew the answer.

■ ■ ■ ■

"I'm seeing more of you these days," Katherine said as she poured coffee.

Alex took the mug she offered. "Is that a good thing or a bad thing?"

She smiled. "Hmm, let me think."

He chuckled. Katherine had the ability to make each of her children feel as if he or she were the only one who mattered. Should he ever have kids of his own, he was hoping to give them the same gift.

It was early, barely after seven, but she looked as she always did. Perfect makeup, casual but expensive clothes. His mother defined class.

She settled back in her chair and picked up her coffee. "I'll admit to being intrigued. It's not often that Mark is afraid to discuss something with me, and I can't remember the last time he sent you in his place."

"I can. I was seventeen. He'd lost Bailey at the mall for over an hour and he was afraid to tell you himself."

She smiled. "You're right. So what has him quaking this time?"

"He wants you to invite Dani along to one of your charities and then have the press there."

151

With someone else, he might have continued with the explanation, but this was Katherine Canfield. She'd been a politician's wife nearly as long as she'd been married. She would do the right thing because it *was* right. Duty defined her.

Nothing about her expression changed. She sipped, then nodded slowly. "If I accept Mark's daughter, then America should, as well. After all, I'm as close to a wronged party as there can be, under the circumstances."

She was calm and rational, which he appreciated. Yet how was that possible? "Doesn't this piss you off?" he asked. "Don't you hate the world getting into your life?"

"Of course, but there's nothing I can do about it. Let me check my calendar and see what events I have in the next few weeks. I want to pick a charity that can use the extra publicity. What is it your father is always calling the press?"

"The jackals."

"Right. The jackals can do some good this time."

"You always say and do the right thing."

Her mouth tightened. "I wish that were true. But I try. I suppose I get points for that."

"This has to be hard for you." Knowing about Dani privately was one thing, but having the world talk about her was something else.

She shrugged. "I don't like being the subject of gossip, but sometimes it can't be helped. In time, people will find something else interesting to talk about. Until then, I'll do what I've always done. Take care of my family and try to make a difference in the world."

"You made a difference with me."

"You were easy."

"I wasn't. They told you not to adopt me. They said I couldn't be socialized."

"They were wrong." She reached across the table and took his hand. "You're the reason we have eight children, Alex. I had a dream and a plan, but I had no idea if I was capable of raising one child, let alone eight."

It wasn't just the volume, he thought, it was who those children were. Children with needs, both medical and emotional. Children other people hadn't wanted.

"When you turned out as perfectly as you did," she said, her voice teasing, "I knew I could do it again."

"I'll remind them at the holidays. They can all buy me extra presents."

His mother laughed.

He studied her for a second. "Are you sorry Dad's running for president?"

Her humor faded. "No. It's what he's always wanted. I think he has a good shot, better than most. Are you worried the news stories will materially damage his chances?"

"I don't know. I'm not an expert."

She released his hand and picked up her coffee again. "Trust the American people. They'll understand. If Mark had had an affair while we were married, then that would be different. But this was before our engagement. Everyone can do the math."

"Marsha Buchanan was married."

"People will think badly of her, not your father. It's not fair, but there it is."

This had to be killing her, he thought. Being at the center of a scandal. Worse was the speculation about why the Canfields really adopted all those children. He'd already heard what people were saying. Maybe Katherine wasn't such a saint. Maybe she simply couldn't have children of her own. She was making the best of a bad situation. After all, Mark obviously didn't have a problem.

The need to protect rose up inside of him. The promise had been made more than twenty years ago, but he still felt the burning intensity of it.

He'd been eight when Katherine had taken him from the foster home. The latest foster home, because there were so many. She'd been patient through his clumsiness, his tantrums, his terrifying dreams. She'd taught him, praised him and gradually found her way into his heart. He still remembered everything about the afternoon she'd sat him down and had told him, if he wanted, he could stay with her forever.

He'd tried not to cry, because he was older and it wasn't right for an eight-year-old boy to cry. Still, he hadn't been able to help himself. She'd held him while he'd sobbed and had asked him to tell her what was wrong. He hadn't. He didn't want her to know what he remembered . . . how he was seeing his birth mother murdered in front of him. How he'd been terrified and alone and he hadn't been able to save her.

When he'd realized what Katherine was willing to do for him, how much she loved him, he'd vowed he would protect her and the rest of her family, with his life, if necessary. No one would ever hurt her.

Yet here she was, in pain.

"There is a condition of my cooperation with Dani," Katherine said, drawing him back to the present.

155

He raised his eyebrows. "That's not like you."

"I know. These are unusual circumstances."

He thought about Dani, about their kiss the previous night. About how he wanted to do more. Was that the condition? Stay away from Mark's daughter?

He knew Katherine would never interfere in his life that way, even if she did know he was interested. But there was a bigger problem. Him seeing Dani would hurt Katherine. She would see it as a betrayal, as if he'd chosen Mark over her. Which he hadn't, but it made for an awkward situation.

"I want you to give Fiona another chance," his mother said.

It had been a morning for remembering, Alex thought grimly. While recalling his early years with Katherine and Mark had been pleasant, not so with memories of his ex-wife. In a single moment of time, he'd become a cliché — a wronged husband who came home early and walked in on his wife fucking another man.

Not in their bed. That would have been too tame for Fiona, who always sought more sensation whenever possible. No, she and her companion had been naked on the din-

156

ing room table — a wedding gift from Katherine's cousin. An antique of some kind. He'd never paid much attention to things like that.

But the image of her naked legs wrapped around the other man's hips, the auditory memory of her screaming for more, her long red hair spilling on to the wood, was locked in his brain forever.

He reached for his coffee. "It won't be a condition. Fiona and I are finished. There's no going back."

"Why?" Katherine asked. "I know she loves you. You must still have feelings for her. You never talk about what happened. I realize you're an adult and you're no longer required to run to me with every problem you have, but I want to help. You were so good together."

They looked good together, he thought cynically. There was the difference. They made a perfect couple — but that was only on the outside. On the inside, they were worlds apart.

"Trust me," he said. "It's long over. We've both moved on."

"She hasn't."

Alex didn't know what stories Fiona had told his mother and he didn't care. He'd made the decision not to tell anyone the truth to save himself the embarrassment of admitting his wife had married him for money and position. She'd played him and he'd let himself be played.

The less painful half of the equation was that after throwing Fiona out, he hadn't missed her as much as he thought he would. Apparently he hadn't been in love with her. At least not at the end of the marriage. Or maybe he'd never loved her at all. Which wasn't a fact that made him proud.

"You seem to have made up your mind," Katherine said. "Are you going to tell me why?"

"No." He softened the word with a light touch. "I appreciate what you're trying to do. I know you care about both of us. My marriage to Fiona is long over. There is nothing anyone can say or do to get us back together."

"I've known you long enough to recognize that stubborn set of your jaw. All right. I'll let it go. It makes me sad, though. I thought the two of you had something special."

"I thought we did, too, but I was wrong."

Alex left shortly before nine. Katherine watched him go. He was a good man and as much as she wanted to take credit for that, so much of who he was came from inside of him. She'd merely offered suggestions.

Sometimes she thought Mark could learn something from Alex, then she shook off the disloyal thought. She accepted Mark, flaws and all. Wanting him to be different would only make her unhappy and snarky, to quote Julie. No man wanted a snarky wife.

She heard footsteps in the hallway and looked up. Fiona stepped into the smaller of the two family dining rooms. She was perfectly dressed, but there was a faint puffiness around her eyes.

"What happened?" Katherine asked. "Are you all right?"

Fiona swallowed. "I'm sorry. I got here about a half hour ago. To finish with the menus. I wasn't trying to listen in on your conversation with Alex. I didn't even know he was here. I just . . ." Tears filled her eyes. "I heard what he said."

Katherine rose and drew the other woman close. "Oh, Fiona. I'm so sorry."

"I still love him. I've been hoping that we could work things out, but now . . ."

Katherine closed her eyes and absorbed the other woman's pain. She knew exactly what she was going through. When Katherine had ended things with Mark all those years ago, she'd thought she would die from missing him. Eventually her pain had pushed her to fly to Seattle and beg for a second chance.

"It's over," Fiona said dully.

Katherine stepped back and shook her head. "It's only over if you stop trying. Alex is a good man. If you give up on him now, then you're not the right one for him. Sometimes you have to love them through the rough spots. It's not easy, but it can be done. Don't give up hope, Fiona. I know you can get Alex back. I know it and I'll do whatever I can to help."

CHAPTER EIGHT

Dani sat at a corner table in the Daily Grind, waiting for Alex. She was reminded of her meetings with Gary — how they'd met at a different Daily Grind and what a disaster that had turned out to be. She still felt guilty for ending things when she'd discovered he'd only recently left the priesthood. Maybe a better woman would have tried harder to make things work. All she'd been able to think was that this was a clear message from God to stop trying to date.

All of which had nothing to do with Alex, but everything to do with the anticipation knotting her stomach. She was eager to see him. Had been anticipating the meeting ever since he'd called and asked if she had a few minutes for coffee. Which was a serious problem.

A relationship between them would be a massive disaster, and she knew plenty about relationships that ended in disaster. But

they'd kissed and she got all quivery whenever she thought about him. The way things
were going, all she needed was an iceberg
and a ship named *Titanic* to complete her
day.

She sipped her latte and tried not to react
when he walked into the shop. He glanced
around, saw her and smiled. Instantly her
entire body went on alert. She flushed from
the inside out, and she desperately wanted
to start squirming like a nervous teenager.
Talk about trouble.

After getting a double espresso, he joined
her at her table. "Thanks for meeting me,"
he said as he settled across from her.

"No problem. What's up?"

"You've been the subject of intense meetings and we have what we hope is a solution
to the problem."

The problem being her. "Will I like it?"

"No. We think you and Katherine should
appear together at a charity function. Something big and splashy, with lots of press. By
showing a united front, the appeal of the
story goes away."

Dani stared at him. Dark soulful eyes or
not, he had to be crazy. The panic was as
sudden as it was powerful.

"You want me to show up in public with
your mother? At a charity event? Like a

ladies' luncheon or something?"

"Yes. You'll both speak and it will —"

She held up her hands in the shape of a T. "Stop right there. I don't *speak* in public. I never have. I'm sorry I've caused trouble for the campaign and I do want to help make things right, but couldn't I just stuff envelopes?"

"No, you can't. This is important, Dani. You're the senator's daughter. This is what his family does."

There wasn't a hint of warmth in his dark eyes. It was as though he was the dragon again and she was an annoying serf who got in the way.

She wanted to protest that she wasn't family, except biologically she was. Talk about inconvenient.

"I can't," she said. "I've never spoken in public. And it would be too weird to be with your mother like that." Not to mention potentially embarrassing. She liked Katherine. She didn't want to do anything to make Katherine not like her.

"Dani, this isn't an option," he told her, his voice almost impatient. "It's the right thing to do. I've already talked to my mother and she's more than willing to move forward. This is much harder for her than it is for you. You're the long-lost child the senator knew nothing about. Katherine is just the wife. Do you realize what your presence has cost her? Two weeks ago she was a respected, admired woman who had taken in disabled children and made them her own. Now there's speculation that she can't have children and she was only making the best of a bad situation."

Dani understood what he was saying, but didn't appreciate the lecture. "I'm not some wayward child," she snapped. "I don't need to be told my responsibilities. I respect Katherine and am sorry for any discomfort this is causing her. But you're missing the point. I didn't ask for any of this and I'm not the one who leaked the information to the press."

"Dani —"

"I'm not finished," she told him. "You come in here and tell me I have to show up for a charity function and speak in front of God knows how many people. Then, when I don't jump for joy, you get on me like I'm a sixteen-year-old who took the family car without permission. I'm not the bad guy. Give me a minute to take this all in, will you?"

She braced herself for the explosion and was shocked when Alex leaned back in his chair, nodded once, then said, "You're right.

I'm sorry."

She blinked. "Excuse me?"

"I'm sorry. I got in your face. I should have given you time to get used to the idea."

Wow. That was unexpected. And very human of him.

"Yes, you should have. I'm going to say yes to the charity, I just need some time to get used to the idea and some space to whine about it."

"Fair enough."

The tension between them eased. She studied him. "Katherine is really lucky to have you on her side. You're loyal."

"I owe her everything," he said flatly.

"That's extreme."

"It's true."

He paused, as if not sure what more he should say. Dani was intrigued and leaned forward.

"Why Katherine?" she asked. "Why not Mark?"

"Because she's the one who saved me." He drew in a breath. "I grew up on the streets of Seattle. My mother did drugs and God knows what else. She turned tricks to pay for food and her fix. I remember growing up cold and wet and scared. We lived in abandoned buildings in the winter and outside in the summer. When she had to do

165

business —" He grimaced. "I still remember that's what she called it. 'Mommy has some business.' I had to go hide. That was the rule. Hide and stay quiet."

Dani willed herself not to react physically. She didn't want to let her horror show. Alex had started life on the streets? Like that? Was it possible?

"One guy got mad. I don't know why. He started hitting her. I ran out to save her and he backhanded me so hard, I passed out. When I came to, she had been beaten to death. I don't know if he meant to kill her or if it was an accident. Either way, she was dead."

His dark eyes stared beyond her, as if seeing a past she couldn't begin to imagine.

"I stayed with her body until the police came. I don't know how long that was. A day? Two? They couldn't find any family. I didn't know anything about where my mother had come from, so I went into foster care." He looked at her. "I never lived in a house or had access to a real bathroom. I didn't know how to read or take a shower on my own. I was a wild animal put in a cage. It didn't go well."

"Alex," she breathed, not sure what to say. The man in front of her was sophisticated, educated, charming and funny. How had he come from that abandoned little boy?

"I bounced around for two and a half years and ended up in a group home. One day a beautiful lady came and read me a story. There was something about the way she looked at me that made me feel safe. I'll never know why, but she applied to be my foster mother that day. A week later, I'd moved in with her and Mark."

"Katherine?"

He nodded. "She spent every minute with me. She taught me to read, how to live in a house. She let me sleep on the floor until I was ready to be in a bed. She came at night when I dreamed about my mother being murdered and she held me while I cried and screamed and waited for the bad man to kill me, too."

Dani's stomach turned over. No child should have to experience anything like that. Not ever. Her heart ached for all Alex had been through.

"She found me in March. By September I was enrolled in a regular classroom. I was behind in everything, but Katherine made sure I caught up. The following year, the adoption was final. She became my mother, my family. I thrived, because of her. I'm here, because of her."

Dani swallowed. "I don't know what to

say. 'I'm sorry' seems ridiculous and inadequate."

"It happened. It's over. I couldn't save my birth mother. I was a kid. But I am perfectly capable of protecting my family now and I will. Against anyone."

She believed him. "She's a wonderful woman. I already figured that out. I don't know what to say about what happened to you, except you've done incredibly well. You're both amazing. I already said I'd do the charity and I meant it."

"I'm not trying to impress you," he said. "I'm trying to explain my position. Why family and duty matter. Most people don't know about my past."

He said it as if he wasn't sure why he'd told her.

"I won't say anything," she murmured. It wasn't her story to tell.

Maybe he'd meant to scare her away. Maybe he had just been explaining his loyalty to Katherine. Maybe he hadn't wanted to impress her.

Too late, she thought. He'd done a hell of a job. She was stunned by what she'd learned and more intrigued than ever by a man who had started with nothing and come so far. It spoke to a strength of character she could admire.

It was one more item on the "reasons to fall for Alex Canfield" list. If there were many more added, she would be in serious danger of losing her heart.

Later that week Dani returned to campaign headquarters for lunch with her father. This time she knew better than to expect any serious one-on-one time with Mark, which was good. It was another lunch by committee.

The suits were back, along with Heidi, Mark's assistant. Unfortunately Alex didn't show up, which made her more than a little disappointed.

"You're tracking well in the polls," John said. At least she thought his name was John.

"I have polls?" she asked.

John nodded. "We put a couple of questions into the field in the Midwest and the results were mixed. Here, we started with falling numbers, but once the senator issued his statement and gave an interview, the numbers started rising."

Dani felt totally out of the loop. She glanced at Mark. "You gave an interview? About me being your daughter?"

He smiled. "It seemed the best way to handle things. Heidi, get Dani a copy of the interview." He turned back to Dani. "You can watch it at home."

"Sure." Because she'd been planning to get to know her father on video. It could be a new hobby.

The other suit-guy said, "The senator always comes across as sincere. The voters like that."

Dani wondered if there was a difference between coming across as sincere and being sincere.

"He told the interviewer he'd wanted some private time to get to know his daughter, but a reporter tricked Bailey into telling him about you. The reporter looked mean, Alex is painted the hero and everyone loves the senator," suit-guy concluded.

"Poll numbers jumped after that," John added with a grin. "Good for us."

"It is good," Mark said.

Dani didn't know what to think. On the one hand, she was sorry her presence had caused a problem. On the other, she felt a bit used — as if her situation had been spun or exploited, which probably wasn't fair. Presidential campaigns weren't won by being retiring. Still, it was overwhelming. Too much had happened too quickly.

"We were thinking you could do an interview."

Dani had reached for her sandwich. Now she left it untouched on the paper plate and stared at nameless suit-guy. "Excuse me?"

"An interview. Maybe with *People.* You're exactly the kind of story they'd jump on."

He kept talking, but Dani wasn't listening. An interview for *People* magazine? All the blood rushed to her head. Or maybe it was away from her head. Either way, she got a little dizzy and her heart started pounding.

"I don't want to do an interview," she whispered. A charity event with Katherine was one thing, but *People* magazine? Not in this lifetime.

Mark met her gaze and grinned. "Breathe, Dani. You don't want to pass out in your egg salad sandwich."

"What?" She sucked in a breath. Her head cleared.

Mark turned to suit-guy. "Let's hold off on interviews for now."

"But —"

Mark shook his head. "No interviews. Leave Dani out of things."

"Fine." Suit-guy scribbled on a pad.

The meeting continued. Dani risked nibbling on her sandwich. She couldn't seem to get a handle on Mark. One minute he seemed distant and totally political, the next he was saying she didn't have to do a national interview. So who was the real Mark Canfield?

A few minutes later, the meeting wrapped up. Mark motioned for her to stay after everyone left.

"How are you handling this?" he asked. "Katherine mentioned it had to be difficult for you."

The door opened and Alex stepped into the room. "Am I interrupting?" he asked.

Dani stared at him. Something was wrong — she could feel it.

"No," Mark said. "What is it?"

"It's official. I'm going to be charged with assault. The particulars haven't been worked out by the D.A.'s office."

Dani stood. "That's just wrong. How can someone do what that man did and it's okay, but when you defend your sister, you're the bad guy?"

"I appreciate the support," Alex said. "But I hit him. Not a good thing."

Mark held up a hand. "Don't worry. Either of you. This isn't about what happened with Alex. It's about the campaign. It's a distraction. We'll get it fixed."

Dani might not be a political expert, but she wasn't sure the charges had anything to do with the campaign. And she didn't think

Alex would appreciate something that could end his career being called a distraction.

"I'll fix it," Alex said.

"We'll talk," Mark told him. "Fortunately we both have access to excellent legal counsel." He glanced at his watch. "I have another meeting." He smiled at Dani. "That's how I spend my days. Going from meeting to meeting. Thanks for coming by. I'm glad we were able to spend some time together."

"Right," Dani said, thinking that thirty-seven seconds alone with her father wasn't exactly bond-building.

"Alex, walk Dani out, will you?"

"Sure."

Dani waited until Mark left before standing and turning to Alex. "I can find my own way to my car. It's daylight, so I should be safe."

"I don't mind."

"Ooh, now I'm going to fall for you, for sure. How smooth and seductive. 'I don't mind.' Words every woman lives to hear."

He smiled. "Have I mentioned you're not easy?"

"Yes, and thank you for the compliment."

He put his hand on the small of her back. "Come on. Let's fight those snipers and get you to your car."

His touch was warm and made her want to step closer. They'd nearly made it out of the building when Heidi called Alex.

"The senator needs you to sit in on the meeting," she said.

Alex looked at Dani. "Think you can make it on your own?"

"I'm wearing body armor."

"Good."

He took her hand in his and squeezed lightly. There was something in his eyes, something that made her think about sex and being naked. Two good things. Dangerous, but good. Then he was gone.

Dani sighed heavily. At least her life was never boring. That had to be worth something, didn't it?

The not-boring continued as she stepped into the parking lot and nearly ran into Fiona, the beautiful. The tall, perfectly dressed stunner paused, a tiny frown drawing her fabulous eyebrows a little closer together.

"Dani?" she asked. "It is Dani, isn't it?"

"Yes. Hi. I was having lunch with the senator."

"Good. I think it's great the two of you are getting to know each other. Family is everything and I'm thrilled to have you part of mine."

Dani stared. Part of hers? As in, the Can-fields were Fiona's family, too? But she and Alex were divorced.

"I didn't think you were married to Alex anymore," she said carefully.

Fiona shook her head. "I know. We went through a bad patch. Have you been mar-ried? You know how that happens, right? We were young and reckless, but so in love. Desperately in love. We've started talking and spending time together again. I'm hope-ful." She held up her right hand, showing her fingers crossed. "Alex is, too."

"That's great," Dani said, feeling sick to her stomach. Fiona had to be playing her. Alex wouldn't be kissing Dani *and* making time with his ex-wife, would he?

She wanted to think the best of him, but honestly, how well did she know the man?

"It's not just Alex," Fiona continued. "It's the whole family. Katherine and I are like sisters. I love working with her. We're mak-ing a real difference. Plus, I've never brought trouble to the family. Trust me. The Can-fields don't like that sort of notoriety. In case you were wondering."

"I wasn't," Dani said as she shifted her purse to her shoulder.

"Don't hate me," Fiona told her. "I'm simply the messenger. It's just everyone would be really upset if you were the reason Mark didn't get the nomination."

With that, she smiled and walked into the warehouse.

Dani was left standing in the parking lot, feeling grateful she hadn't eaten too much at lunch. It meant there was less for her to throw up later.

When Dani's cell phone rang, she considered ignoring it. She didn't need any more hits in one day. But when she glanced at the number, she didn't recognize it and curiosity won over apprehension.

"Hello?"

"Dani? It's Katherine. How are you?"

Katherine should be the one person Dani was avoiding these days, yet she actually felt pleased to hear her voice.

"I'm good. How are the kids?"

"Great, and they're why I'm calling. They know about you. Obviously. Poor Bailey is sick about what happened. When I think about that reporter, I want to jam him in my microwave and hit full power. It makes me furious. Which is not the point of my call. It would be so nice if you could get to know the children."

Dani didn't know what to say. "I — I'd love that."

"Perfect. How about dinner one evening? I'll check my calendar and get back to you. I believe Mark mentioned you work?"

"I'm an assistant manager at a restaurant. Bella Roma. I mostly handle the lunch shift, but I do work a couple of evenings a week."

"All right. Let me get some dates and we'll find a time for you to come over."

"Thank you, Katherine. For everything. You're being so gracious and kind. I appreciate that."

"You're family, Dani. What else would I be? Bye."

Dani hung up, then stepped out of her car. So much was happening so quickly. She felt as if she were living inside an emotional tornado.

Taking a second to relax, she stared at the restaurant in front of her.

Buchanan's was the steak house in the family restaurant empire. It had been around longer than she'd been alive and it had always been her secret dream to run the place. She loved everything about Buchanan's, including the glass and wood doors that welcomed guests to a unique steak house experience.

She glanced at her watch and saw she was right on time for her meeting with her brothers.

The interior was cool and cozy. There were booths rather than tables, plenty of wood and fresh white linens. The smell — a combination of leather, steak and great wine — was a heady perfume. Afternoon light sparkled through the windows, but at night candles flickered at every table.

Back home, buried in the back of her closet, was a notebook filled with ideas. Ways to improve the service, the menu, the wine list. She'd even played with a few recipes and had asked Penny to work them up for her.

Foolish dreams, she told herself. She wasn't truly a Buchanan anymore and this restaurant would never be hers. Her words — not theirs. As far as her brothers were concerned, nothing had changed.

She saw her brothers seated at a booth in the back. As she approached, they slid out and each hugged her in greeting. Cal held on a little longer before kissing the top of her head.

"How's it going?" he asked.

"I'm hanging in there."

He stared into her eyes. "You need anything?"

If she did, he would be there in a heartbeat. They all would. As they'd told her over and over, she might have a different father, but she was stuck with them for life. Thank God.

"I'm fine," she said. "I believe we're here to talk about Walker's wedding in the land of twinkle lights."

Walker passed her the open bottle of wine and a glass. "I'm not talking about twinkle lights. That's Elissa's thing."

Dani poured herself some wine, then glanced at Reid. "Rumor has it you're eloping. Is that true?"

Reid nearly choked. "Who said that?"

"Lori."

Cal and Walker leaned forward. "When were you going to tell us?"

"There's nothing to tell. We've talked about it. There aren't any plans yet."

Dani sighed happily. "I love knowing something first. It never happens. This is a good moment."

"Brat," Reid grumbled good-naturedly.

"That's me. Just don't elope before Walker's wedding. That would distract everyone and not be fair to Elissa."

"I already know that," Reid told her. "We're waiting."

They discussed wedding details until Walker said he couldn't take it anymore. Cal turned to Dani.

"What about you?" he asked. "You've

been in the paper. How's that working for you?"

"Ugh. I hate it. I'm normal. Normal people do not make the front page of a newspaper. Do you know the campaign people have been running polls on what my appearance means to the American people? Because they now get a vote in my personal life."

"But it's worth it?" Cal asked. "With Mark?"

She shrugged. "I have no idea. I'm happy to know who my real father is. Sure. But it's not what I thought. Mark isn't . . . He's just different."

"Different how?" Walker asked.

"I thought we'd bond or feel a connection. I like him, but I don't know him. I'm not sure I ever will. I had unrealistic expectations, I guess. I blame television. Too many family sitcoms. Maybe if we had a soundtrack when we were together."

"It takes time," Reid said. "It's only been a few weeks."

She eyed him. "I'm not comfortable with you being the emotionally sensitive one."

"It's just how I am. A real special guy."

Cal nearly choked and Walker made a gagging noise. Dani smiled at her brothers. At least she had them. This part of her life was totally secure.

"Somebody said something to me earlier," she said. "About the campaign. That I could lose it for Mark."

"Not possible," Cal told her. "His ability to govern has nothing to do with having a kid he didn't know about."

"But will anyone else agree with that? More than one presidential hopeful has been derailed by a scandal."

"You're not a scandal."

"Not yet. But if I became one . . ." Dani hated that Fiona had planted that particular seed in her head, but she couldn't seem to get rid of it.

"Let it go," Walker told her. "Worry about what you can control."

"Where Mark's concerned, that's exactly nothing." She drew in a deep breath. "His wife, Katherine, called. She's invited me over to get to know the family better. I want to go. I like the kids and she's great. She could have joined the ladies who lunch crowd. Instead she's taken in all these special needs children and made them her own. That takes a kind of courage not many people have."

Reid put his arm around her. "You have good qualities, too. I can't think of any, but I'm sure you have them."

She punched his arm. "Gee, thanks. I feel so special."

"You are," Cal said.

Walker nodded and raised his glass to her. Reid did the same.

Dani felt a tightness in her chest, but it was a good sort of ache. It was as if her heart was so full of love, it couldn't possibly hold any more.

CHAPTER NINE

The dining room table at the Canfield house looked about a hundred years old. It was solid wood, with elegantly carved legs and space for twenty. But instead of a sophisticated dinner party, schoolbooks filled the surface.

Ian sat at one end, his wheelchair replacing a regular chair. He worked slowly, carefully recording his answers on a pad of paper. Bailey had a sheet of math problems in front of her. Trisha read a history book. Quinn practiced his writing, Oliver looked at a picture book while five-year-old Sasha colored.

"Controlled chaos," Katherine said over the din of six children working and talking. "It's like this all through the school year."

"I'm impressed," Dani said and meant it. "That they are all so willing to do their homework and that they do it together."

"Sometimes Ian goes to his room when

he has to concentrate."

"It doesn't happen often," Ian said, without looking up from his paper. "I'm pretty smart."

Katherine rolled her eyes. "I can see we need to have another conversation about grace and humility."

He glanced up. His mouth twisted in what Dani had come to realize was a smile. "Hey," he said. "It's me. Isn't that enough?"

Dani grinned. Ian looked at her and winked.

Dani walked to where Trish was reading her book. When she looked up, Dani carefully signed, "You like your class?" At least that's what she hoped she signed. She wasn't totally sure.

Trish stared at her for a second, then smiled and nodded while making a fist with her hand and rocking it up and down.

"That means yes," Katherine said. "I didn't know you signed."

"I don't," Dani said hastily. "Please, don't quiz me. I'll fail. But I know Trish is deaf and I wanted to be able to communicate with her so I went online and looked up a few phrases. There's an online dictionary that has video clips, so you can see how the signs are supposed to be done. I had trouble figuring them out from reading the description."

Dani shrugged, suddenly feeling silly. "You probably knew that."

"We have a CD-ROM dictionary that shows the signs. I agree, it makes it easier to understand the directions, especially on the more complicated signs." She touched Trish's shoulder. "She's in a special program for deaf students where she's learning to read lips and vocalize, as well as sign. We want her to be comfortable in both the hearing and the deaf world."

"Makes sense," Dani said.

"It's complicated," Katherine admitted. "There's a big debate in the deaf world about keeping their culture strong, focusing on their language. I want to respect that, but I also want Trish to be able to be happy and successful. It's something I can get passionate about, as can the deaf community. It makes for interesting debates."

Oliver tugged on Dani's hand. When she looked down, he handed her a large picture book. "Read, peas."

"I would love to read you a story." Dani glanced at Katherine. "If that's all right?"

"Of course. I'll start dinner."

Dani felt her eyes widen. "You cook? Oh. Sorry. That came out wrong. I'm sure you can, but when do you find time? You're so busy with your work and the children."

Katherine laughed. "Don't get excited. I rarely cook anything from scratch anymore. I have dinners delivered. They're prepared and ready to be grilled or popped in the oven. If it's a big party, I use a caterer. I still make soups and stews on weekends, when I have a free afternoon, which isn't often. Okay, there's a big overstuffed chair in the family room, assuming you don't mind cuddling while you read."

Dani smiled at Oliver. "I love cuddling."

She took the book and his hand and let him lead her to the family room. It was a huge open space with a big television at one end and seating for twenty. Oliver pointed at a dark blue chair with a large, squishy ottoman.

Dani settled down, then lifted Oliver onto her lap. He wiggled until he was wedged between her and the side of the chair, then he put his head on her chest and sighed. Sasha walked over and stood by them.

"I want a story, too," she said.

"Absolutely. You want to sit with me?"

Sasha nodded, then crawled over to Dani's other side.

" 'Once upon a time there were two kitties named Callie and Jake. They were brother and sister and lived in a blue house with a green lawn. They liked to play in the sun and take long baths.' That *is* a green lawn. I wish my lawn looked that good."

Sasha giggled. "You need a gardener."

"I probably do."

Oliver, who was a few years older, but hampered by Down's syndrome, pointed at the book. "Kitty," he said.

Dani put an arm around each of them and continued reading. As she told the story of two cats welcoming a human baby into their home, she wondered at the heartbreak of having a child who would always have challenges. Would Bailey or Oliver ever get to live on their own, get married, grow old?

What about Quinn, who looked like other children, but couldn't learn as quickly? Or Ian, who was brilliant, but trapped in a body he couldn't control?

The blessings of this family overwhelmed her, as did the potential for heartache.

When Dani finished the story, Oliver and Sasha ran off to play. Dani wandered into the kitchen to see if she could help.

"You were gracious enough to invite me to dinner," she said. "I'm prepared to earn my place at the table."

Katherine laughed. "Oh, but you work in

187

a restaurant. How do I know you're not going to silently mock my skills?"

"Never. I'm in management. I don't do actual cooking."

Katherine wore wool slacks and a blouse that was probably silk. With her hair pulled back and tasteful pearl earrings, she looked as if she'd just stepped out of the pages of *Town & Country.* Yet when Sasha came running in the kitchen, Katherine caught her easily and pulled her close for a hug.

"I could be very good if I had a cookie," the little girl said.

"I'm sure you can be very good without a cookie. Dinner's in less than an hour."

Sasha sniffed. "That's a very long time and I'm very hungry."

"I suspect you'll survive."

Sasha glanced at Dani. "Do you want to give me a cookie?"

Dani shook her head.

Sasha sighed heavily and left.

Katherine picked up the knife she'd been using to slice broccoli. "She's in a 'very' stage right now. Everything is very something. She's so dramatic. I won't be surprised if she ends up on the stage." She glanced at Dani. "You know Sasha is HIV positive."

Dani nodded.

"You're not afraid to touch her? You had her on your lap while you were reading."

Dani had the sense of being tested. "No. I'm not concerned."

"People have a lot of misconceptions about HIV."

"Among other things," Dani said quietly. "You must deal with it all the time."

"I do. A lot of people think I chose these children because they have problems. That's not true. I chose these children because they touched my heart."

Dani understood how that could happen. They were already making inroads into her heart.

She'd put off thinking about children when she and Hugh were first married. Taking care of him had been all she could handle. Eventually, he'd become more autonomous, so she'd explored different options, including in vitro fertilization. Then Hugh had said he wanted a divorce and it had all hit the fan. Now, for the first time in her life, Dani understood what people were talking about when they mentioned a biological clock. There was some serious ticking going on with hers.

"Alex mentioned the charity event to me," she said. "I'm sorry you have to deal with me in public."

"Don't be," Katherine told her. "We'll be fine."

"I've never done anything like that. Spoken in public, been to a fancy charity."

"It sounds worse than it is," Katherine said with a smile. "I'm thinking we'll go to a luncheon. It's more low-key. As for speaking, one of Mark's people will prepare a few remarks and go over them with you. We're talking ten minutes, tops."

Ten minutes sounded like a lifetime to Dani. "Great," she murmured, wondering what the headline would be when she projectile vomited halfway through her speech.

"You'll be fine. I'll help. When it gets closer we can talk about what you should wear and how to make sure you don't have anything in your teeth when you smile for pictures."

Dani felt both pleased and awkward. "You didn't have to do any of this. You could have thrown me out of your home. Instead you've made me feel welcome."

"You're Mark's daughter, Dani. That means something to me."

"You're an amazing woman."

Katherine laughed. "How I wish that were true. I'm just like everyone else, trying to get through the day."

Dani doubted that. Katherine was class. Dani didn't think she could have been as kind if the situations were reversed.

"Who knows," Katherine said as she scooped the broccoli into a steamer. "You may find you enjoy the charity work. Some women find it very satisfying. I do, as does Fiona. You met her, didn't you? Alex's wife."

Dani's insides went cold. "His wife? I thought . . ."

"They're divorced," Katherine admitted as she poured water into a pot. "I don't know what's going on. Honestly. Alex won't talk to me about specifics. Fiona is devastated. I've asked him to rethink his decision. I'm getting through to him, at least that's what I tell myself."

Dani didn't know what to say. When Fiona had gone on about being a member of the Canfield family, Dani had thought it was just cheap talk. Now she wasn't so sure.

But Alex had kissed *her,* Dani reminded herself. He wasn't the kind of man to play around, was he?

She swore silently. Not again, she told herself. She would not be played again. So how to be sure?

"Marriage is difficult," she murmured, because a reply seemed expected.

"I agree. I've told Alex it's important to

take the time they both need to be sure. As it is, we're hopeful."

Hopeful. Fiona had used the same word. Did that mean anything? Was Dani looking for trouble where there wasn't any or was the truth staring her in the face? Was Alex too good to be true?

Gloria put her feet up on the coffee table and pointed the remote control at the television. "It's unrated. But as it is a political interview, I doubt we have to worry about graphic violence and sexual situations," she said as she pushed Play.

The video started.

Dani took a handful of popcorn from the large bowl between them. "If there is graphic sex involving my biological father, I'm so out of here. That's not an image I want planted in my brain."

"I doubt the junior senator from Washington interviewed naked. Although if he looked good in a thong, that could help his campaign."

Dani didn't know if she should laugh or be shocked. "Gloria Buchanan, I can't believe you said that."

"Why shouldn't I appreciate a handsome man in a thong? I'm not dead. At least not yet."

"Still, it's borderline icky."

"So I'm supposed to go blind as well as break my hip?"

"No, but let's not talk about thongs."

Gloria winked. "I'll only sin in my heart."

"A good place for it."

Dani ate the popcorn. Six months ago she never would have believed that she could have enjoyed living with Gloria. Six weeks ago it would have been a stretch. But here she was, in her house and feeling perfectly comfortable. It was a miracle.

"Our interview tonight is with Senator Mark Canfield. The senator is considering a run for president, although a recent revelation about an illegitimate child might present a challenge to the campaign."

Dani grabbed another handful of popcorn. "I never thought of myself as illegitimate. How Victorian."

"You have a father listed on your birth certificate," Gloria told her. "You're fine."

"So reality doesn't matter? It's all about perception?"

"Naturally. You should already know that."

Dani had a good sense of it. She turned her attention back to the interview.

Mark let the other man talk himself down,

then began to calmly explain how a member of the media used a puppy to get a child with Down's syndrome to betray a family secret.

He was good, speaking slowly, conversationally, painting a vivid picture of a pretty little girl who could never really understand the harsh cruelty of the world. Mark made Alex's intervention sound like a knight riding to the rescue, and the discovery that Dani was his long-lost daughter a miracle.

"He's good," she said when she'd chewed and swallowed. "Better than good."

"He's a professional. What did you expect?"

Dani wasn't sure. "The smoothness is off-putting," she admitted. "Sometimes he doesn't seem fully human."

"Don't judge him because he's good at his job," Gloria told her.

"Why couldn't he be a plumber or a math teacher?"

"Life isn't that convenient."

"Whose decision was that?" Dani reached for more popcorn. "I can't figure Mark out. I can't figure any of them out. They're living in a world I don't understand."

"Don't be sorry you met him," Gloria told her. "He's your father. It hasn't been very long. Give both of you a little more time. It will get easier."

"I hope you're right," Dani said. "Sometimes I think I should just disappear. That if I stay around, we're all headed for a massive disaster. What if I'm the reason he's not elected president?"

"Don't be a quitter. You have nothing to do with the election."

"You don't know that."

"Neither do you. I like a good worry as much as the next person, but give this one a little time off. You can always come back to it later if you need to."

"How rational," Dani murmured, not feeling very rational at the moment. Still, her grandmother was right. Dani couldn't be sure her presence had done any harm. After all, she was tracking well. She would just wait and see how it all played out. What's the worst that could happen?

Katherine finished putting night cream on her face, then pulled off the scrunchie that held her hair back. She looked up and saw Mark getting undressed in their walk-in closet.

As always, the sight of him thrilled her and watching him take off his clothes made her want to make love to him. Instantly her mind filled with images of them naked, touching, kissing. Her body tightened.

So many of her friends talked about sex being a chore, something to get through so they could get to sleep, but it wasn't that way for her. She wanted Mark as much today as she had when they'd first been together. She had a feeling they could be eighty and toothless and he would still turn her on.

She walked to the doorway of the closet. "I talked to Dani about both of us appearing at the charity event. She's a little nervous, but I think she'll do well."

"Good," he said, not even looking at her. "Is my black pinstripe suit at the cleaners?"

An innocent question that brought tears to her eyes. "That's it?" she asked. "All you can say is *good?* Don't you have any idea of how this is hurting me? Don't you know that I'm devastated by her presence and what it means?"

He frowned. "What do you want me to say?"

That he would love her forever. That she was the most important part of his life. That he'd never loved anyone but her. Words he would never speak.

She turned away. "It doesn't matter," she whispered, knowing this was a battle she could never win. Mark would never love her as much as she loved him. He would never want her the same way. She'd tried to make peace with that truth for years. Tried and failed.

"It does matter." He moved close behind her and put his hand on her shoulder. "You matter. I don't know what to say. Katherine, you're the one who broke off our engagement all those years ago. You're the one who dumped me. You sent me away."

She nodded, because it was true. Still tears burned in her eyes. "You weren't supposed to fall in love with someone else. You were supposed to miss me."

"I did miss you."

"Not enough to keep from having an affair with that woman. I was devastated, Mark." She turned to face him. "I couldn't stand the thought of telling you I couldn't have children. Rather than see your pity or watch you walk away, I let you go. But I never stopped loving you. That's why I came back. That's why I flew out here and begged for a second chance. Do you know how hard it was to tell you I couldn't have children?"

He took her hands in his, his blue eyes dark with confusion. "And I was fine with it. I said it didn't matter and it didn't. I loved you, Katherine. I still do."

"But you loved her, too."

"It's over."

Was it?

She pulled away and walked into the bedroom. The questions haunted her. Why had Mark really married her? He'd been ambitious and she'd been rich. Until she'd known about Marsha, she'd assumed he'd really missed her. Now she knew he'd easily moved on and had gotten involved with someone else in a matter of days. That simple fact changed everything.

What would have happened if Marsha hadn't ended things? Would Mark have been willing to come back to her, Katherine, then? She would never know.

He came up behind her and drew her against him. "I hate to see you hurting."

"I'm fine," she lied.

He turned her until she faced him, then put one hand on the back of her neck and kissed her.

She had a feeling he was trying to distract her. She willed herself to be strong, but it was impossible. She'd never been able to be strong where he was concerned. The second his mouth touched hers, all she wanted was to surrender. Wanting overwhelmed her and she gave herself over to the man and how he made her feel. The pain would still be there in the morning, but for now, this was enough.

Alex knew it was going to be a long day when the only nonlawyer in the meeting was his father.

Peter Aaron flipped through the folder in front of him. "We have some time before the charges are filed. If we talk to the D.A., we'll find out what they're planning."

"They're planning a circus," Mark grumbled. "This is all political. They want to hurt the campaign. The damn press."

"There are a lot of ways this can play out," Pete said. "We need a few details before we can come up with a game plan. The partners are very interested in the outcome of all of this."

Alex kept his expression neutral and calm, but on the inside, he wanted to throw something. Or hit something, which is what had gotten him in trouble in the first place. He didn't usually have trouble controlling his temper, but when he'd decked the reporter, something inside him had snapped.

He hated all this. He hated that there was no good outcome for him, with the exception of the charges simply going away and that wasn't going to happen. However this fell, he was screwed.

Pete Aaron was a partner in Alex's law firm. He was working Alex's case for only one reason and that was Mark's bid for the presidency. If Mark was elected, then Alex would have a place at the White House and the firm would benefit. If Mark didn't run, or wasn't elected, Alex had a feeling he could kiss his corporate law career goodbye.

What frustrated him the most was that it didn't matter why he'd hit the guy. No one wanted to talk about an asshole using a kid to get private information. Oh, sure, it would come out at the trial, but now it was simply incidental.

The other two lawyers talked, with Mark adding a few comments but he, Alex, didn't listen. They were coming up with a plan and it would be his job to go along with it. After all, there was a presidency at stake.

He thought about the hurt in Bailey's eyes when she realized she'd done something wrong and knew that given the same set of circumstances, he would do it all again, regardless of the outcome.

He studied his father. Mark loved the political arena. If he won, they were all going to be in it for a long, long time.

CHAPTER TEN

Dani drove down a lengthy driveway, not sure what she would find at the other end. A mansion? A trailer? She smiled and then caught her breath when she made a turn and found herself in front of a large, two-story log home.

It was all wood and glass and shaped a little like a fairy-tale castle, which should have looked strange but instead made her feel as if she'd stumbled into someone's private architectural fantasy.

There were stone steps leading to a long porch that had both chairs and a swing. Old-growth trees soared toward the sky, while lush landscaping added to the dream-like quality of the place.

Not exactly what she'd been expecting, she thought as she grabbed the bottle of wine she'd brought and got out of her car. But then she hadn't known what to expect when Alex had called and invited her over for dinner. At least the press had stopped following her a few days ago. She hadn't had to use James Bond driving to keep them at bay.

She walked up the stone steps. The door opened before she could knock and there was Alex. He looked good. She'd only ever seen him in suits, so the jeans and sweater came as a surprise. While she appreciated fine tailoring as much as the next woman, there was something to be said for a man who looked hot in jeans.

The worn denim emphasized narrow hips and long legs. He'd pushed the sweater sleeves up a little, leaving his wrists bare, which was oddly sexy. Funny how that had never turned her on before. Wrists weren't anything all that exciting, except on him. Or was it more about the man himself?

"Hey," he said as he motioned for her to step inside. "Thanks for coming."

"Thanks for asking me. An interesting invitation, if unexpected."

"I had a hell of a day," he said. "I needed to see a friendly face."

Simple words. Casual words, yet they hit her hard and fast, stealing her breath and leaving her weak at the knees.

She was the friendly face he wanted to see? Her? Not family or friends or that annoyingly beautiful ex-wife of his?

"Great place," she said. "Have you lived here long?"

"About five months. I bought it after the divorce was final. I wanted privacy and quiet. This has both."

"Plus it's a cool place to bring the ladies."

She was determined to keep things light. It was her only way to stay sane. An excellent plan that turned to dust the second Alex pulled her close and kissed her.

There was no warning, no niceties, no asking for permission. Just his mouth on hers in a kiss that took and offered all at the same time.

His breath was hot and faintly minty, his body hard in all the right places. He took the wine from her, set it on a table and nipped at her lower lip.

His hands were politely at her waist. As she leaned in to him, she wanted him touching her everywhere. She wanted to writhe and moan and be taken so hard that she didn't have to think. She only had to feel.

Apparently he couldn't read minds or he wasn't interested in her that way because he stepped back and smiled faintly.

"You look great," he said.

"Thanks." She'd come straight from work,

but she was willing to accept the compliment.

"For the record, I don't bring ladies here, as you put it. Except for family, you're my first dinner guest."

Really? In five months there hadn't been anyone else?

A thrill swept through her before she reminded herself that just because he hadn't brought anyone *here* didn't mean he hadn't gone somewhere else to get naked. It was unlikely Alex had been celibate since his divorce.

"How'd you find this place?" she asked.

"I got lucky. My agent brought me to see it the day it went on the market. There was a bidding war and I won."

That's right. He was a Canfield. His financial resources weren't limited to his impressive lawyer salary.

He grabbed her hand and led her through the entryway into a large, open great room. There were walls of glass, with French doors leading to a covered patio about the size of her rental. To the right was a massive kitchen, to the left a big television and lots of electronic equipment — the kind designed to make a man very happy.

The room was decorated in earth tones, subdued but welcoming.

"Impressive," she said. "Did you do this all yourself?"

He chuckled as he set the wine on the granite counter. "You can't believe that. My mom helped, as did Julie. She's the next oldest in the family. She's a sophomore at UW, living on campus. She's studying psychology, but has a great eye for this kind of stuff."

"Which you don't?"

"I'm a guy."

He was, and an excellent representation of the entire gender.

She set her purse on a stool in front of the counter that separated the open kitchen from the living area in the great room. While he took care of the wine, she sniffed delicately.

"I'm not smelling any food," she teased. "Should I be worried that I'll starve?"

"It's here, in the refrigerator. All it requires is a little heating. Are you hungry or can you wait a little?"

She looked into his dark eyes. Food wasn't a problem. The thing she didn't want to wait for was him.

Danger, she told herself. Big, burly, sexy danger. Hadn't she learned her lesson? Was she one of those sad women destined to repeat the same mistakes over and over again when it came to men?

"I can wait," she told him. The longer, the better.

He handed her a glass of wine, then led her out onto the patio. The floor was some kind of stone . . . maybe slate. On one side was a steer-size grill, a built-in sink and under-the-counter refrigerator.

"You could throw a great party out here," she murmured as he turned on a propane heater and gestured to a wicker sofa lined in soft-looking cushions.

"That's the plan. When I get the time."

"Famous last words. You have to make the time. I know from personal experience."

He settled next to her, angling toward her. "Do you?"

"Not as much as I should. My excuse is that I'm in a new job and trying to learn as quickly as possible. Of course your excuse is that you're part of a national campaign. I guess you'd win that contest."

"It's crazy," he admitted. "Today I sat in on a meeting of lawyers all discussing how to handle the problem of me being charged with assaulting that damned reporter. I've never been the subject of a meeting before."

"I'm guessing you didn't like it."

He looked at her, his eyes dark and un-readable. "Not my style. The thing is, I don't want to be involved. But I am involved. If this screws up the campaign . . ."

She shook her head. "Sorry. I already have that guilt sewn up. You're going to have to find something else to feel bad about."

"You have nothing to do with the campaign."

"Oh, please. I'm being tracked. So far the American people are delighted to know about me. What happens when that changes? What if I say or do something I shouldn't? I'm really not the right person for the job. I have a past."

He smiled. "Not much of one. I know. I had you investigated."

"How comforting. So nothing about my life is a mystery to you?"

"I know broad strokes. Not details."

That was something. "Would you be impressed if I told you some of the details are really juicy?"

"I'm already impressed."

Oh my. "Good to know," she murmured, then sipped her wine.

He set his glass on the low table in front of them. "Dani, you need to know that as the campaign moves forward and you become a public figure, you may hear from people in your past."

She was so stunned to hear the words

"public figure" associated with herself that she nearly missed the second half of the sentence.

"Like who?"

"I don't know," he said. "Maybe Hugh."

"You mean because he'll want something?"

"He might want you back. Being married to the daughter of a president is a big deal."

She immediately flashed to Fiona, then pushed the image away. "Hugh isn't that stupid," she said. "He knows it's totally over. I won't forgive the cheating and I don't want to go back. I've mourned the marriage, listed my regrets and moved on."

"Just be aware that it could happen."

She thought about the other men so recently in her life. Gary would never bother her but Ryan? He was stupid enough to try.

"What are you thinking?" Alex asked.

"About who else might suddenly show up."

"Are you going to name names?"

His voice was low and teasing. Sexy. He made her want to spill state secrets, or make them up if she didn't have any on her own.

"After Hugh, I got involved with a guy at The Waterfront. It's one of the family restaurants."

"I've eaten there. Good place."

"Thanks. We hired a new general manager. Ryan. He was funny and charming and really good-looking."

"Jerk."

She laughed. "Actually, he was. He said and did all the right things. I decided he could be my rebound guy."

"Was he?"

"That and more. Just when I thought he might be someone I could really care about, his wife and toddler showed up. Literally. She came in looking for him and had the kid with her."

"Ouch."

Alex stared at her and she met his gaze directly. She had nothing to hide. She might still be dealing with a few regrets for being such an idiot, but there weren't any secrets.

"The thing that got me the most, more than the lies and betrayal, was what he said. He told me he was sorry I had to find out that way. It was stunning. How did he want me to find out? The point was he was upset I had the information, but not the least bit remorseful that he'd been a cheating weasel dog."

"Some guys are like that."

"Did you ever cheat?"

"No."

His gaze was steady, his voice calm. She

209

believed him.

"I didn't think so." She set her wineglass next to his. "So my Ryan relationship was dumb on my part."

"Why? How could you know?"

"I could have asked more questions. He was playing me. Shouldn't I have sensed that?"

"You don't play people, why would you expect others to play you?"

"You're right. I just felt so stupid. I vowed to never get involved with a guy again."

"But you did anyway?"

"Oh, yeah. His name was Gary. He's a quiet, unassuming, sweet sort of guy who made me feel safe."

"Did I mention he's a jerk, too?"

"That was Ryan. Gary is fairly jerk-free. I liked him but there wasn't any chemistry. I thought that might be a good thing, what with chemistry getting me in trouble with Ryan. For a while I thought he was gay."

Alex chuckled. "Not exactly what a guy likes to hear."

"Tell me about it. Still, he handled it all with grace and style and when he asked me out, I said yes." She paused, not sure if she should have started down this particular conversational path. It was one thing to have secrets, it was another to spill the details.

"What happened?"

She drew in a deep breath. "We went to a lovely little neighborhood restaurant he knew about and before we were even seated, this woman walked by and called him Father."

Alex looked confused. "You got mad because he had kids you didn't know about?"

"No, I got upset because he used to be a priest."

Alex started laughing. Dani narrowed her gaze.

"It's not funny," she told him.

"It is. Come on. A priest? Were you his first date?"

"No, he'd been out before, but I'm not sure he'd . . . you know. I couldn't deal with it. I'm sure it shows a lack of moral fiber or character on my part. But the second I figured it out, I knew God was giving me a message from the great beyond. I was not supposed to be with Gary, so I left. Ran, actually. Like the wind."

He laughed again and this time she joined in.

"I almost feel sorry for the poor guy," he admitted.

"Almost?"

"I wouldn't want you with him."

Right, she thought, her mind going fuzzy with possibilities. Because then she couldn't be here . . . with him. That's what he was talking about, right?

"So that's my sorry love life, the recent years, anyway," she said. "Tragic and funny and nothing I ever expected."

"It's been interesting," he said, reaching for his wine. "Better than boring."

"Oh, I don't know. Boring sounds good. Now you know all my secrets. What about yours?"

His eyes darkened slightly. "No one since the divorce. A few dates that didn't go any-where."

Did he count seeing Fiona as dating? Was he seeing his ex-wife? "What ended the mar-riage?" she asked, knowing it was an in-tensely personal question but figuring he'd seen hers, so he could show his.

"She cheated," he said flatly. "I walked in on her screwing some guy." He frowned. "I don't even know who he is. I never bothered to find out."

Dani stared at him. She couldn't believe she and Alex had cheating in common. "I'm sorry. I know how that feels. I walked in on Hugh. It's how I found out."

"They were doing it on the dining room table," he said.

"Hugh and his groupie were in his office. Equally tacky." She shook her head. "I hated the betrayal of it. If we hadn't already started divorce proceedings, I would have left him then."

"That's what I did. Once Fiona broke my trust, it was finished. She wanted to talk things over, to give the relationship a second chance. Like your Ryan, I suspect she was only sorry she'd been caught."

Dani drew in a breath. "So you're not seeing her?"

"Hell no. Why would I?"

"I ran into her recently and she implied you were getting back together, or at least talking about it." As had Katherine, although Dani didn't want to go there.

"She's one of those people I told you about," he said. "The kind who want to be close to the seat of power. She's interested now that my father is running for president."

"Okay. Good. Thanks for telling me."

There were only a few lights on the covered patio. In the dimness, Dani's eyes looked more brown than hazel. Still, Alex could read a lot of emotions flashing across them, the last one being relief.

Had she been worried about Fiona? God knows what the bitch had said. Fiona would

213

do just about anything to get what she wanted. At one time he'd admired her single-minded determination. These days — not so much.

Dani was different. There was an honesty about her that he appreciated. She seemed to lead with her heart, which could get her into trouble if she wasn't careful. Not with him — he had no plans to hurt her, although he wouldn't mind getting to know her better. Especially if that involved them being naked.

His body tightened as the image filled his mind. There had been a couple of casual sexual relationships after he and Fiona had split up, but they'd been little more than a way to scratch an itch. He hadn't thought he was looking for anything more, but maybe he'd been wrong.

"What are you thinking?" she asked. "You have the strangest expression on your face."

"That you've changed everything in a very short period of time."

She sighed. "That's not a good thing, is it?"

"Why not? Maybe we needed a change."

"What your mother needs is a vacation," Dani said. "I hate that this has upset her. Dealing with the reality of me can't be easy for her. She's so fabulous. I want to be her when I grow up."

"You're grown-up now."

"Don't say that. Then I can't have her as a goal."

He liked that Dani respected Katherine and that she was sensitive to what his mother was going through.

But talking about his mother wasn't how he wanted to spend his evening.

"Are you hungry?" he asked. "Want me to start dinner?"

She stood. "You mean heat dinner?"

"Whatever works."

"Sure."

She led the way back into the kitchen. As she put her glass of wine on the counter, she turned and they bumped.

He held out his arm to keep his wine from spilling. She reached for it at the same time, but instead of grabbing the glass, her hand ended up on his chest.

Desire hit him with the subtlety of a bomb blast. Need consumed him, made him hard and threatened any self-control he'd learned in the past thirty-plus years. Her eyes widened, her breath caught and he would swear she was just as interested as he.

"I know what you're thinking," he said as he put his glass next to hers and then grabbed the hand touching him. "That I lured you to my cabin in the woods so that I could have my way with you. Just so you know . . . there really is a dinner."

One they could easily eat later rather than sooner.

"Yes, well, food is good," Dani mumbled. "It's not that I'm not interested. You're very appealing and nice and I like you."

Appealing and nice? Nice? He dropped her hand. Great. So he'd imagined her reaction to him. She probably thought of him as a brother.

But what about their kisses? She'd been aroused. He'd felt her interest. He refused to believe their chemistry was all one-sided.

"It's not that I don't want you to have your way with me," she continued. "I'm tempted. But we have family issues. The potential for scandal. Not to mention my past. I've learned to be very cautious. Relationships are bad, at least for me."

"You're comparing me to two assholes and a priest?"

"Ex-priest and I'm not exactly comparing you. It's just I don't want to make another mistake. I know it's unfair that you're stuck paying for my mistakes, but there we are. I'm starting to think the only way I'll ever be comfortable getting naked with a guy again is to be totally in charge. I'd probably have to tie him up first."

Alex leaned against the counter and nodded slowly. "I've never done that, but I'm open to the possibility."

Dinner was delicious. A spicy chicken dish with mashed potatoes and vegetables. Dani didn't know where Alex had picked up the meal, but she wanted the restaurant's phone number. Not that she'd been able to eat that much. She continued to be in shock, first by the fact that she'd blurted out bondage would be required for her to have sex and second because Alex hadn't run screaming into the night at the thought.

She knew he could be dangerous to her. Now she had a bad feeling she was in way over her head.

They sat on the sofa in his great room. The lights were low, the music seductive, the man irresistible. Hmm, she might have a problem here. So what was she going to do about it?

Before she could make a decision, mature or not, he put his hand on the back of her neck. Just a light touch, fingers barely grazing her skin. Yet goose bumps broke out on her arms and she found herself wanting to shift so she could rub against him.

She turned to him and found him closer

than she'd realized. Close enough that leaning in and kissing him made all the sense in
the world.

His mouth was an impossible combination of firm and soft. It was a perfect mouth
for kissing and maybe other things, she
thought, imagining how it would feel to
have him press his lips to her everywhere.

He slid his hand up the back of her neck
until his fingers threaded through her hair.
He put his other hand on her waist. Again,
a light touch, nothing demanding. Just
tempting . . . very tempting.

She strained to get closer, which was probably his plan all along. To make her want
him so much that making love would be her
idea rather than his. Smart man.

Despite the gentle brush of his tongue
against her lower lip, she drew back.

"Alex, I . . ." She stared into his dark eyes.
Fire burned there. Hot fire that made her
want to be swallowed in the flames. "I really
want to do this."

"Good. Me, too."

"There are complications."

"I have condoms."

"What? Oh, not that, although I appreciate that you're willing to use them. I meant
us. Who we are. The fact that our lives are
oddly intertwined. My hideous past."

He smiled at her, then kissed her again. "I'm totally open to your terms."

That took her a second. "My terms?" Then she shrieked. "Bondage. Are you saying bondage?"

"You're the one who wanted to tie me up."

"If you have velvet handcuffs in your nightstand, I am so out of here."

"Ties," he said as he kissed her again. "Really nice ties. Silk."

His teasing felt almost as good as his mouth. She gave herself over to his kiss, letting desire sweep through her, the heat of it melting away lingering good sense.

Alex was so much of what she wanted and nearly nothing she didn't. He was single, funny, open to new experiences and interested in her. He cared about his family, did the right thing, respected vows and hadn't cheated on his wife. He'd also never been a priest. All pluses.

He wrapped both arms around her and pulled her close. She sank into him, loving the feel of his hard body against hers. She put her arms around his neck and gave herself over to the kiss, parting for him, letting him sweep her away. She needed a good sweeping away.

She let her body sink into his, enjoying the differences a man brought to the table . . . or the bed. She liked how he was all hard planes and jutting arousal. She liked how her insides got squishy and wet in response. She liked imagining what it would be like to make love to him.

He swept his tongue across hers, exploring, pushing, taking. Then he pulled away from her mouth and began kissing his way along her jaw. He nipped, then licked, making her gasp. He nibbled his way down her neck, pausing to suck on her earlobe. When he dipped lower, along the V of her sweater, she had the sudden thought that she should have worn something much lower cut.

He shifted so he was stretched out on the sofa and she was on top of him. The position gave her the feeling of being in charge, which she liked.

"It's warm in here," he murmured as he tugged at the hem of her top. "You must be hot."

"In a thousand different ways," she joked.

She helped him pull off the sweater, then bent over him, kissing him as he ran his hands up and down her back.

His touch skimmed over her skin, heating her from the inside out. He moved to her rear and cupped the curves. The action made her rub against him.

There were too many layers of clothing

for her to feel much, but the pressure of his hardness against her moist, swollen center made her want him.

He eased his hands up to her waist, then around to her back where he unfastened her bra. She pulled it away and bent over him, letting her breasts hang free.

"Hell of a show," he whispered as he placed his hands on her breasts.

He moved slowly, discovering her curves, teasing her, circling around and around, getting close to her nipples without actually touching them. She nearly whimpered in anticipation. But instead of using his fingers, he raised his upper body and drew her right nipple into his mouth.

He sucked gently, tugging just enough for her to feel the connection to that place between her legs. Her skin puckered, her toes curled. He used his hand on her other breast which was nice, but not nearly as good. Need built inside of her and she began to move back and forth against his arousal, riding him in an attempt to ease her own tension.

He switched to her other breast, sucking and licking and biting just hard enough to make her breath catch.

More, she thought desperately. She needed more.

"Alex."

He opened his eyes and looked at her. "We should probably move the party."

She nodded, then slid off him. She was topless, but not self-conscious. Not when he could barely keep his eyes off her.

They both kicked off their shoes, then he took her hand and led the way down the hallway. As they entered the bedroom, he grabbed a remote that turned on a gas fireplace.

Flames provided enough light for her to see the large bedroom. The furniture was big and masculine and the bed was massive. Then Alex pulled her close and she didn't care about anything but what they were going to do to each other.

He jerked off his sweater and pulled her closer. Bare skin to bare skin, she thought with a sigh. Now that worked for her in a big way.

He unfastened her slacks and pushed them down, along with her panties. Then they were kissing and she stepped out of her clothes and tried to move backward, only she couldn't get her legs to work right, probably because he'd slipped his hand between them.

Get to the bed, she told herself. It would be better there. But it was hard to think about anything but the back-and-forth motion of his fingers on her swollen center.

He explored her, finding that one magic place, then worshipping it with a gentle, rhythmic touch. She moaned, then nipped at his bottom lip.

"You're driving me crazy," she whispered.

"That would be the point."

But he released her long enough for her to pull back the covers and scramble onto the bed. She yanked off her socks, then stretched out on the cool sheets.

Alex did a little prep work of his own. He stripped off his clothes in about an eighth of a second and joined her.

"Where were we?" he asked before pulling her close.

She went into his arms, aroused, yet more at ease than she would have thought possible. She was making love with Alex for the first time and didn't feel nervous or apprehensive. What was up with that?

A silly question, she thought as he stroked her breasts. What mattered was how the man made her feel.

He shifted her onto her back and began to kiss his way down her body. She closed her eyes and gave herself over to him, both tensing and relaxing as he brushed his mouth against her belly, her hips, her thighs, before parting her damp curls and kissing her intimately between her legs.

His tongue was warm and sure, stroking her with just enough pressure to make her catch her breath. He moved slowly, explored thoroughly, circling and licking, pausing until she wanted to scream, then going just a little faster.

He made love to her like a man who enjoyed what he was doing, which made her want him more.

Pleasure shot through her. As he continued the easy pressure, the bottoms of her feet began to burn. She pulsed her hips in time with his movements, urging him on.

More, she thought through a veil of passion. She needed more. But he seemed in no hurry to finish things up. He continued to tease her with his tongue, barely increasing his speed. Her muscles tensed in anticipation of an orgasm that still seemed so far away. She reached for her release, straining, wanting, but it wasn't time.

He went on and on, driving her crazy in the best way possible. Ribbons of pleasure wove their way through her body. Her skin was tight and sensitive, her breasts ached. Inch by inch she got closer and closer still. So close that coming seemed inevitable and yet she hung there, just shy of the edge, desperate to fall.

"Alex," she breathed. *Do something!*

But she didn't say it. The journey was too exquisite.

He shifted slightly and she felt him slide a finger inside of her. At the same time he sucked on her very center while flicking her with his tongue.

Her release exploded like thunder. One second there was only expectation, the next her entire body was lost in sensations so intense, she thought she might never find her way back.

She cried out, then gasped for breath. She writhed beneath him as he touched her perfectly until the very last ounce of pleasure had flowed from her body.

Dani couldn't move. She might never move again, which wasn't a bad thing. Not if she could experience something like that a second time.

He pushed himself into a kneeling position and reached for a condom. After slipping it on, he eased inside of her, filling her, stretching her, making her quiver. Then he slipped his hand between them and slowly rubbed her.

She opened her mouth to tell him he didn't have to bother. She'd already had her fun. Besides, she would be too sensitive.

But there was something about the gentle touch of his fingers that was surprisingly erotic. Before she could get out the words, she found herself eager for more of what he was doing.

He stayed where he was, inside of her and touching her. He was barely moving, but there was just enough friction to get her attention. Back and forth, back and forth, little pulses that teased. She wanted more.

So when he pushed in, she pushed down, drawing him all the way inside of her. His eyes dilated, his body stiffened. The fingers rubbing her fumbled slightly.

She smiled. "Better."

"I want you to come again. If I get going too soon . . ."

She was already halfway there. "I think we should be able to time it right." She was still sensitive from her recent orgasm. He'd pushed her close; it wouldn't take much to get her over the edge once more.

"I want you inside of me for real," she told him. "Stop playing."

He shifted onto his knees and braced himself over her. Then, as he stared into her eyes, he took her at her word and got serious.

He filled her hard and fast, pushing into her with an intensity that made her nerve endings want to sigh. The sensation of being taken was nearly as exciting as it was arousing. She wrapped her legs around his hips, pulling him in closer, holding him in place. He lowered his head and kissed her.

Pressure built inside of her. The deep thrusts shoved her closer to another release. She tried to hold back, to enjoy what he was doing for as long as possible, then she felt him stiffen. He broke the kiss.

"I can't hold back," he said through gritted teeth.

"Good."

He pushed in once more, then groaned. She felt the first shudder claim him and it was enough to send her over the edge. She clung to him as her second orgasm swept through her. She gasped, she might have screamed. Honestly, she didn't care one way or the other. The man deserved a scream or two after what he'd done.

Seconds, or maybe minutes, later, Alex rolled onto his side. He touched her face, tucked her hair behind her ear, then kissed her. Then he started to laugh.

"What?" she asked.

"I forgot to have you tie me up. Remember? It was supposed to make you feel safer and more in charge."

Oh, yeah. She'd been worried about trusting another man. "I guess we can let that go."

Humor brightened his eyes. "But I was looking forward to trying something new."

"Next time," she promised, wondering if he was really as amazing as he seemed and hoping that he was.

Dani figured she caught her breath sometime close to one in the morning. They'd left the fire going, giving Alex's bedroom a soft glow. She lay curled up against him, her head on his shoulder in a classic postsex pose.

"You okay?" he asked as he stroked her back. "You've been quiet."

"I'm basking in contentment."

"Basking is good."

"Better than good," she said, remembering how he'd made her tremble and shudder and scream. Again.

"For me, too."

So she could add chemistry to the plus side of the list, she thought. The complications of that chemistry would have to sit on the negative side.

"If anyone knew . . ." she began.

He chuckled. She could both hear and feel the sound.

"Tell me about it," he said. "It would

make for some interesting copy."

"They aren't getting it from me," she told him.

He looked at her, then bent close and kissed the tip of her nose. "You didn't have to tell me that, Dani. I trust you."

She felt heat inside, but this time it had nothing to do with sexual arousal and everything to do with how she felt about this man. Based on what she knew about his past, he didn't trust easily.

"I'm glad," she said. "Maybe we could —"

A faint but distinctive ringing interrupted her. Dani raised her head. "That's my cell phone."

It was late. A call at this hour was never good.

She jumped up naked, grabbed what looked like Alex's shirt and ran back into the great room where she'd put her purse.

"Hello," she said as she opened her flip phone. "What's wrong?"

"Dani, it's Kristie."

Dani's body got cold. Kristie was Gloria's night nurse. The only one still on duty.

"What happened?"

"Your grandmother collapsed. I've called 9-1-1 and the paramedics are here. They're taking her to the hospital. She's breathing and her vitals are okay. I don't think it's another heart attack, but I'm not sure."

Dani felt the room sway. Then Alex was at her side, urging her to sit on the sofa.

"Okay," Dani said, not able to think through the panic. What if Kristie were wrong? What if Gloria had had another heart attack? Dani couldn't stand to lose her. Not now. Not when they'd just found each other after all these years.

"I'll be right there," Dani said. "Thanks for calling."

"No problem. I'll phone your brothers from the ambulance."

Dani hung up. "My grandmother," she said. "She collapsed. She's going to the hospital. I have to get there now."

"I'll go with you," he said.

She wanted nothing more than having him around to lean on. But before she agreed, she remembered who he was, who his family was and how interested the world was in her.

"You can't," she told him. "What if the press found out?"

His mouth twisted, as if he was about to tell her he didn't give a damn about the press. But they both had to.

"Call me," he said. "Let me know what's going on."

"I will."

Five minutes later she was dressed. Alex walked her to her car, then cupped her face and kissed her.

"If you need me, I'll be there."

She believed him. "My brothers will be at the hospital. I won't be alone. I'll let you know as soon as we hear anything."

He stepped back. She got in her car and started the engine.

As she drove down the long driveway, she felt both worried about Gloria and happy about her evening with Alex. The emotions fought for dominance — and in the end, concern for her grandmother won.

She was thinking more about what could have gone wrong than anything else, so she didn't pay attention to the odd, moving shadows at the end of Alex's driveway. It wasn't until it was too late to turn back that she saw cars and people. People holding cameras.

They parted for her, but she still had to drive slowly. Slowly enough for them to take her picture and yell out questions about her spending the night with the senator's son.

Chapter Eleven

When Dani arrived at the hospital, her brothers, Penny, Elissa and Lori were already there. Lori sat with a sobbing Kristie, who stood up when Dani entered the waiting room.

"I'm so sorry," she said, her voice thick with tears. "Oh, Dani, she just collapsed. She was doing so well. Just a couple of days ago we were talking about when my contract would end. With you staying there, Gloria was feeling comfortable being on her own at night. She's planning her own meals, scheduling her physical therapy, handling her meds. She's fine. Or she was."

Dani knew the other woman was just trying to help and maybe make herself feel better, but for Dani, the conversation was a one-way ticket to Guilt Land.

She had moved into Gloria's house. The expectation was that she would be home at night. But last night she hadn't gone home . . . she'd gone to Alex's. To be honest, after she arrived, she never once thought about her grandmother.

Okay, sure, she'd told Gloria about her plans and the older woman had teased her about having too good a time but neither of them had expected her to stay out all night.

Dani glanced at her watch. It was barely after two in the morning, but it was close enough to all night for guilt purposes.

"It's not you," Dani told Kristie. "It's me."

Lori shook her head. "Let's not argue about it. Neither of you could have prevented the collapse. Not unless you're secretly psychic and could have predicted what happened. In which case, it would be nice if you could tell us what's wrong with her, so we know how much we should worry."

Kristie wiped her face. "You're using logic."

"It seems like the right time," Lori said.

"You don't have to be so smug about it," Kristie muttered.

The two women hugged.

Dani was glad they'd worked things out, but she was still feeling like crap. She walked over to Cal and let him pull her close.

"I should have been there," she murmured.

"Want to tell me where you were?" he asked.

"Not really. I was off having fun, which is all that matters."

Penny came over and punched her lightly in the arm. "Stop it. You didn't make this happen and feeling bad won't help. Let's wait and see what the doctor says."

Dani scowled. "You sound like Lori."

"Really?" Penny looked pleased. "Because I like her a lot. She's so together."

"Meaning I'm not?" Elissa grumbled as she joined them. "I'm tough."

"You're practically titanium," Walker said as he put his arm around his fiancée.

"At least we can be neurotic together," Dani said, doing her best to hang on emotionally. The need to start crying was strong, but she was determined to beat it. She wanted to stay in control so she could be ready in case there was something she could do.

"Look at the bright side," Reid said. "Last time Gloria collapsed, no one gave a damn. Now we all care about what happens to her. That has to be good."

Dani nodded slowly. She understood his point, but in some ways it was easier when she hadn't cared. Last time, there hadn't been so much to lose.

Alex was at his parents' house by six that morning. Dani had phoned to say there wasn't any news on Gloria and right after her call, his phone had rung again. He sure as hell hadn't expected it to be his father.

"It made the morning papers," Mark had said by way of greeting. "How soon can you get here?"

Alex sat across the breakfast table from his parents. He hated feeling as if he was sixteen and had gotten caught doing something stupid. The need to squirm and explain kept rushing through him but he ignored both. More difficult to push aside was the sense he'd been a disappointment.

He reminded himself he was a successful lawyer in his thirties. He didn't have to answer to anyone. Too bad he couldn't believe it.

He wanted to defend himself, but against what? So he accepted the cup of coffee his mother gave him and waited for her or his father to make the first move.

Neither of them seemed in a hurry to speak. There was something in Katherine's eyes — a lurking accusation, as if asking why he had to pick Dani from all the women available to him.

This had to be hurting her. Dani represented so much failure to her. Now if Alex got involved with her, would that make the wound deeper?

If he got involved? Wasn't he already there and beyond?

"Is it true?" Mark asked. "There's a picture of Dani leaving your place around one-thirty this morning. Is it really her?"

"Yes."

Mark glanced at Katherine, then back at Alex. "We'll take care of the situation. I'll call a meeting first thing. Please be available." Mark stood and left.

Alex didn't like the sense of being handled, but what was he supposed to say? Sure, his personal life was his business, but as his father was running for president and Dani was Mark's long-lost biological daughter, there were questions and realities to be dealt with.

"Good to be a member of the staff," he said when Mark was gone.

His mother picked up her coffee, then put it down. "He's in crisis mode. He's not angry."

"I got that." Mark hadn't been anything. But his father had never been emotionally involved with his family. Not the way Katherine was.

"So you're seeing her," she said, her voice carefully polite, as if she didn't want to give anything away.

"Yes."

"Is it serious?" Her mouth tightened slightly, her hands trembled.

"Mom, I'm sorry all this is happening and that it's upsetting you."

"But you're not sorry about your relationship with Dani."

It wasn't a question. "No."

He was reminded of his conversation with Dani earlier that evening. How they'd discussed that both their previous spouses had been sorry about being caught, but not about the act itself.

This was different, he told himself. Yet someone was still hurt.

"You didn't say if this was serious or not," Katherine pressed.

He shrugged. "I don't know yet."

"You're sleeping with her."

His mother was the most amazing woman he'd ever met. She had determination and class and more love than any three people he knew. He would take a bullet for her, but he wouldn't let her run his life.

"I'm not discussing Dani," he said quietly. "Not in that context."

"I see."

Two words. Easy, simple words said in a tone that hinted he'd broken her heart. That by shutting her out, he was saying she didn't matter.

"I know Dani is a complication," he said, trying to give a little.

"For all of us. You're aware of the difficulties this relationship presents."

He nodded.

She drew in a breath. "Alex, I don't want to run your life or judge you. You've been an adult for a long time. You've made good decisions and bad ones. I thought you knew the difference."

"I do."

"I don't think so. Why her? Why now? There are so many other women out there. Women like Fiona."

His concern and compassion turned to anger. "My marriage with Fiona is over. I've let it go, I wish you would. I've made my position clear."

"Yes, you have," she snapped. "Although you haven't said why. Fiona is far more appropriate than Dani Buchanan. Of course that's not a very high bar to get over. Is it asking too much for you to have a relationship that doesn't tear this family apart?"

More guilt, which wasn't Katherine's

style, he thought as his anger faded. "Are we torn apart? You matter to me, Mom. You always will. I don't want to hurt you."

"Then don't," she said, almost pleading. "Don't hurt me."

Which was another way of saying "Don't do this." But it wasn't her decision to make.

Long ago he'd vowed to protect his family, no matter what. It had been a vow born of pain and fear as he'd watched his biological mother die on the street. He'd never been in this position before with Katherine. Never felt he was doing the wrong thing.

But being with Dani wasn't wrong and he refused to let circumstances control his personal life.

"I need to get to the office," he said. He stood and kissed Katherine on the cheek. "I'll call you later."

She nodded, but didn't speak. There was still tension between them. Unresolved issues. It had never been like that with her and he didn't like it now.

Dani woke up with a stiff back and cramped arm. Somehow she'd managed to curl up in a corner of a sofa at the hospital waiting room. She straightened and saw Cal talking with a doctor. She stood and hurried over.

"What?" she asked. "Is she all right?"

The doctor, a pleasant-looking woman in her late thirties, smiled. "She's fine. There was a mix-up in her medication. Everything worked its way through her system, so she'll be perfectly all right. We're going to be releasing her in a few hours. There aren't any special instructions. Just make sure she knows what she's taking."

The relief was as quick as it was powerful. Dani turned to Cal and hugged him.

"She's okay. It's fine."

"I know." He pulled her close and kissed the top of her head. "Let's tell everyone else."

They turned back to the full waiting room. Dani looked at her other brothers, their fiancées, and wondered when her family had gotten so big. For years it had seemed like her and her brothers against the world. But not anymore. With Penny's, there was even a second generation beginning.

It was more than she could take in on an hour of sleep. "You tell them," she said. "I want to go to her room."

Dani hurried down the hall and walked into her grandmother's room.

Gloria lay on the narrow bed, her face pale, her eyes closed. Dani stopped next to her and lightly touched the back of her hand.

Gloria opened her eyes. "I'm not dead," she said. "That's something. Of course if you've been looking for an excuse to lock me away due to mental incompetence, you've found it. I can't believe I did that. Even an idiot should be able to handle three or four medications. I must be getting old, which I hate to admit."

Dani felt her throat closing. Emotions flooded her, making it impossible to speak. This was her *grandmother.* Whatever complications and biological connections might or might not exist, Gloria had been her family her whole life.

"I don't want you to die," Dani said, then shocked herself and possibly Gloria by bursting into tears. "I d-don't want you to die."

"Hush, child. I don't want that, either. I have a lot of things to atone for and that's going to take some time. Being an idiot isn't fatal. Well, I suppose it could be if I continue to take the wrong pills. But I'll be more careful. Does that work?"

Dani covered her face with her hands and nodded. Gloria patted her arm for a few seconds, then said, "Bend down so I can hug you. You'll feel better and so will I."

Dani did as she asked. Gloria put thin arms around her and squeezed.

"I've been a horror to you," she said, her voice soft and shaky. "So cruel. There's no excuse, although I'm likely to try to give you one. You're like me. Oh, not the bad things. You're better than that. You have a lot of your mother in you. I always liked Marsha. I hated her, too, for being strong. My son was never strong. There was too much of his father in him."

Dani sniffed and straightened. She wiped her face. "What are you talking about?"

Gloria smiled and blinked away a few tears of her own. "I'm saying I was hard on you. Too hard. I wanted you to be better than me, but I never knew how to say that. You didn't run away, like your brothers. I kept waiting for you to, so I pushed and pushed and then one day you were gone. I've missed you so much."

Tears trickled down Gloria's sunken cheeks. "I'm sorry. I know that's a useless thing to say, but I mean it. I'm so sorry, Dani. I love you. I have from the moment your mother handed you to me and I held you." She smiled. "Even then you were feisty. You grabbed onto my hair and you wouldn't let go."

Dani didn't know what to think. There

was too much information, but in the best way possible. She felt happy and confused and connected with the woman she'd most admired all her life.

"I love you, too," she said. "I wanted to be like you."

"Perhaps you need a more inspiring goal. Maybe you should be like Katherine Canfield. She's a saint, isn't she? Everyone says she is."

"She's very special, but you're my family."

Gloria took her hand and squeezed. "They're your family, too. That could make for very interesting holidays."

Dani laughed. "I hadn't thought of that." She drew in a deep breath. "The doctor says you're fine. You're going home in a few hours. I'll be there to keep watch on you."

"I live to be a prisoner in my own home." But she was smiling as she spoke.

The door to her room opened and Dani's brothers spilled into the room. Dani stepped back to let them reach Gloria, but she didn't leave. She needed to stay close.

The irony of the situation didn't escape her. A year ago, she'd felt alone in the world. Only her brothers had been there for her. Now she had Gloria and the Canfield family. What was that old saying? An embarrassment of riches?

Speaking of embarrassment, she had a bad feeling that when she checked out the morning papers, her personal best on the humiliation level was going to sink to an all-time low. She hadn't said anything yet — not while they didn't know what was going on with Gloria. But she should probably tell them before they saw it themselves.

She waited for a lull in the conversation, then stepped in front of Gloria's bed and said, "Guess what I did last night?"

It was midafternoon when Alex showed up at Gloria's house. Dani let him in and led him to the kitchen.

"How's she doing?" he asked.

"Good. She's sleeping. The doctor said she would be drowsy for the rest of the day. I'm staying here to keep an eye on her. Kristie wanted to. She's flogging herself with guilt — something I can relate to."

He leaned against the counter. "What do you have to be guilty about?"

"I was off having hot monkey sex while my grandmother was messing up her medication."

"Hot monkey sex?" He grinned. "Is that what it was?"

"Don't get all macho and smug. It's your fault I wasn't here in the first place." Not that she actually blamed him, but he was looking too pleased with himself at the moment.

"Because you always check her pills before she takes them?"

"No."

"Because she's not capable of managing her own medication?"

"She's perfectly capable. It was an honest mistake, one she won't make again. For the record, I deeply resent you using logic at a time like this. You should simply accept the blame and promise never to do it again."

"Never make love with you?"

Oh. Right. "Well, maybe not that, but something close."

"I shouldn't think about making love with you?"

"Did I mention I hate the logic?" she asked. "Plus you have an unfair advantage. You probably got more sleep than me."

"Not by much." He closed the distance between them and kissed her. "Want to start over?" he asked.

She rested her forehead on his chest. "Yes. Hi, Alex. Thanks for stopping by. I've had a hell of a day."

"I bet. But Gloria is better now and that's what matters."

"It is. I just feel like I've been on an

emotional roller coaster for weeks. My life used to be boring. I miss boring."

"Me, too."

She looked up into his dark eyes. "How was your day?"

"Not one I want to repeat. I had a meeting first thing this morning with my parents. I don't, as a rule, enjoy discussing my sex life with them. Then there were a series of meetings both with and without the senator, all on how to 'handle' the situation."

Dani pointed to the paper on the table. She'd left it open to the photo and article about her leaving Alex's place in the pre-dawn hours. No one knew exactly what had happened in his big house, but there was plenty of speculation.

"We can't even deny what they're saying. Sex was had by all."

"More than once," he agreed.

She fingered the paper. "I haven't really made it to the big time, though. They're still accusing me of having sex with a man. Now if we move on to aliens, then I'll have hit the big time."

"Good attitude."

"Really? It's all that stands between me and a major meltdown." She stepped away until the table was between them. "I hate this. I hate that my life is being scrutinized.

I know, I know, it's because of who my father is. But I don't want this. I don't want to have to worry about being followed and photographed. I'm not a celebrity. I don't want to be news."

"Me, either. It comes with the territory."

"But you've been living this way for a while. You're used to it. Your whole family expects it. Mine doesn't. My grandmother is going to read this."

"My mother asked me if it was true. It's not comfortable, it's not what anyone wants, but it's reality."

Again with the logic. If Alex had a flaw, this was it. "I don't want this reality," she said, fighting the urge to blame him for everything. It wasn't his fault, she reminded herself. They were in this together.

"It's the one we're dealing with. Unless you want to go away somewhere." The edge to his voice told her what he thought about anyone running away.

"I'm not giving up my life so easily. I just hate that I don't have any choices. That because of the press, I'm on the defensive."

"You live your life and the hell with them."

"Is that what you told Katherine?" she asked. "I know this is hurting her and I hate that, too. She doesn't want to be the subject of speculation, yet she is. Like all of this.

Why on earth does Mark want to run for president?"

"Because he thinks he can make a difference. I'm sure he's sorry that his goals in life are getting in your way."

She frowned. "Why are you angry with me? I'm the innocent party in all this."

"We're all the innocent party. You're just more vocal than the rest of us."

She bristled. "What? I'm complaining too much? Is it uncomfortable? Am I expected to just smile and wave, no matter what happens? I don't get an opinion? I don't get to complain that my bad luck with men continues on."

The second the words fell out of her mouth, Dani knew she'd gone too far. Her excuse, if one could be made, was that she'd been on the emotional edge for too long and really needed to get some sleep.

"So I'm just like Ryan and Hugh?" Alex asked coldly. "Good to know."

"You're not," she said quickly. "I'm sorry. I didn't mean it like that. I'm just running out of energy here. Why can't I meet a nice guy and have it be easy? Why can't things go well?"

"They're not going well?"

He was deliberately misunderstanding her. She hated that, too. "Not by my definition," she said pointing at the paper. "This is awful."

"It's an outside circumstance that has nothing to do with what's going on between you and me. If you back away because of publicity, you let the press win."

"I never said I was backing away."

"You said I was like the other jerks in your life. If that's true, why would you stick around?"

When had this conversation spiraled out of control? She folded her arms over her chest. "Alex, stop. I don't want to fight with you. I'm having a hard time coping. I'll deal with it."

"You're not yet. You want an instant solution. There isn't one. You came looking for your father and you found him. It's not going to be easy. Are you willing to see it through, or are you going to disappear at the first sign of trouble?"

"What? That is totally unfair. I have never walked away from trouble. Do you think it was easy being married to Hugh? I'm not the one who ended that relationship. You don't know me, so who the hell are you to judge me?"

"Right back at you."

She was seriously pissed off, but she was also hurt. This was not how she wanted things to go with Alex. Last night had been so amazing and wonderful. Shouldn't they be thinking about that instead of fighting?

"I have to go," he said and walked out of the kitchen.

She started to follow him, then stopped herself. What was there to say? Then she shook her head. No. She wasn't going to leave things hanging like this.

She went after him, but by the time she reached the hallway, it was too late. She heard the front door close. He was gone.

CHAPTER TWELVE

Katherine parked in front of Oliver's school. She knew her attention should be on the coming meeting, but it was hard to focus on anything but the sick feeling in her stomach.

She was losing Mark. She tried to tell herself she wasn't, that nothing had changed about her situation, that only the information was new, but she couldn't quite make herself believe it. She had a strong sense of him drifting away and knowing that he might be lost to her forever tore at her heart.

Had he ever gotten over Dani's mother? She tried to tell herself that Mark hadn't been in that deep. But she knew that if something happened to him today, she would mourn him the rest of her life. She only ever wanted to love him. Perhaps he felt that way about Marsha Buchanan.

If so, Dani would be a constant reminder of what he'd lost. She would make the past live again. Was that why Katherine felt such a distance from him lately? If only Dani had never come looking for her father.

Katherine tried not to blame the young woman. It wasn't her fault, but could the timing have been worse?

She glanced at her watch and realized if she didn't hurry, she was going to be late. So she gathered her briefcase and walked into the school.

Individual education plans or IEPs were the backbone of the special education system. Parents and teachers sat down together to discuss and agree on goals for the coming year. The battle Katherine frequently fought was to push the goals so the child was asked to do just a little bit more than expected. It was the only way to get real growth.

The teachers were committed professionals who saw what was possible. Katherine prided herself on believing in what was impossible.

Ten years ago she'd been told Ian would never survive a regular classroom. That the constant teasing would destroy his spirit and that he wasn't physically capable of keeping up. Today he was being courted by excellent universities on both coasts, including Stanford and MIT.

But it was always a battle. Her friends told her to stop fighting, to put her children into private school. The family could certainly afford it. But for Katherine, there was something more at stake than making her life flow more smoothly.

She was a high-profile parent. Every time she was able to win a battle, she believed she made things easier for a parent without her connections and resources. So she sat through IEPs and fought for more than the school wanted to give.

She entered the small conference room. Oliver's teacher, Miss Doyle, was there, as was the school administrator and the special ed counselor.

They worked through the pleasantries, then got down to the logistics.

"Our main focus for next year is Oliver's reading," Miss Doyle said. "We think by the end of the year he should be reading at the first grade level."

Katherine slipped on her glasses and flipped through the pages she'd brought with her. "That was the goal for last year. Along with helping him interact better in new situations."

The other women exchanged glances, then Miss Doyle sighed. "Mrs. Canfield, Oliver is developmentally disabled. He has limitations. Wanting him to be different isn't going to change who he is."

The teacher was maybe twenty-five or twenty-six. Katherine was genuinely torn between feeling old and tired and wanting to point out that she had been raising children nearly as long as Miss Doyle had been alive. She knew a whole lot more about what her kids could and could not do.

"What I want," Katherine said slowly, "is targets that stretch us both. Oliver gets help at home. He can get more help. But I do not accept that after two years of reading he should still be at the first grade level."

"Oliver is a lovely little boy," the administrator said. "But he will never be normal. As Miss Doyle said, there are limitations."

"Agreed. But if we all decided he can't be more, then his fate is sealed right now. I won't do that. People rise to the level of expectation. It has been proven time and time again. Expect more and you will get more."

Katherine suddenly thought of Mark. His limitations weren't about his intelligence, but he sure had them.

"Have you considered Oliver might get more personalized attention in a private school?" Miss Doyle asked.

The administration winced.

Katherine stared at Oliver's teacher. "Are you telling me you're not capable of instructing my son?"

"No. Just that . . ."

"I appreciate this is a challenge for all of us. You have said yourself that Oliver is very well behaved in the classroom. He's not disruptive or difficult. So there is no reason to move him. I am confident we can come up with a plan that makes us all stretch and is in Oliver's best interest."

The administrator leaned over to Miss Doyle and said something Katherine couldn't hear. She'd been through this enough times to know that a compromise would be reached, but it would take some fighting on both their parts.

It wasn't that the school didn't want to give Oliver an excellent education. She knew they had his best interests at heart. Yet special education children were a financial burden on a school district. Despite the increased state funding for each child in the program, the district had to pour in more resources, which came from other programs. It was always a balancing act.

Three hours later, she left and drove to meet Fiona for lunch. Her former daughter-in-law had called to request the lunch the previous day. While Katherine didn't have the energy to deal with her right now, she understood that Fiona was going through a difficult time. Katherine briefly wondered when anyone stopped to think about her going through a rough time, then pushed the thought away as both selfish and unproductive. She'd been raised to believe it was her duty to give back, regardless of how she felt that particular day. With wealth came responsibility. But just once she would like to call in sick, where her life was concerned, and spend the day curled up with a great book and a pint of Ben & Jerry's.

She met Fiona in the restaurant of what had been the Four Seasons hotel, until it had been sold. The food was excellent, as was the service. As the lunch crowd was mostly businesspeople, they were unlikely to run into anyone they knew. An important consideration, Katherine thought as she handed her keys to the valet. Alex was probably going to be a topic of conversation.

Fiona was waiting in the lobby. Tall and beautifully dressed, as always, Fiona was put together in a way that made Katherine feel as if she should check her makeup.

"Have you been waiting long?" Katherine asked. "I was at an IEP for Oliver. It ran over."

Fiona smiled, then leaned in and kissed

her cheek. "They always do."

"You're right. I fight and fight and hope I'm doing the right thing. Let's go in to lunch. I'm starving."

The women linked arms as they walked. Fiona mentioned a blouse she'd bought at Nordstrom and how they should go shopping sometime soon.

The idea made Katherine tired. Mark frequently told her she should hire more help, which probably made sense. But what, exactly, was she supposed to give up to a stranger? Her afternoons with her children? Her evenings with Mark? Her charity work? What she needed was a clone. The thought made her smile.

"You're in a good mood," Fiona said. "The IEP went well."

"It went, which is about the best it can be. I want the moon and they can't give it to me without giving it to every other parent. It's a question of resources."

"I don't know how you do it," Fiona admitted. "Raise those children. You're so busy. One or two special needs children would make sense, but all of them. Not Alex, of course," she added. "At least he's normal."

Katherine stared at the other woman. There were so many thoughts in her head, she didn't know which one to deal with first.

Normal? Fiona was defining normal? How dare she? Yes, some of Katherine's children had issues, but they could all be dealt with. As for Alex not having problems, hadn't Alex told her how difficult things had been when he'd first come to live with them? He'd been as far from "normal" as any of the others.

"I'm not sure I could give any of them away," Katherine said lightly, sure that Fiona hadn't meant anything bad by what she'd said.

"Of course not." Fiona laughed. "They're all so precious."

Were they? In her eyes? Katherine wasn't so sure. There was something about Fiona's tone and body language.

The waiter appeared. They both ordered without bothering to look at the menu. Fiona asked for a glass of chardonnay. Katherine settled on iced tea. She was so tired that if she had any alcohol, she was likely to collapse face-first in her salad.

Maybe it was the exhaustion or the stress in her life or just a streak of bad breeding showing up, but she found herself saying, "Alex and Julie always used to argue about who would take the kids when Mark and I got older. I remember heated discussions about having to split them up so they would each have a couple. It made me so proud of both of them."

Fiona's expression tightened. "Yes. I remember. Julie being female makes her the more likely choice."

"I'm not so sure. Alex has a soft spot for his siblings, especially Bailey, Oliver and Quinn. Ian, Sasha and Trisha are likely to be fully independent."

Fiona pressed her lips together. Katherine wasn't sure if that was to keep from saying something or to stop herself from shuddering. It was obvious the other woman didn't want anything to do with Katherine's "non-normal" children. Had Alex known about that? Was it one of the reasons for the divorce?

She remembered how Alex talked about so much with her, yet he'd been completely closemouthed about the reason for the divorce. He would never say anything bad about the woman he'd been married to. She'd thought he hadn't been specific because there hadn't been anything to say. But maybe there was another reason.

The waiter appeared with drinks and the bread basket. Katherine usually ignored it, but today the carbs and sweet butter called to her. She could do an extra ten minutes on the elliptical in the morning.

"I saw the pictures in the paper," Fiona said quietly, nearly ruining Katherine's first bite of the fresh bread. "I was devastated. How could he do that? And with her of all people. I thought of you, of course. How are you holding up?"

The words were all there. The tone was perfect. Yet Katherine had the sudden impression that Fiona was putting on a very well-crafted show.

Which wasn't fair. Fiona obviously wanted a second chance at her marriage. From Katherine's perspective, the other woman had been a good wife. But what secrets did Fiona and Alex keep between them? What had really happened when the two of them were alone?

"I didn't know what to think," Fiona continued.

"I would guess that he's seeing someone else," Katherine snapped, then sighed against the wash of guilt. She patted Fiona's arm. "I don't mean that to sound harsh. I'm saying this for your own good. It might be time to move on."

Tears filled Fiona's eyes. "Why are you saying this? Has he told you something?"

Katherine hesitated. "He said nothing will ever change his mind. He doesn't want to be with you anymore."

"I see."

"Maybe it's for the best."

"No, it's not. I still love him. He's the only man I'll ever love. He's my Mark."

Katherine was less sure. Of the two people involved, the one she trusted implicitly was Alex.

"I'm sorry to hear you say that," she told Fiona. "I don't think my son is going to change his mind."

Fiona nodded. The tears disappeared, as if they had never been. "I see. Thank you for being honest. It's because of Dani, isn't it? He's infatuated by her."

"I wouldn't say that. They're involved." They were obviously having sex, as the entire world had recently discovered.

"You can't be happy about their relation-ship," Fiona pressed.

"I accept it, as you should. There's noth-ing either of us can do to change things."

Fiona hesitated for a second, then said, "Of course. You're right. I wouldn't dream of coming between them."

Alex met Pete outside the courthouse. The hearing was scheduled for nine.

"Nervous?" the other man asked.

"No," Alex told him. He had done as

much as he could to prepare for the hearing. There was little else he could do to influence the outcome.

Even if the D.A. decided to use him as an example and charge him with everything possible, it was unlikely Alex would be spending the night in jail. He had a clean record and close ties to the community. He wasn't a flight risk.

But knowing he would continue to sleep in his own bed didn't change the fact that his future was on the line. If he was convicted . . .

He didn't want to think about that, about having to find a new career. He didn't want to think about how it would be wrong for that sleazy reporter to get away with using Bailey. No matter the outcome, Alex refused to regret what he'd done — he'd protected his own. That was much more his job than being a lawyer.

Pete checked his watch. "Let's go," he said and they walked into the courtroom.

Alex's specialty was corporate law. He'd assisted on a couple of court cases, but spent most of his time in an office. It was considered bad form to let a corporate case go to trial. While he'd sat at the table for the defense, it had never been as the defendant. He wasn't looking forward to it now.

There were already several spectators in the courtroom. Reporters, of course. Neither of his parents were there — he'd asked his family not to come. It would only give the press more to write about. There were a few junior members of his law firm, a member of the campaign and Dani.

Alex stared at her, surprised she would show up. They hadn't talked in nearly a week — not since they'd fought. As she turned and her hazel eyes met his, he couldn't remember what they'd argued about.

He paused by the wooden half wall separating the main aisle from the seats.

"What are you doing here?" he asked.

She stood. "Showing support for truth, justice and the American way." She smiled slightly. "I thought you could use a friend. You don't have any family here yet."

"I asked them not to come. I thought it would give the media too much to write about."

Her smile faded. "Damn. So now they're going to write about me."

He didn't bother to look around at the reporters, knowing they would be typing furiously on Palm Pilots and laptops.

"Probably," he said, "But I don't care."

"Then I won't, either." She touched his

arm. "I hope it goes well."

She was beautiful. Her wide eyes perfectly balanced her full mouth. She wore a conservative pants suit and could have easily passed for a lawyer. Not that she would consider that a compliment.

He wanted her. Not just in bed, although he wouldn't say no if she asked, but to talk with. To spend time with. He'd missed her this past week. He'd gotten used to having her around and then she'd been gone.

He introduced Pete, then they left her and walked to the defendant's table. Alex took his seat and waited for the judge.

Thirty minutes later, his fate was sealed, but not in a way he'd expected. The assistant D.A. explained that due to lack of evidence, they were dropping all charges. The judge dismissed the case and left the courtroom.

"Way to go," Pete said as he shook Alex's hand. "Congratulations."

"I didn't do anything."

"Still, this solves a lot of problems. I'm going to phone the other partners. They'll want to know."

Pete walked out. Alex stared after him, then turned to watch as Dani approached.

"This is good," she said happily. "You're free. I'm so happy. I was worried that horrible reporter would totally screw up your life." She paused and frowned at him. "Why aren't you more excited?"

Alex wanted to hit something. Despite having grown up with money and privilege, he'd done his damnedest to never use that to get something he hadn't earned. He'd prided himself on working hard, on doing the right thing. With a couple of phone calls, Mark had taken it all away from him.

"It has nothing to do with lack of evidence," he said grimly. "My father did this."

"What do you mean? He talked to the D.A.?"

"He talked to someone. I don't know who, but I'll find out."

Dani sighed. "I don't know what to think. I'm happy you're not facing charges or being arrested or whatever they would have done. That's good. But him getting involved like that. It's just not right."

He stared at her. She got it. He didn't have to explain why he wouldn't have wanted this. She knew — because of who she was.

"What are you going to do?" she asked.

"Hell if I know. I can't go to the D.A. and demand he try me."

"It would make for an interesting conversation."

"I have to talk to the senator."

"Another interesting conversation," she said.

He put his hand on the small of her back and led her out of the courtroom. He'd thought there might be press waiting outside, but no one was there. Had Mark taken care of that, too?

"He did it because you're his son," she said. "That has to mean something."

"He did it because of the campaign."

"You don't know that."

"Yeah, I do."

She faced him. "Alex, he's your father. Do you really want to have this fight with him?"

"I have to."

"You're very stubborn."

He managed a slight smile. "It's one of my best qualities."

She looked as if she didn't know what else to say. He touched her cheek.

"I'm sorry about before. About what I said."

"Me, too." She shook her head. "I know you're not like Ryan and Hugh. You're a good man. My life isn't easy right now. I was reacting to that. Not to you."

"I get it. I pushed too hard."

"Yes, you did."

She smiled as she spoke.

He nudged her back into a small alcove, then leaned in and kissed her.

She kissed him back, her mouth soft and yielding, her hands resting against his chest. She smelled of flowers and tasted of coffee and that sensual essence he remembered from making love with her.

When she parted for him, he swept inside. Wanting moved through him, but he ignored the need to have her. This wasn't the place or the time, but soon, he thought. Very soon.

They pulled back at the same moment.

Dani glanced around, then looked at him. "This might be illegal."

"Not technically, but it's frowned upon." He rubbed his thumb across her lower lip. "I want to see you again."

"Good thing. I'm worming my way into your world. You won't be able to escape me."

"I don't want to."

She trembled slightly and her breath caught. "You're really good," she murmured. "And dangerous. Dragon-boy."

He grinned. "That's me. How's your grandmother?"

"Doing fine. She's being very careful with her medication, so all is well." She glanced at her watch. "I hate to say this, but I have to go. I'm guessing you have places to be, too."

He nodded. He had to deal with his father. Although he was thinking he should put that off until he could face Mark without wanting to hit something . . . or someone.

CHAPTER THIRTEEN

Dani arrived at the Canfield home for her appointment with Katherine. They were supposed to discuss the charity event. As Dani rang the bell, it occurred to her that she didn't even know what charity they would be supporting. It was probably a good question to ask.

Katherine opened the door. For once she wasn't perfectly groomed. Her hair was down, she wore a University of Washington sweatshirt over jeans and had on socks, but no shoes.

"Is it three already?" she asked as she smoothed the front of her shirt. "I wasn't watching the time. The kids are all home today so it's been hectic."

"We can reschedule, if it would be easier for you."

"No, no. This is fine." Katherine stepped back to let her in. "I wouldn't want you driving all this way for nothing."

Mussed and in casual clothing, Katherine seemed more approachable. Not that she wasn't always nice. But like this she made Dani less nervous.

Dani followed her into the family room. Sasha, Oliver and Quinn were sprawled on the floor playing with interlocking building blocks. Bailey sat in a chair, reading a Nancy Drew book.

Bailey bounced up when she saw Dani. "Hi. Mom said you were coming by."

"Here I am." She waved to the other kids, then turned back to Bailey. "Don't you love Nancy Drew? My grandmother gave me the whole set one summer and I read one after the other."

Bailey nodded shyly. "These were my mom's, but I'm real careful with them. I wash my hands and everything."

"I'm sure she appreciates that," Dani said. "It's so nice that you get how important books are."

Bailey smiled broadly.

Katherine put her arm around Bailey. "You make me proud in so many ways."

Bailey leaned against her.

Katherine hugged her then sighed. "Dani, I have to make a phone call. Can you stand me to leave you with my herd while I'm gone?"

"Of course. I can build with the best of them."

"It should only be a few minutes. Then we'll discuss that luncheon we're going to."

Honestly, Dani would rather play with building blocks for days than finalize luncheon details. She sank to the floor where Sasha promptly crawled on her lap

"Hey, you," Dani said.

"Hey, you, back." Sasha giggled. "This is a boy game. We should play a girl game. Like dress-up."

Bailey pressed her lips together. "That's for kids."

"I'm a kid," Sasha said proudly. "I'm the baby. Mom doesn't want me to ever grow up. She told me so."

Dani wondered how the differences in the children affected the dynamics in the family.

"I was the youngest, too," Dani said. "And the only girl. It's fun to be the baby, but Bailey is becoming a young woman."

Bailey looked pleased by that. "I'll be fifteen soon."

"Wow. Fifteen," Dani said. "I remember that. It's kind of an important birthday."

"I'll be six," Sasha told her.

"Six is also important, but there's something about being a teenager. My best friend was only three weeks older than me. I remember her mom took us shopping for our first pair of high heels when my friend turned fifteen. It was a lot of fun. I still have those shoes."

Not that she would wear them anywhere. They were pretty out of date. But they were a good memory.

"Boys don't wear high heels," Quinn said.

"You're right. They don't." As a rule. This wasn't the time to discuss drag queens.

Katherine returned. "That's all done. Did they torture you?"

"Not at all."

"Good." Katherine glanced at her watch. "I think it's about time for your snack. Who wants to see if Yvette has it ready?"

The boys and Sasha raced off. Bailey hesitated. "Dani, would you like something to drink?"

Katherine smacked her own forehead. "Thank you, Bailey, for being so polite. I can't believe I forgot to ask. Dani, you want anything?"

Dani smiled at Bailey. "I'm good, but thanks for asking."

"You're welcome."

Bailey followed the other kids out of the room.

Dani moved to the sofa. "They're wonderful. All of them. They're also a handful, so I'm not sure how you stay sane."

Katherine laughed. "Sanity is not required. Just a lot of patience and love."

"You obviously have an excess of both."

"You're good with them, as well."

"I adore them," Dani admitted. "I kind of have a soft spot for Bailey. She's a sweetie. Her hair is so beautiful."

"I agree. A natural redhead. When Alex and Fiona were still married, and people saw us together, they thought she was Fiona's daughter or sister." Katherine frowned for a moment, then shook her head. "Part of that is Alex was always so close to Bailey. They have a special bond."

Dani was more excited to hear about Alex's connection with his sister than to have information about his ex-wife.

"I'm close with my brothers," Dani said. "Especially Cal, who's the oldest. I guess he's always looked out for me."

"Family is important," Katherine said. "As is raising money for breast cancer research, which is what our luncheon is about. I believe I mentioned you'll be expected to speak."

Dani swallowed. "Yes, you did. In return I might have murmured something about projectile vomiting."

"Not to worry. You'll be fine. We're talking about five or six minutes of remarks."

It might as well be a century of remarks, Dani thought, telling herself it was silly to panic now. She should wait until they were closer to the event and then freak out.

"We should coordinate what we wear," Katherine continued. "We don't want to match and we don't want to clash. I don't usually worry about this sort of thing, but we'll be photographed. A dress with a nice blazer is always good. A suit works. If you aren't sure what would be appropriate, I'm happy to look over your choices and give you the benefit of my experience, such as it is. Of course I'm much older, the thought of that might scare you."

"I'd love your opinion," Dani said. "You're always so stylish."

Katherine glanced down at her sweatshirt. "Not so much today. But that's all right. Okay, back to the event. The reality is you should eat before you come. So many people will want to talk to you there that you won't get a chance. Plus, you don't want to have a picture taken with something in your teeth."

"Should I be taking notes?" Dani asked, as her apprehension turned to outright fear. "What if I can't do this? I don't want to embarrass you or your family. I'm not really good at this sort of thing. I don't have the experience."

Katherine touched her arm. "Take a breath. You'll be fine. It's not that hard. I'll admit it can be a little terrifying, but you'll get through it and the next time will be easier."

The next time? "I don't think so," she murmured, addressing both the possibility of getting through it and any thoughts of there being a next time.

Katherine smiled at her. "Trust me."

"You don't have to do this," Dani said impulsively. "You don't have to be nice to me or help me or even accept me. Yet you are. I'm sorry. I mean that. I never meant to cause any trouble. I never meant to hurt anyone."

"Of course you didn't," Katherine told her. "I'll admit that there are some challenges in the situation, but you're the innocent in all this and I know that."

"You're amazing," Dani breathed.

"I have my moments," Katherine admitted. "There are times I'm not very proud of what I've done, but this is something we all have to deal with. You want to know your father. Why wouldn't you?" She frowned. "Speaking of Mark, I have something I wanted to show you."

She stood and crossed to a built-in unit with cupboards on the bottom and bookcases on top. She opened one of the low cabinet doors and pulled out a couple of photo albums, then she returned to the sofa and sat next to Dani.

"Pictures," she announced. "I have hundreds, so any time you can't sleep, feel free to come over and I'll bore you into a stupor. Mark's late mother put this one together." Katherine looked at her. "She would have loved to know she had a granddaughter. Leslie died about ten years go."

Grandparents. Dani hadn't much thought about extended family. Were there others she was related to?

Before she could ask, Katherine said, "Mark's father passed away when Mark was five or six. There isn't any other family that I know about."

"Oh." Dani didn't know how she felt about that. Mark was kind of enough to deal with for now.

Katherine opened the older of the two photo albums. "Mark's baby pictures," she said as she pointed.

Katherine flipped through the pages, explaining who the people were. Dani tried to relate to them as family, but in truth they were strangers she would never meet.

"There you are."

Dani looked up and saw Mark walking into the room. Katherine rose and crossed to her husband. As she leaned in and kissed him, Dani caught a flash of emotion in her eyes.

She really loves him, she thought, oddly pleased by the information. As if Mark and Katherine having a happy marriage somehow made things better.

Mark smiled at his wife, then turned to Dani. "Tell me she's not making you look at old pictures. Katherine is very big on documenting life."

"I'm enjoying myself," Dani told him.

"Good. Good." He looked back at Katherine. "How long until dinner?"

"An hour."

"Dani, want to join me in my study? We can talk about family. I'll even go through those old pictures with you." He turned back to Katherine. "Is that all right?"

"Of course."

Mark kissed her again, then patted her butt.

"This way," he said, motioning for Dani to follow him.

She grabbed the photo albums and trailed behind him.

Bailey stepped out into the hallway. "Dani," she called. "Can I talk to you?"

"Sure. What's up?"

Bailey ducked her head. "It's my birthday soon."

Dani smiled. "I know."

"Could I have high-heeled shoes, like you did?"

Dani hesitated. She had no idea what Katherine would think of the idea. There were degrees of Down's syndrome and Bailey seemed to be highly functional. It made sense that a fifteen-year-old girl would want to feel a little more grown-up.

"You'd have to clear it with your mom," Dani said. "But if she agrees, I think it's a good idea."

"Could we go shopping? You and me?"

Dani's smile widened. "I'd really like that. Ask your mom and if it's okay with her, then we'll set something up. We'll go to the mall and eat at the food court and make an afternoon of it. How does that sound?"

"Really cool," Bailey breathed. "I'll go ask right now."

She turned away and started to run down the hall, then turned around, ran back and hugged Dani.

"You're the best!"

"I think you're pretty great, too," Dani

said, hoping Katherine agreed to the shopping trip.

She continued into Mark's study. The room was large and lined with bookshelves. The dark colors and leather furniture made it feel masculine.

Mark sat behind his large, wood desk. He motioned for her to take one of the chairs in front of it.

"Damned pictures," he said easily as he pointed to the albums Dani held. "They make me feel old."

She set them on the desk and settled into the chair. "Katherine has everything so well organized."

"I met her while I was in law school. I thought I was hot shit. I had my future all mapped out. Then I met her. She's from old money. Her family goes back generations. She liked me but her parents weren't impressed by some poor kid who grew up on the wrong side of the country."

He leaned back in his chair, as if staring at memories only he could see. "She was beautiful. Still is. A strong woman, much stronger than me."

Dani was intrigued by his assessment of himself. She agreed with the statement, but was surprised he would admit it.

"But you're not here to talk about Katherine," he said as he glanced at her. "You want to hear about your mother."

"That would be nice," Dani said, even as she felt a flicker of disloyalty. As if by discussing Marsha, she was somehow disrespecting Katherine. What was up with that?

"Marsha didn't want anything to do with me," he admitted. "She was married and didn't want to cheat. I convinced her." He shrugged. "I'm not proud of what I did, but I don't regret it. Not knowing her or having you. I do wish I'd known about you sooner."

"Me, too," Dani said, but even as she spoke, she wondered if it was really true. Mark would have complicated her life. Looking back, she couldn't find a good time for him to have shown up.

"She was terrified we would be caught," he continued. "When she ended things, I thought the stress of the affair had finally gotten to her. I never thought she might be pregnant."

"It makes sense. My grandmother would have made her life a living hell." Gloria might be different now, but twenty-eight years ago, Dani was willing to bet she'd been the queen bitch.

Except Gloria had known. Or guessed. She'd known Dani wasn't a Buchanan for years. How had she found out? Had she just figured it out? As Mark could have?

She had the foolish sense that her father should have known about her. That somehow he should have sensed that she was alive, living only a few miles away.

Foolish little girl dreams, she told herself. She knew better. But knowing didn't seem to make them go away.

"So much has changed," she said. "For all of us. You're running for president. That still shocks me every time I think of it."

"Me, too," he said with a grin, then his humor faded. "Dani, I'm an influential man. You're my daughter. I want to help you in any way I can. Money, introductions, whatever. I'm here for you."

She blinked several times, not sure what to say. "Ah, thank you. I'm good."

"The offer stays open. I'm always here for you."

Is that what he'd told Alex about getting the charges dropped? While she was sure Alex appreciated not having his future ruined, she knew he wouldn't have wanted Mark to get involved.

She didn't want that, either. Rather than having her father do things for her, she wanted an emotional connection. Ironically she had a feeling it was the one thing he couldn't provide.

Katherine was the heart of the Canfield family. For a second, Dani knew everything would have been different if Katherine had been her missing parent.

Crazy, she told herself. And impossible. Katherine never would have walked away from a child. Not that Mark had — he hadn't known. Still, Katherine was the one she'd connected with and being around the other woman made her miss her own mother.

Dani didn't remember Marsha Buchanan. She'd been a baby when her mother had died. Gloria had raised her and her brothers. How different life would have been if Marsha had lived. Or maybe it wouldn't have been different at all. Gloria still would have run their lives.

Families were a complication, Dani thought. Now she had two. What on earth was she going to do with them?

Cal walked into Walker's office a little after three in the afternoon. Reid was already there, lounging on the dark leather sofas his brother had brought in. The room was now done in earth tones — a positive change after Gloria's white-on-white space.

"What's so important that it couldn't be handled by a phone call?" Cal asked as he settled across from Reid.

"The manager of Buchanan's is leaving," Walker said. "We need a replacement."

"Dani's the best choice," Cal told him. "She's always wanted to run this place."

"Agreed, but she's not going to take the job. She would think I was offering it because she's my sister and I don't know that she'd leave Bella Roma so soon after hiring on."

He had a point, but there had to be a way to convince Dani this was where she belonged.

"Have Gloria ask her," Reid said. "Dani will believe her."

Walker smiled slowly. "That just might work."

Dani sipped the champagne. The taste was subtle but refreshing, with a hint of something. . . . "What did you do to it?" she asked Penny, who sat in an oversize chair with Allison in her arms.

Penny looked up innocently. "I have no idea what you're talking about."

"You infused the champagne with something. A hint of . . . Damn, I can't place it." Dani stared at the slender glass. "You can't infuse champagne. You'd lose the bubbles. But you didn't."

"I'm intensely gifted."

"What did you do?"

"I'm not going to tell you. You'll use it for Bella Roma and this is my private secret."

"You're evil, do you know that?"

Penny grinned.

Elissa held up her glass. "I don't care how you did it, I just want more of it. This is fabulous."

"I agree," Lori said. "Plus I've never had champagne at two in the afternoon. I like your style."

"Thank you," Penny said graciously. "Style is important."

"She's tempting you so you'll want to have this at the rehearsal dinner," Gloria said. "Plus, she wants you to regret not having her cater the wedding."

Dani eyed her grandmother. She would bet Gloria was right on both counts.

"I am interested in having this at the rehearsal dinner," Penny admitted. "But for the rest of it, I have no idea what you're talking about."

Elissa sighed. "You're never going to forgive me, are you? Even though I'm trying to let you enjoy the wedding."

"I'll get over it," Penny said with a sniff. "Eventually."

"Don't let her bully you," Gloria said.

"She's a total bitch when she doesn't get her way."

The room went silent. Lori and Elissa exchanged glances, as if not sure how to handle the comment. Penny stared at Gloria, probably plotting her response.

Dani wasn't sure if her grandmother was trying to be funny or if this was one of her infrequent sarcastic bursts. After all, no transformation was complete.

Determined to keep the mood light for Elissa, she looked at Gloria and said, "Takes one to know one."

Gloria sipped her champagne. "Indeed it does."

Penny laughed and raised her glass to the older woman. "I learned from a master."

"You learned totally on your own, but I'm willing to take any credit being handed out." She turned her attention to Elissa. "I have some ideas about the wedding. I don't want to push them on you, so please tell me to take a hike if you don't like them." She frowned. "Young people don't say 'take a hike' anymore, do they?"

"Not really," Lori said cheerfully. "But that's okay. I'm quickly falling behind on what 'young people' are saying."

"Me, too," Elissa added. "Unless you want to count the things Zoe tells me. Of course she's only five. So what ideas do you have for the wedding?"

She sounded a little nervous as she asked the question.

"Too much input?" Dani asked.

"My mother," Elissa told her. "We're making up for lost time in a hurry. I love her desperately and I know she's just trying to help, but sometimes I want to scream."

"Hopefully this won't make you scream," Gloria said as she braced herself on her cane and pushed herself to her feet. "I don't know why I even kept it, but I did and it's yours if you want it. You're a bit taller, but I wore impossibly high heels with it."

They followed Gloria into the living room. The furniture had all been pushed aside and in the middle of the room stood a dressmaker's form wearing a stunning ivory wedding gown.

The dress was silk and lace, with long sleeves and a sweetheart neckline. The lines were exquisite, the lace incredible. Dani didn't know a whole lot about designer clothing but she recognized an extraordinary gown when she saw one.

"It's French," Gloria said from the doorway. "Couture. You are welcome to it, if you want it."

Elissa went pale. "You can't mean that.

It's too wonderful."

"I was impossibly horrible to you, Elissa. I accept that I'm rude and difficult, but I threatened you and your child and that is unforgivable. You've been very kind to me. Wary, but kind. This is my way of apologizing."

Elissa shook her head. "You don't have to do that."

"I know, but I want to."

"The dress should go to Dani."

Dani took a step back. "I'm good with this." The dress was amazing, but not her style. Besides, Dani liked Gloria making the effort. She *had* been awful to Elissa.

"Dani already knows I love her," Gloria said.

"I do," Dani said, knowing a year ago it never would have occurred to her that the other woman even liked her.

"But you're so skinny," Elissa murmured. "I'm not even close to that thin."

"I hadn't been sick back then. Now if you don't like the dress, just say so. I'll understand. But if you're interested, try it on. We can get it altered to fit you."

Elissa made a sound low in her throat, then rushed at Gloria. The two women embraced.

Penny moved close and hugged Dani, then

pulled Lori into the embrace. Baby Allison cooed between them.

"Hell of a family," Lori murmured. "Gloria's got me tearing up. I hate that."

"Me, too," Dani said happily as she sighed. "Me, too."

Dani returned to the Canfield home to take Bailey shoe shopping. The teenager had called the previous evening with the exciting news that her mother had said yes, and that she had a Nordstrom gift card in her possession as an early birthday present.

But the person who opened the door to let her in wasn't Katherine or even Bailey. Instead it was a tall, handsome man she'd recently seen naked.

Alex grinned at her, glanced over his shoulder, then stepped out onto the porch and closed the door behind himself. He grabbed her by the shoulders and pulled her close.

She raised her head in anticipation of the kiss and when his mouth touched hers it was every bit as hot and tingly as she'd hoped.

She loved the feel of his lips against hers. She loved the firm pressure, the way he smelled and tasted and how right they felt together. She loved the way her body melted

288

from the inside out and that all the worries of her life just disappeared. There was only the man, the wanting and the kiss.

She reached up and wrapped her arms around his neck. The position had the added advantage of allowing a full body press. He was hard to her soft, and very hard in really interesting places. She rubbed against him. He groaned, then stepped back.

"Trouble," he said as he stroked her cheek. "You're nothing but trouble."

"It beats being boring."

"Yes, it does. Bailey asked me to come along on this historic shopping event. Is that all right?"

"Sure. But are you up to an afternoon of shoe shopping?"

He grimaced. "Not my idea of a good time, but Bailey wants me along and it was a chance to see you."

"I like that."

"Good." He put his arm around her and led her inside. "Give me five minutes to change out of this suit and I'll be with you. Bailey's changing, as well. Katherine's in her office. Why don't you go say hello to her?"

She considered her options. "I think I'd rather help you change clothes."

"My first choice, as well. If I say yes?"

She shook her head. "It was cheap talk. Getting naked in your mother's house is a level of tacky I'm not comfortable with."

He leaned in and kissed her again. "Then I'll see you in a few minutes."

Dani watched him head upstairs. She glanced around the foyer, but none of the other children were around. While she wanted to say hello to Katherine, she didn't want to intrude. Still, saying hello shouldn't be too much of an interruption.

She walked down the hallway that led to Katherine's office. The room was on the south side of the house and got a lot of light. She remembered the warm yellow walls and blue pattern furniture from the tour Katherine had given her the last time she'd been there.

The door was partially open. She reached up to knock but lowered her hand when she heard her name mentioned.

"Of course I'm delighted about Mark's daughter," Katherine was saying.

Dani shifted slightly and saw Katherine was on the phone. She started to back up, then paused, wanting to hear what the other woman said.

She was going to hell for sure, she told herself. Talk about childish and disrespectful. Yet, there she stood.

"Of course," Katherine continued. "Yes it was a shock, but not a bad one. Mark is thrilled." There was a pause, then. "Oh, no. He knew Dani's mother long before we were engaged. Things ended, I came to Seattle and the rest is history. Uh-huh. I think Dani is very happy to have family. Yes, she was very young when her mother died."

Katherine turned. Dani took another step back. Okay, she really had to leave. Only before she could, she saw Katherine touch her face. Then the light caught her skin and Dani realized the other woman was crying.

"You know Alex," Katherine said with a chuckle that sounded forced. "He's always been unconventional. As they're not related by blood and we adore her, of course we're happy. It keeps things all in the family. We could be connecting our families in more ways than one."

There was pain on Katherine's face. Her expression and her tears were in stark contrast to her words. Dani wondered who she was talking to. Obviously someone she couldn't be honest with.

Dani backed away from the room and regretted pausing to eavesdrop. It had been rude and selfish. For her lack of character, she'd learned an uncomfortable truth. That she'd deeply hurt someone she only respected and short of going away — something she wasn't prepared to do — there was no way to ease Katherine's pain.

CHAPTER FOURTEEN

Alex could think of several things he'd rather be doing than shopping at Bell Square, yet the thought of spending the afternoon with his favorite sister — not that he would ever admit that to anyone — and Dani, had been irresistible. If nothing else, he would be distracted from the fact that he knew he had to confront his father about what he'd done but wasn't sure what to say.

In his heart and his gut, he wanted to walk away. The political world wasn't his and he didn't belong. But he owed Mark and he'd been taught the importance of duty from the moment Katherine had adopted him. So leaving wasn't an option. Which meant he had to figure out a way to make his current situation work for him. If Mark won the nomination and subsequent election, nothing would ever be the same.

After lunch at P.F. Chang's — ordered by Dani, to keep up their strength — they headed to Nordstrom.

"The perfect place for shoes," Dani informed him as she linked arms with Bailey and led the way. "They have a fabulous selection and the employees are always great to work with. You'll love it."

Bailey's big smile widened. "Can I get any color I want?"

"Of course," Dani told her. "These are your birthday shoes. They have to be special. Maybe red or purple or something with a cool pattern? I always wanted red suede pumps when I was a teenager. My grandmother said they were tacky, but I still wanted them. Maybe I should buy some now."

Alex walked just behind the women and briefly allowed himself to enjoy the fantasy of Dani in high-heeled red suede pumps and nothing else.

It worked for him in a big way.

They entered the store and found their way to the shoe department.

Alex also shopped at Nordstrom, although usually at the downtown store. He walked into the men's department, told them what color suit he wanted, tried it on, was fitted and gone in less than thirty minutes. If he needed shirts or ties, Frank, the man he worked with, had a selection ready for his approval. For him, shopping for clothes was about as interesting as shopping for groceries. Wasn't the point to get what you needed and get out?

But women were their own country, he reminded himself, with different expectations and different customs.

"Look around," Dani told Bailey. "I need to check on a couple of things."

She walked toward the counter in the corner. Alex smiled at his sister. "Are you having fun?"

Bailey nodded but didn't smile. Instead she pressed her lips together, then drew in a shaky breath.

"Are you mad at me?" she asked, sounding terrified to hear the answer to her question.

"No," he said quickly. "Why would I be mad at you?"

"Because. Before. I talked to that man and you hit him and got into trouble."

"Honey, no." He walked over and hugged her. "Bailey, that had nothing to do with you. You didn't do anything wrong. I love you."

She gazed up at him, her eyes filled with tears. "You sure?"

"I promise."

She had never been the problem and he

hated thinking that she'd been worried all this time.

"I love you," he told his sister.

She smiled. "I love you, too. But you're not my favorite brother."

The start of their familiar game let him know she was okay now. "Sure I am. Who else could be your favorite?"

"Ian."

"No way."

"Way."

"Crazy girl."

She grinned. "That's loco to you."

"Loco it is."

He put his arm around her. He loved all his siblings, but he had a special place in his heart for Bailey. He had no idea why, but he welcomed his need to take care of her.

Suddenly the combination of hugging Bailey, the store setting and a sense of protecting his own caused him to remember another time in a store. He couldn't remember how long ago it had been. Two years? Three?

He'd been married to Fiona at the time and the three of them had gone to some store. Bailey had tripped and banged her arm. She'd been in tears from the pain and he'd been holding her. Fiona had offered a tissue from her purse when an older woman had stopped.

"Your daughter is lovely," the stranger had told Fiona. "She has your hair."

"That is not my child," Fiona had said forcefully. "She's my husband's adopted sister."

Later he'd wondered why Fiona had felt it so necessary to distance herself from Bailey, both by biological and familial connection. Had she been afraid someone would think she was flawed?

It had been a small thing, but it had stayed with him. Finding her on the table, having sex with another man might have been the end of their marriage, but it hadn't been the only reason he'd left her.

Dani returned with a handful of shoes. "What do you think of these?" she asked. "Now before you say anything, I want you to know that there will be much trying on of shoes. This is an important decision and not one to be made lightly." She eyed him. "No whining from the male contingent."

"Yes, ma'am."

"Good. Bailey, we're going to need some help." She pointed at the two men who stood just behind her. "This is Eric and this is Cameron. They are your shoe slaves."

Bailey covered her mouth with her hand and giggled before ducking behind Alex.

Dani reached for her and dragged her toward the leather chairs.

"Sit," she said sternly and pointed. "You're the princess today, young lady. We're here to make you happy."

Bailey continued to giggle. Eric winked at her, while Cameron said her hair was a beautiful color of red. Alex slid close to Dani.

"Your doing?" he asked, nodding at the two guys.

"I said today had to be exceptional. They'll flirt in a nice, safe way. I want her to feel special."

"You've gone to a lot of trouble for a girl you barely know."

Dani stared up at him. "I know as much as I need to. I like Bailey. I'm not a saint, Alex. Don't get any weird ideas. I'm acting selfishly because it makes me happy."

"I get that."

He also got that she wouldn't see her actions as anything extraordinary. But he knew better. He knew exactly what kind of person bothered and what kind didn't.

Dani collapsed next to Bailey and kicked off her shoes. "I'm thinking something flashy," she said as Eric, or maybe Cameron, slid a pair of magenta suede pumps on her feet.

"Me, too," Bailey said. She had on the same pair.

Dani pushed herself into a standing position. Bailey tried to do the same, wobbled, then collapsed back into her chair. Dani sighed. "I see we have some work to do. Gentlemen?"

Eric and Cameron each took a hand and drew Bailey upright. When she was balanced, Dani walked in front of her.

"The trick is to keep your weight forward and low. Those skinny heels will kill you if you let them. But you don't want to go too far forward or you'll fall on your face and that's never pretty."

With Bailey laughing, Dani demonstrated an exaggerated walk, complete with swinging hips and fancy turns. Bailey followed her, staggering only a little. She nearly fell on the turn, but one of the guys caught her and held her arm while she straightened.

"I'm walking!" she cried as she moved through the center of the shoe department. "Look, Alex. I'm really walking in high heels."

His baby sister was growing up, he thought as he watched Bailey get more confident with each step. She and Dani returned to their chairs and tried on another pair of shoes.

Two hours later the decision had been made. Both Bailey and Dani had purple suede pumps with impossibly high heels. They elected to wear their shoes out of the store. He trailed behind, holding their shopping bags.

He liked Dani a lot. He wouldn't have slept with her otherwise. But today he saw a side of her he hadn't expected. A side that impressed the hell out of him. She was more than a pretty face — she had a giving heart. She was smart, sexy and she cared about people. Which made her an amazing woman. Someone he shouldn't let get away.

"We really shouldn't be doing this again," Dani said as she followed Alex into his kitchen. She had the pizza they'd stopped for and he carried a six-pack of beer. "We're going to get caught."

"We've already been caught."

"Interesting point." She wasn't about to challenge the Fates by saying it couldn't get worse. It certainly could and that was a place she didn't want to go. "So long as we don't get caught again."

He put the beer on the counter. "Are you worried? Would you rather leave?"

"No, I'm good." She liked spending time with him and the potential for another close encounter in his bed was enough to make her stroll across hot coals. "You survived our shopping expedition. You must be so proud."

"It was easy duty," he told her. "I like hanging out with you and Bailey."

She was sure he meant the words casually, but they still caused her to get all squishy inside. "Your sister is a lot of fun. I hope she loves her shoes."

"Do you have any doubts?"

Dani smiled, remembering Bailey's excitement. "Probably not. Those guys at the store were really great. I'm going to send a letter to their boss and tell her what they did."

Something flashed in Alex's eyes.

"What?" she asked. "Are you mad I had them be extra nice to her?"

"Why would I be mad about that?"

"I don't know. What were you thinking? You looked weird."

"How flattering."

"You know what I mean."

He shook his head. "It was something totally different. Something I should let go."

She set the pizza on the counter and moved toward him. "Want to talk about it?"

He shrugged. "I'm still pissed about Mark getting those charges dropped. I have to

301

deal with him — I just don't know what to say. I'm not willing to leave the campaign. I owe him my loyalty. But what he did was wrong."

"Even though it helped you?" she asked, already knowing the answer.

"In my book."

She put her hands on his chest. "Maybe doing the wrong thing for the right reason is okay sometimes."

"Do you really believe that?"

She sighed. "No, but it sounds good." She stared into his dark blue eyes. "While we're on a vaguely uncomfortable topic, I have a subject of my own."

He covered her hands with his. "Which is?"

"Your mother. I kind of overheard her talking to someone earlier. They were talking about me, about us. She said all the right things, but she seemed . . ." Dani hesitated, then decided she wasn't about to tell Alex his mother had been crying. "She was sad," she said instead. "I'm hurting her, aren't I?"

"She's dealing with a lot. You're one more thing. But you didn't do anything wrong. You were just looking for your father. The rest of this is incidental."

It felt like more than that to her, Dani

thought. "I don't want to make her life harder. I admire everything she does. I don't want to be responsible for anything bad in her life."

"You're not."

Dani didn't agree with that. "But if she could have children of her own — birth children — don't you think she would have? Aren't I a reminder of what she couldn't have?"

"No more than any of us."

Which she didn't believe. "I don't know the answer," she admitted. "Sometimes I think about just disappearing."

He tugged her a little closer. "Running away won't fix the problem."

"I'd be less visible."

"Is that really what you're going to do?"

"No," she admitted. "I don't want to leave. I just hate that she's in pain because of me. This whole family thing is complicated."

"Especially our family."

She laughed. "We *are* totally twisted. If someone tried to write a movie of the week about us, all the producers would say it was too unrealistic."

"Some of it is real enough," he said before bending down and kissing her.

She closed her eyes in anticipation of the

gentle yet firm brush of his mouth against hers. The contact was as warm and welcoming as she remembered. She raised her arms so she could wrap them around his neck and pressed her body to his.

He was hard. Hard and confident and deliciously sexy. He was everything she'd ever wanted and exactly what she needed. A strong man with a sense of right and a need to take care of what was his. Did that include her? Because she could sure use a little being taken care of.

He teased her lower lip with his tongue and rational thoughts faded away. She gave herself up to simply feeling the long, slow strokes of his hands as he moved them up and down her back. She surrendered to the wicked marauding of his tongue as he slipped it inside her mouth, moving lazily to kiss him back.

When he reached for the buttons on her blouse, she stepped out of her shoes, then went to work on his shirt. They bumped into each other, laughed and kept on working. He moved to her skirt next. When it fell to the ground, he swore.

Dani glanced down at the thigh-high panty hose she'd worn that day. Normally she would have wrestled her way into regular panty hose, but on the off chance that she and Alex might do the wild thing, she'd gone for sexier lingerie.

The bikinis were second cousin to a thong and matched her lacy bra.

"You're killing me," he murmured as he pulled her close and cupped her rear. "Seriously. I'll be dead soon."

"No, you won't. But I can keep the stockings on, if you'd like."

He squeezed her curves, then bent down to touch the stockings on her legs. As he straightened, he dipped his tongue between her breasts, arousing her with damp heat.

"You're a fantasy I didn't even know I had," he said before kissing her again.

She got lost in the passion stirring between them, but also couldn't get his words out of her head. Was she his fantasy? She'd never really considered herself fantasy material. Still, a girl could dream.

He nudged her backward a few steps. She took them, then turned and led the way into his bedroom.

The space was as she remembered. Clean and masculine with oversize furniture and a fireplace big enough to live in. He hit the remote as they walked past. Flames jumped to life and provided soft, sexy illumination.

The bed was still huge. Dani stretched out on it, then patted the space next to her. Alex pulled a package of condoms out of his nightstand, moved next to her and began to kiss her.

He moved his tongue in a dance so erotic, she didn't realize he had reached behind her until her bra fell away. Cool air caressed her breasts, making her shiver. He dipped his head and took her right nipple in his mouth. He sucked gently, then circled the tip, moving around and around until she felt herself get wet and swollen.

She clung to him, wanting him with a desperation that took her breath away. She wanted his weight on top of her, his erection between her legs, stretching her, taking her. She wanted to surrender to this man in ways she never had before. Giving herself, exposing herself. The need was so strong, it frightened her . . . but not enough to stop what she was doing.

She reached between them and tugged at his belt. After unfastening it, she eased down his zipper then drew his trousers down his hips.

He paused long enough to push them off. He'd lost his shoes on the trip into the bedroom and now removed his socks.

His arousal strained against his boxers. She reached for him, but before she could touch him, he grabbed her around her waist and flipped them so she was on top.

"You weren't willing to tie me up last time," he said with a smile. "How about being in charge?"

"I live to be in charge."

"Good."

She was kneeling, straddling his midsection. When she would have gone back to allow him to enter her, he urged her forward.

"All the way up," he said.

"Why?"

"You'll see."

She did as he requested, slowly moving up his body. He shifted, sliding his shoulders between her legs, then running his hands up and down her stocking-clad thighs.

She was about to protest that she felt too uncovered this way when he told her to, "Hang on."

She grabbed the only thing she could — the headboard — then nearly screamed as she felt his tongue between her legs.

He used his fingers to part her flesh so she was totally exposed to him. Then he moved against her, licking, sucking, but letting her set the rhythm with her hips.

She held on to the headboard for support and rode him, rising up when she needed less pressure and sinking down when she needed more. Blood rushed to her groin, engorging her. Every inch of her felt sensitized. Heat and need and pressure built faster than she'd ever experienced before. She was close in seconds, yet desperate to prolong the pressure and not come — even though coming was inevitable.

She moved faster as she got closer. He grabbed her hips and dug in his fingers as he helped her move, urged her on. She gasped, then cried out as her orgasm claimed her.

She stiffened and parted her legs even more, wanting him to touch her everywhere. He sucked her until raw nerves made her shudder, then he backed off, kissing her, licking her, drawing out every last ounce of her release.

She knelt there, leaning heavily on the headboard as she tried to catch her breath. Alex moved away. She heard the rustling of a plastic wrapper, then he was back, turning her to face him.

She shifted and settled herself over him. He filled her, stretching her, making already sensitive nerves sing with excitement.

Passion darkened his eyes and pulled at his features. A smile turned up the corners of his mouth. She braced herself on her slightly trembling arms and rocked back and forth. They both groaned.

She was still swollen from her release, yet as he moved in and out of her, she felt her muscles begin to tighten again. He reached up and began to stroke her breasts. When he brushed against her nipples, her entire body squeezed around him.

She rode him until they were both gasping and reaching, until he pushed in so deep, she couldn't help coming again. As the first shudder claimed her, he stiffened and rose toward her. Their eyes locked as they lost themselves in their mutual release.

Dani hummed softly as she took the elevator to Walker's office. She'd stayed at Alex's the previous night and hadn't seen a single reporter as she'd left. Maybe the reality of her personal life wasn't so interesting anymore. Wouldn't that be thrilling?

Even better had been the night of lovemaking, broken by a few hours of sleep and cold pizza. She loved sleeping in his bed with his arms around her. She felt safe there. Being with Alex was something she could get used to but there were still thousands of complications.

She reached Walker's office and half expected to see Cal and Reid there. But her brother was alone.

"Just us?" she asked as he stood and

walked around his desk to hug her. "I was braced for another explosive family secret. Not that I think I could take another one. It might push me over the edge and send me screaming into the night."

"It's barely two in the afternoon," Gloria said as she entered the room. "You'd have to wait to scream and run."

Dani felt the space-time continuum shift and fold. Her grandmother wore a suit Dani had seen before. Elegant, perfectly fitted and in a shade of gold that was both fashionable and flattering. Gloria looked like what she was — a powerful matriarch.

For a second Dani felt swept back a year, to when she'd been doing her damnedest to impress Gloria by making Burger Heaven the best it could be. She could almost feel the burning on her forehead from pounding it against a wall she couldn't see or understand, but also couldn't break through.

"Is it bad?" she asked before she could stop herself. "The reason for the meeting? Is it really bad?"

"It's not bad at all," Gloria said, pointing to the leather sofa in the corner. "It's good. Have a seat. Walker and I want to talk to you about something."

"If you're going to tell me I'm not my mother's daughter, either, I'm not sure I can take it."

Gloria smiled. "You can be very dramatic. I think you get that from me." She looked at Walker. "Do you want to tell her or shall I?"

"It should come from you," Walker said.

Dani felt as if she was going to throw up. Was someone dying? Was there a genetic disease that was going to eat her flesh? Was the sky falling?

"We want you to run Buchanan's," Gloria said. "The manager is leaving and we need someone brilliant in charge. We've all been talking about it and you're the most logical choice. Not to mention the best one. You've always loved the restaurant, you're good at what you do and you're family. So, what do you think?"

Dani opened her mouth then closed it. She'd never expected anything like this. Buchanan's?

"No one's sick?" she asked.

"We're all fine. Say yes."

Say yes? Just like that?

While it was true Buchanan's was her favorite of all the family restaurants, the offer was totally unexpected. "I just started working for Bernie," she said, more to herself than them. "I love it there. I'm learning a lot. It wouldn't be right to leave so

311

quickly."

"She's a good negotiator," Gloria said to Walker. "We haven't even started talking money and already I'm going to have to increase my offer."

"This isn't about money," Dani said, even as she wondered what the opening offer would be. How much did her grandmother think she was worth?

"Of course it's about money," Gloria said. "Get as much as you can. Walker's no kitten to work for."

Dani laughed. "Hey, I survived you."

"Yes, you did. You were wonderful at Burger Heaven. I probably never told you, did I?"

Dani was humiliated to feel tears burning in her eyes. "No, you didn't."

"I'm sorry about that. I'm telling you now. You did an incredible job and I was always proud of you. While Bella Roma is a perfectly fine restaurant, it's not enough for you. Besides, Buchanan's is family. We need you, Dani."

Dani looked at her brother. "You're being very quiet."

"She's doing a good job of explaining my position. I figured if I said it you wouldn't believe me. But coming from Gloria, it has to be true."

"Interesting point," Dani murmured.

"You're the only one on the list," he continued. "You're the one we want."

She was seriously tempted, but there was a lot to think about.

"Give me a few days," she said as she stood. "I'll get back to you by Friday."

"We should talk money," Gloria insisted.

Dani grinned. "If I decide to take the job, we will. Don't worry. I'm going to make you pay for the best."

Gloria smiled. "That's my girl."

Dani figured her day couldn't get much better than it was. Last night had been spectacular, the morning relaxing and now she had a shiny, new job offer.

Running Buchanan's was tempting. Honestly, the only thing holding her back was the fact that she'd only worked for Bernie a few weeks and she hated to hire and run. Of course, if she gave him a lot of notice, that would help.

She laughed out loud as she realized she'd already made up her mind — she wanted the job at Buchanan's. In some ways it would be like coming full circle.

She walked toward Bella Roma and didn't notice the woman lurking by the front door until she nearly ran into her. Dani hastily backed up, then stared.

"Fiona? What are you doing here?"

The beautiful redhead drew Dani to a bench by the front door. "We have to talk."

Dani didn't like the sound of that. "Actually, we don't. I need to go. I'm due inside in about thirty seconds."

"What I have to say won't take much longer." Fiona clutched her small purse to her midsection. "It's about Alex. Based on what I read in the paper I'm guessing he hasn't been honest with either of us."

Dani instinctively tensed, then told herself not to be crazy. Fiona was trying to make trouble for her own reasons, but there was no way she was involved with Alex. She couldn't be. He wasn't the kind of guy to play someone. Plus, he would never forgive Fiona for cheating on him.

"He's been honest with me," Dani said flatly.

"Oh, really. So he told you he's still seeing me? That I was over there two nights ago, and the previous week and so on?"

Dani took a breath. She would stay calm. Fiona was bluffing. "That's bullshit."

Fiona tilted her head. "Don't you love the fireplace in the bedroom? How it turns on with a flick of a remote? So romantic. Have you used the jetted tub in the bathroom yet? I have."

Cold thickened Dani's blood until it nearly felt frozen in her veins. "You're lying."

Fiona's expression turned pitying. "Actually, I'm trying to save you while there's still time. My problem is I can't help loving him, no matter how much of a bastard he is. Maybe there's still time for you to save yourself. I sure hope so." She reached in her purse, then passed over a digital photo. "I'm about twelve weeks along. It's sort of hard to tell what's what, but everything is progressing nicely."

Dani stared at the picture. It was a blob, but the kind of blob she recognized from Penny's pregnancy. "You're having a baby," she breathed.

"With Alex." Fiona stood and smoothed the front of her shirt. There was a definite bump. "We're reconciling. I know I'll have to live with the other women, but that's the fate of the Canfield wives. To love their men, no matter what. Look at what Katherine has gone through for Mark."

A dig at Dani's mother. Compared to Fiona being pregnant with Alex's child, it was a poor follow-up. She handed over the picture and stood.

"I have to get to work," she said numbly, barely able to form the words. She couldn't think, couldn't focus. None of this was real, she told herself. It couldn't be.

Of course she hadn't thought it was real, either, with Hugh or Ryan.

She'd thought Alex was different — that he wasn't like the other men in her life. She'd trusted him, given her heart to him. But she'd been wrong and he'd been nothing but a lying, cheating, weasel bastard.

CHAPTER FIFTEEN

Dani curled up in the corner of the sofa, Gloria holding her and rocking her back and forth.

Everything hurt. She could barely breathe because the sobs were too harsh and frequent. She felt as if she'd been beat up and left for roadkill, only this was worse. She'd done it to herself.

"I trusted him," she cried. "I t-trusted him. I know better. They're all bastards. Every one of them. I thought he was different. I thought he was better than Ryan or Hugh, but he's not."

Gloria smoothed her hair. "Shh. It will be all right."

"Will it? Really? Can you know that?"

"I know you're too strong to let this setback break you."

Dani tried to laugh, but the sound that came out was more of a gargle. "I don't think so. I feel completely broken. Worse. I feel shattered. I can't keep doing this. I can't keep leading with my heart only to have it stomped on."

She grabbed a handful of tissues and blew her nose, then began to cry again.

There was a huge open wound right in the middle of her chest. She wondered if her very essence was going to spill out onto the rug and evaporate. She was hurt on a level that was past anger. She'd believed in Alex. That's what really killed her. She'd totally believed in him.

"He said all the right things," Dani said. "Like Ryan, only better because they weren't about me. He always talked about his family and being so damn loyal. Like he was this incredible guy."

"You don't know that he's not."

"He cheated on me with his ex-wife after telling me this whole story about how she'd cheated on *him*. We bonded over slimy ex-spouses."

"So why would he say all that if he was really still sleeping with her?"

"To suck me in."

Gloria smiled sadly and touched her cheek. "That's a complex plan, Dani. Do you really think you're worth all that?"

Despite everything, Dani laughed. Then she collapsed in her grandmother's arms and began to cry again.

"She's having his baby. I saw the picture. I saw her stomach."

"Maybe she has gas."

The sob-giggle combined into a snort. "Women like Fiona do not have gas."

"Everyone has gas. You don't know she's pregnant and if she is, you don't know it's really Alex's baby. Fiona has an agenda. You said she wanted Alex back. Getting her competition out of the way is going to make that go more smoothly."

"Maybe," Dani said, unwilling to give Alex the benefit of the doubt.

"Someone else could be the father."

Based on how beautiful Fiona was, Dani was willing to bet there would be thousands of volunteers.

"I don't know what to think," she admitted. "I want to believe it's all a game she's playing, but she knew stuff about the house. Specific stuff and he said she'd never been there. So he has to have lied about that."

"I'm sure there's a logical explanation for how she knows that."

Dani sniffed. "You're taking his side. That's not allowed."

"I'm trying to help you see that you don't have all the facts. If it turns out he's betrayed you, then I'll have Walker hire some mercenary type to grind him into dust."

There was a fierceness in Gloria's voice that made Dani feel safe and loved. It was no match for the ache inside, but it helped a little.

"I like that plan," Dani admitted.

"So we're in agreement. In the meantime, you need more information. You have to talk to Alex."

"Not today," Dani said. She'd barely gotten through her shift at Bella Roma before escaping to Gloria's house where she'd collapsed. "Not for a long time."

"Eventually."

"Maybe."

Dani wiped her face and wondered how she would get over this if Alex was the cheat she suspected. Were there really no good men out there or was she just cursed to never find one of her own?

Alex waited until everyone had left the meeting. Mark picked up the phone in his office, then glanced at Alex. "Did you want something else?"

"I want to talk about how you got the charges against me dropped."

Mark shook his head. "There's no need to thank me. I was happy to do it." He looked at his watch. "I need to make this call."

Alex ignored that. "I'm not here to thank you. I'm here to ask you what the hell you think you were doing, messing in my life? You didn't even have the courtesy to talk to me first. You just fixed everything. Like that was the right thing to do."

His father straightened in his chair. "You could show a little gratitude. If you'd been charged, you would have had to leave the campaign. Your old law firm wouldn't have wanted you back, so what would you have done? If you'd been convicted, the likelihood of you ever practicing law again would have been close to zero. I saved you, Alex. Don't forget that."

"I wanted to handle things myself."

"Give me a break. How were you going to do that?"

"By working through the system."

"The system? The only system that matters is the one we control. You're acting like a child. Did you want to go to jail?"

"If necessary," Alex said, determined to keep his temper. He knew Mark's style well enough to recognize the technique of trying to make his opponent feel foolish enough to walk away without finishing the discussion. Alex wasn't going to be sidetracked. "I want to do the right thing."

Mark stood and walked around his desk.

"The right thing is for you to live up to your potential. You have an outstanding career and why should some pissant reporter get to screw that up? Did I make a few calls? You bet. Would I do it again? In a heartbeat. You're so big on family loyalty and protecting those you care about. So am I, and that's what I did. I protected you."

Alex stood. "You got involved in a legal matter that didn't concern you. You used your position to influence a district attorney. Doesn't that bother you? Because it sure as hell bothers me."

Mark leaned against his desk. "I keep forgetting how idealistic you are. Look around. This isn't an intellectual discussion in some Ivy League law classroom. This is the real world. Do you know why you're on my campaign right now? On my staff? Because your law firm wants you to be here. They let you go because they're hoping I'll win the election. Then they'll have a connection to the White House. You know it and I know it. All of life is politics, son. It's a reality and you have to accept that."

"Political reality has to stop somewhere."

"Why?" Mark asked, sounding genuinely confused. "Why does it stop anywhere?"

Alex got it then. He'd never seen his father before — not as he really was. Mark wasn't evil or power-hungry. He simply saw the world in the way that made his life easier.

He thought of Katherine, who lived her life doing the right thing — not only because it was expected but because doing the right thing defined her. Yet she loved Mark with every fiber of her being. How did she reconcile the two?

If she were here now, she would tell him that loving someone meant accepting them as they were — good points and faults. He could love his father, but accept the faults? That was going to be tougher.

He had two choices. He could accept what had happened, or he could walk away. His gut told him to walk. That he wasn't the man to be a part of that.

But his heart remembered standing next to his birth mother's dead body, sobbing because he hadn't been able to save her. His heart remembered his vow to be loyal, no matter what. That if he ever found a family again, he would stand with them, protect them and never walk away. His heart remembered Katherine teaching him that duty was everything.

He didn't have a choice. He would stay, because it was the right thing to do.

Dani didn't even know which channels carried political shows on Sunday morning, but she flipped through the national networks until she saw men and women in suits looking serious. Then she poured herself a cup of coffee and prepared to become informed about the American political scene.

She'd never been interested before, but then she'd never had a parent running for national office before, either. Better late than never and all that. At least she always voted.

She sipped the coffee and listened to the guests talk about the latest crisis in the Middle East. Her mind wandered, probably because she was so tired. She hadn't been able to sleep in four days. Not since she'd spoken with Fiona.

Dani had been dodging Alex's calls — something she couldn't do forever. But she didn't know what to say to him. Part of her was afraid of the confrontation because it would be ugly, but mostly she didn't want to hear him admit that yes, he was a bastard and she'd been fooled yet again. Until there was confirmation, she was weak enough to want to believe the best of him.

"Shame on me," she murmured into the quiet of the room, as the show shifted into a commercial break. "I need to be stronger than this."

And she would be. In time. Wasn't she allowed a little weakness, at least in the short term?

The show resumed with a shift in topic. She saw a picture of Mark Canfield and turned up the sound.

"While the presidential election is nearly eighteen months away," the host said, "already things are heating up in the state of Washington. Bill?"

The camera panned to one of the other men in suits. "It's true. Senator Canfield, always a voter favorite, is facing a unique and uncomfortable situation. Trouble in his own home. Nearly two months ago we learned about his daughter from a previous relationship."

Dani nearly dropped her coffee when her own picture flashed onto the TV screen. She swore.

"Danielle Buchanan arrived unexpectedly and turned around the whole campaign. The senator was up-front with the public and the poll numbers showed the American people respected his honesty. Experts believe the main reason for that is the

325

senator's wife, Katherine Canfield. She's seen as the perfect wife and mother. She has embraced Dani, both literally and figuratively. If the wife can forgive the husband, then the nation can, too."

"It didn't work for Hillary," one of the other guests said.

"Different situation," Bill went on. "The senator's relationship with Dani's mother predates his marriage. But while the numbers were climbing, they've taken a sudden downswing in the past couple of weeks, ever since the public discovered that Dani and the senator's oldest son — who is adopted — have formed a romantic relationship."

Dani knew what was coming and braced herself to see that horrible picture of her driving away from Alex's house. Sure enough it was put up in a corner.

"The problem is," Bill said, "the American people have a limit to what they can tolerate and they're not willing to accept the love child of a presidential candidate dating his adoptive son."

"But they're not related," the host said.

"That doesn't seem to matter to the polls. The senator's numbers have been dropping steadily. If this continues, there's not going to *be* a Canfield bid for the presidency. The campaign will be over before it even begins."

"Your young man is here," Bernie told Dani the following day shortly after two. "Go on. I'll finish up here."

Dani's stomach tightened with dread. "No, it's okay. I'll tell him I can't see him now. I want to work my whole shift."

Bernie grinned. "I just said 'your young man.' Now I'm talking like my mother. I need work to distract me. Go. It's fine."

Trapped by a kind man with good intentions, Dani nodded, then walked through the main dining room of Bella Roma.

The lunch crowd had faded to only a few diners. She easily saw Alex standing by the front door. He didn't look happy.

"You've been avoiding me," he said as she approached.

She hadn't seen him in nearly a week. Despite everything, she found herself wanting to step close and have him hold her. She wanted to feel his arms around her and breathe in the scent of his body. She wanted to kiss and be kissed and have all the bad stuff go away. Which only showed that she was spineless, weak and in need of a feminist intervention.

"I haven't known what to say," she admitted, then nodded toward the back. "We can talk in my office."

He frowned. "So there's a problem."

"Let's talk in private."

He followed her into the small, crowded space. There was a desk, a file cabinet and not much extra room. Especially with them both standing.

"What's going on?" he asked. "You haven't returned any of my calls. I went by your grandmother's place this weekend and she said you were out of town."

She'd hated to ask Gloria to lie for her, but she hadn't been ready to face Alex yet. She still wasn't.

"I'm not ready to deal with this," she admitted.

"Deal with what? What are you talking about? Dammit, Dani, why are you avoiding me?"

"Because I don't want to see you," she snapped back. "Can I make it more plain than that? I don't want to see you."

He stiffened as if she'd slapped him. "All right. You going to tell me why?"

She couldn't. She couldn't say the words without crying and she refused to break down in front of him. She turned away.

"Just go," she said softly. "It will be easier that way."

He grabbed her by the arm and turned her to face him. "Maybe I'm not interested in easy. Maybe I want the truth."

"You want bullshit, because that's where you live," she snapped.

"What the hell are you talking about?"

His eyes were the color of a midnight sky. She hated that she could be angry and hurt and still notice that.

He swore then and crossed his arms over his chest. "I can't believe it," he said. "I expected better of you."

"What?"

"You saw the shows on Sunday. You've been reading the papers. You know the numbers are falling and you're running away, just like you said you would. You're taking the easy way out. I never thought you'd get political so fast."

She went from sad to furious in two nanoseconds. "Welcome to *my* world of disappointment. That's what I've been thinking about you. For starters, I haven't gone political, but how kind of you to judge me. As for why I've been avoiding you, here's the reason. I'm tired of lying, cheating, rat bastard men in my life, of which you are apparently the latest in a long chain.

You talk a great game. You played me like a pro. Congrats on that, by the way. You make Ryan look like an amateur."

He dropped his arms to his side. "I have no idea what you're talking about."

"Drop the act. I've talked to Fiona. I know the truth."

"What truth? There's no truth."

"Right. You're a lawyer. Everything is relative. If that works for you, great. But it doesn't work for me. How incredibly pedestrian of me to expect the man I'm sleeping with to sleep with only me. I suppose you can get out of it on a technicality. We never had the 'it's exclusive' conversation. My bad. No, wait. *Your* bad. You're a disgusting person. I'm sorry I got to know you, I'm sorry I slept with you and I can't tell you how much I regret that because Mark's my father, I can't just walk away from you and never see you again."

He took a step toward her. "You think I'm seeing someone else?"

"I know you are. Fiona. She told me. Are you excited about the baby?"

He stiffened and looked stunned. "She's pregnant?"

Dani stared at him. "She didn't tell you? Gee, I spoiled the surprise. Yes, Alex. You're going to be a daddy. In the end you get

330

everything."

"I'm not sleeping with Fiona," he said, but he sounded distracted.

"That's convincing. Look, you don't have to play the game. She told me everything. It's obvious she's been in your house and in your bed. I'm too tired to keep fighting this battle. I give up. I'm so over men. I thought you were special. Better . . . But you're not."

"I don't deserve that. I haven't done anything."

"Let me guess. You're sorry I had to find out this way."

His gaze narrowed. "If that's really what you think of me, then we have nothing to talk about."

"Didn't I tell you that when you first walked in?"

He stared at her for a long time. She braced herself for the apologies, the explanations. She desperately wanted him to prove her wrong. That's how gone on him she was. She wanted him not to have cheated so they could be together again. Talk about sad.

But in the end he didn't say anything else. He walked away and never looked back.

It was the worst possible time to be practicing a speech she didn't want to give, but Dani couldn't come up with a good excuse for changing her appointment with Katherine. It was only after she'd parked and walked to the front of the house that she realized she could have simply phoned and said she wasn't feeling well.

Apparently, along with her heart, she'd also lost her brain.

The thought flashed in and out of her head so quickly that it took her a second to understand its meaning. When that sank in, she slowed, then stopped, right in the middle of the walkway.

She'd lost her heart? Was that possible? Did she love Alex?

She stood there, waiting for the answer to the question, then realized she already knew the truth. Of course she loved Alex. Not loving him would have made what he'd done so much easier to take.

"The hits just keep on coming," she murmured to herself, then continued up the wide path to the front door.

All she'd ever wanted was to find where she belonged. Instead she'd made a mess of everything.

As she knocked, she did her best to clear her head. She had to focus on her meeting with Katherine. She would deal with Alex-pain when she got home.

"Dani!" Katherine opened the door and

smiled. "Come in, come in. Are you nervous yet? I hope not. You're going to do great and I'm going to be able to say I knew you when."

Dani stepped into the large house and instantly felt the welcoming warmth reaching out to comfort her. Katherine was lovely and gracious as always.

"I'm trying not to think about the speech," she admitted as she followed Katherine into her office. "When I let myself go there, I feel like I'm going to throw up. It's not pretty."

"Vomiting rarely is. Can I get you something? Coffee? Soda? Water?"

"I'll take a water."

Katherine walked to an antique chest which opened up to reveal a small refrigerator. "One of my indulgences," she admitted as she removed two bottles of water. "When I get working on a project, I hate to break my concentration. I'm terribly spoiled."

"You're great," Dani said and instantly felt stupid. As if she was babbling around someone she admired. Which she kind of was.

"Thank you," Katherine said. "You're very kind." She pointed to the folder on the coffee table. "There it is. The infamous speech."

Dani held in a groan. She picked up the folder and flipped through the pages. There were only five of them, double-spaced. The opening told a story of a working single mother who found out she had stage four breast cancer and her quest to find the right family to take her children.

Maybe it was the placement of the moon or the fact that she was due to get her period in three days or the hellish trauma she'd been suffering, but Dani found herself suddenly fighting the need to cry.

She sank onto the sofa as she struggled to keep from bursting into tears. Breathing slowly didn't help, nor did swallowing or thinking about something else.

Katherine moved closer. "Dani? Are you all right?"

"I'm fine. It's just stress." She blinked several times and tried to smile. "Sorry. I won't be like this when I give the speech. I'll be too frightened."

Katherine handed her a box of tissues. "Don't apologize. You feel what you feel. Is there anything I can do?"

It was a simple question, but the kindness in the other woman's voice was too much. One tear escaped, then another. Dani did her best to hang on to the little dignity she had left.

"I'm sorry," she repeated. "I'm, ah, dealing with a lot right now. Not that I need to tell you. You have your own issues. I've made things worse. I know that. I didn't mean to. I really admire you and I'm so sorry I've screwed up your life."

Katherine sat down next to her. "You haven't screwed up my life."

"How about challenges?" Dani asked with a sniff. "I've brought those along. You don't deserve that."

"You haven't done anything. We're all fine."

"I never wanted to hurt you."

Katherine's mouth tightened. "I'm not hurt."

She was lying, but Dani understood that. Under the circumstances, why would Katherine trust her with the truth?

"I've made a mess of everything," Dani said. "Without even trying. Imagine what I could have done if I'd been working at it."

"What mess?" Katherine asked.

"The poll numbers. I was watching one of those political shows on Sunday and they said the poll numbers were down because of me and Alex. They said the Canfield campaign was already over."

Katherine patted her arm. "You can't believe everything you hear. Of course the

335

campaign is going forward. If this is the worst of it, then Mark will win by a three-quarter majority. Poll numbers go down, then they go up. This week it's you. Next week it will be something else."

She sounded so calm. So confident. Was it really that simple?

"I haven't damaged Mark's chances?"

"Never."

"Okay." Dani wiped her face. "That's good." She straightened and patted her cheeks. "I'm healed. At least for now. Do I look scary?"

"You look fine."

"Thanks. I want you to know I didn't mean for any of this to upset you. For what it's worth, I won't be seeing Alex anymore."

Katherine tried not to react to the news. Despite everything, she'd found herself liking Dani. The young woman seemed sincere and Katherine had always been a sucker for anyone suffering.

As for Dani and Alex not seeing each other, she tried not to be happy about it, but relief flooded her. If they weren't together then maybe Katherine wouldn't get so many questions about them all the time. She was tired of the questions and the humiliation those questions brought.

There was a knock at the door.

336

"Come in," Katherine called.

Bailey walked into the room. "Dani! I heard you were here."

Dani smiled at the teenager. "I am. How are you? Do you still love your shoes?"

"More than anything."

Katherine drank her water and tried to be mature. It didn't matter that Dani had taken Bailey shopping for high heels. Honestly, she, Katherine, had never thought to make the offer. It was good for Bailey to get out with other people — people who weren't family — and experience the world. She was fine with it.

Okay, maybe there had been a tiny twinge that she hadn't been the one to share that experience with her daughter, but she would get over it.

"I have a dance," Bailey said. "For school. It's the night of my birthday and I get to wear a beautiful dress."

"Lucky you," Dani said. "I'll want to see pictures."

Bailey sank onto the floor and grabbed Dani's hands. "Will you please take me shopping for my dress? I want you to help me find it. Please?"

The words cut through Katherine like a laser.

She'd wanted to be the one to go shopping with Bailey. She'd wanted to be the one making those memories. Although she and her daughter had never talked specifics, she'd assumed she would be the one going with her.

Jealousy burned hot and bright, making her want to attack the woman responsible for this situation.

"Bailey, I'd really like that," Dani said, sounding as if she meant it. Which she probably did. "Katherine, would that be all right with you?"

Katherine knew her jealousy was misplaced and that she was acting like a child. The lessons she'd learned from her mother came back to her. Always be calm, no matter what she was feeling inside. Always do the right thing, the proper thing.

"Of course. You're so sweet to take her. I know Bailey will have a wonderful time."

It hurt to speak the words. It hurt to smile. She wanted to hiss and scratch like a cornered cat.

Bailey sprang to her feet, then hugged them both. "I can't wait! I can't wait!" She spun in a circle, her hands in the air, her face bright with pleasure.

Katherine looked at her daughter and tried to find happiness in the moment. She just couldn't. She wasn't that big of a person.

When Bailey left, Dani sighed. "She's so great. I adore her."

"Me, too," Katherine said, doing her best to keep the sharpness out of her voice.

"Thanks for letting me take her shopping."

"It's not a problem. Now what were we talking about?"

Dani's face shifted until she looked as if she'd lost everything. "Alex," she murmured. "That we won't be seeing each other anymore."

"I see," Katherine said. "What changed your mind? The poll numbers?"

She should point out to Dani that she couldn't let other people's opinions run her life. That was the right thing to do. But before she could decide if she was that mature or not, Dani said, "No, it's not the poll numbers. Alex accused me of that, too."

"Really?"

Dani nodded. Her eyes were dark and filled with pain. "I'm sorry about the numbers, but that's not the reason. He thought I was running away. To make things easier."

"You're not?"

"No." Dani swallowed. "I think . . . I think he might still be seeing Fiona. She came to talk to me and she made a really good case for that."

Katherine could feel Dani's pain. The other woman looked at her.

"You know them both. Is it possible? Could Alex still be seeing Fiona?"

It was like an out-of-body experience, Katherine thought as she seemed to stare down at the room. She could see herself sitting on the sofa. So perfect, she thought, taking in the cashmere sweater, the pearls. She was a cliché. A cliché whose life had been turned upside down by the proof that her husband could father children when she couldn't have them herself.

She argued that it wasn't Dani's fault. That she hadn't knowingly brought this humiliation to Katherine. That the fact that she and Bailey got along was a good thing. She could hear her mother's voice telling her to always be a lady.

Screw that, she thought bitterly. For once she was going to do exactly what she wanted to do. What felt right and would make her hurt a little less.

She looked at Dani and lied. "I don't want to hurt you, but I do think it's very possible Alex and Fiona are seeing each other."

CHAPTER SIXTEEN

Alex walked into his father's office at campaign headquarters. He knew Mark was in a meeting and that Katherine had come in for a photo shoot. She stood in front of the wall map of the country.

"Do you have a minute?" he asked.

She turned and smiled at him. "Of course. I'm stuck standing until the photographer is ready. I can't muss or wrinkle. I can barely make an expression at all, so don't be funny or all this makeup will crack."

He grinned. "Makes me want to ruffle your hair."

"Naturally. Why is it that the small boy always lives inside the man?"

"One of my gender's many charms."

"Yes, it is." She tilted her head. "What's going on? What do you want to talk about?"

His humor faded. He closed the door for privacy and moved toward her. "What would you say if I told you I wanted to leave the campaign?"

Her blue eyes widened. "Alex, no." She reached out and put her hand on his arm. "Seriously? You hate it that much?"

"Yeah. This isn't me or what I want. I'm not a political animal. But I said I'd help and he's my father."

She nodded. "Right. Loyalty to family. Doing the right thing." She dropped her hand. "I'm the wrong person to ask about this."

"Because you're too close to what's going on?"

"That, and . . ." She drew in a breath. "I know about doing what's expected. Sometimes when we go the other way we feel free and sometimes we just feel like crap. Do you know which it's going to be for you?"

"I'm not sure it matters," he told her. "I never thought I'd get caught in the middle of something like this. I know where my loyalties lie and I still can't make myself want to stay."

"This campaign is a complication in all our lives," she said. "Especially now."

He looked at her. "You mean because of Dani?"

"She keeps things interesting. Not that it's her fault. It's just uncomfortable timing."

"She's hurt you, hasn't she?"

Katherine turned back to the map and touched the center of Texas. "Not really. She isn't responsible for what people say or how I react to it."

"She'll be less of an issue now. We're not seeing each other."

His mother tensed slightly. "What happened?"

"I don't know. That's the thing of it. I really thought she was someone I could care about. After Fiona I didn't want to get involved again. I didn't want to trust anyone like that. But Dani was different."

More than different. There'd been something about her. He'd wanted to spend every moment with her. He wanted to know everything about her. He could see a future with her.

"And now?" his mother asked.

"She got upset about the poll numbers, which I get, but then she accused me of still seeing Fiona." The accusation burned. Dani *knew* what he thought of his ex-wife's betrayal. She knew loyalty was everything to him and yet she'd still claimed to believe he was screwing around. With Fiona of all people. What the hell was up with that?

Katherine turned back to him. "Are you seeing her?"

"No," he said flatly. "I would never cheat,

and I'll never go back to Fiona. I just don't get it. Why her? Why would Dani think I was seeing her?"

Katherine knew exactly why. Because that's what Fiona had told her.

Her stomach twisted and she fought the need to vomit. How could she have lied to Dani like that? How could she have gotten in between Dani and Alex? She loved her son and if Dani made him happy . . .

But the relationship was already over, she reminded herself. She hadn't really destroyed anything.

A feeble attempt to pass the blame, to not accept responsibility.

She told herself that the right thing to do was to confess her part in all this and ask for forgiveness. She opened her mouth, then closed it. Right now her world was already askew. Seeing disappointment in Alex's eyes, knowing she'd lowered herself to lying because of her own hurt feelings, was more than she could bear.

"She thinks Fiona's pregnant," he said, his voice thick with disbelief. "What kind of crap is that?"

"Maybe she is."

He looked at her, then swore. "Pregnant? Fiona? She never wanted kids."

Katherine blinked in surprise. "What are

you talking about? She always said she wanted a family."

"It was just talk," Alex told her. "I bought into it, too. But when we were married, every time I pressed her to get started on our family she had a reason we should wait. She didn't want children. So if she's pregnant now, it's got to be an accident."

"Or a way to make trouble," Katherine murmured, wondering how far her former daughter-in-law would go to get Alex back. Would she get pregnant by another man and try to pass that child off as Alex's?

"You really haven't slept with her recently?" she asked, then waved her hand. "Forget I'm your mother. I'm serious, Alex. Have you been seeing her at all?"

He met her gaze. "No. The day I moved out of the house was the day I walked in on her with someone else. I didn't want you to know that — you're still friends with her. But that's what finally ended our marriage."

Her heart tightened with pain. She ached for her child and what he'd gone through. Tears filled her eyes.

"Oh, Alex."

She walked over and hugged him.

"You'll muss," he told her.

"Screw that."

He chuckled. "You're getting feisty. It's

charming."

"Oh, please. Don't treat me like I'm old and infirm. I'll get there soon enough."

"You'll never be that."

She stepped back and stared into his handsome face. How she loved this man. She'd loved the boy and every day her feelings had grown. She couldn't have loved him more if she'd given birth to him herself.

That was her absolute truth, she reminded herself. That she loved her children completely. No one could take away the specialness of their bond — not without her letting them.

"I have to tell you something," she said as the tears once again burned. "I did something awful."

He smiled at his mother. "Not you."

"I'm serious. And I'm sorry. What I'm about to tell you could damage our relationship. I can't tell you how much I regret that. I was hurt and angry and I wanted to hurt someone. I wanted to hurt Dani. That was deeply wrong of me. I know that. I'm ashamed of myself. I don't expect you to forgive me right away, but I hope that in time you won't hate me."

Alex stared back at her. She knew he'd probably never seen her like this. His face reflected his unease.

"Mom, it's okay," he told her. "Whatever it is, we'll fix it."

"I can't fix this, but maybe you can." She swallowed. "Dani came to see me a couple of days ago. We went over the speech, or we tried to. She was upset about a lot of things, but mostly you. She told me Fiona had come to her and told her you were still seeing each other. Fiona had information that seemed to only come from her having been in your house."

Alex swore. "She's never been there. I haven't had her over."

"I know that, but there are other ways. She could have found out you had put in an offer on the house and then gone to see it herself. Who knows? The point is she convinced Dani she was pregnant and that the child was yours."

Katherine folded her arms across her chest. "I'm sorry, Alex. I'm so sorry. Feeble, feeble words. I've always prided myself on being a good person. It's a joke. All of it. I'm living a lie."

"You're not." He grabbed her shoulders. "You're the best person I know."

"I'm not. Oh, God. I'm so scared to tell you."

She looked at him. Tears darkened her eyes. Her pain and regret was a tangible beast in the room.

"There's nothing you can say to make me turn away from you," he told her, meaning every word.

"You don't know that. Dani wanted to know if I thought it was possible you and Fiona were still seeing each other. I told her it was."

He stepped back. Of all the Canfields, Dani most trusted Katherine. Hearing that from her would make it all the more real.

"I know," Katherine said, tears spilling down her cheeks. "I know it was horrible and wrong and I have no excuse or explanation. I was hurt and I lashed out. I . . ." She turned away. "I'm sorry."

He didn't think he could have been more shocked if she'd told him she'd murdered someone. Katherine didn't act out of anger or impulse. She wasn't deliberately cruel. He would never have guessed her capable of hurting Dani . . . or him.

He didn't know what to think or say. While a part of him knew he had to find Dani and talk to her, explain the complexities that had conspired against them, the rest of him wrestled with the uncomfortable truth that his mother was not the saint he'd always believed.

"Alex?" Her voice was a whimper. "I'm sorry."

"I know," he told her, knowing being sorry wasn't going to fix anything.

"This was a hard decision for me to make," Dani said earnestly, wondering if knowing she felt guilty would help. "You've been so great and I've loved working here. I really want to stay until you find someone else. I'm not leaving you short-staffed."

Bernie shook his head. "You're worrying too much. We'll be fine. I have family I can guilt into working here temporarily." He grinned. "I learned from the best."

"I adore your mother," she murmured, knowing she would miss hearing Mama Giuseppe's constant comments on everything from the weather to the state of the cannelloni.

"She adores you. I'll bet you won't miss hearing about how perfect I am."

Dani sighed. "If only you were a few years younger."

He chuckled. "Or you were older." He put out his hand. "Go with God, Dani. You're taking a job with family. That's always the right decision. Give me a couple of weeks to start looking, but no longer. You need to start on the next chapter of your life."

"You're being a lot nicer than I deserve."

He shrugged. "I'm a nice guy."

He was. Perfectly nice. Despite the age difference, she should have fallen for him instead of Alex. Bernie wouldn't cheat and lie and break her heart.

She forced her mind away from thoughts of Alex because thinking about him was too painful.

She shook hands with Bernie, then rose. "You're a good man. Thank you for everything."

He released her hand and pointed to the door. "Now get out of here before I change my mind."

She waved and left.

She would miss Bella Roma, but working at Buchanan's felt right. She was grateful she'd made up her mind before finding out the truth about Alex. She didn't have to worry that her decision was too much like giving up and running home.

A quick glance at her watch told her she had to leave right away or she would be late picking up Bailey for their shopping trip. She'd nearly made it to the back door when one of the waitstaff yelled for her.

"Phone call. A guy. Alex somebody?"

It was the first time she'd heard from him in four days. She hated that her first reaction was pleasure. How bad did it have to get before she was willing to see him for the snake he was?

"Tell him I've already left," she said.

"Will do."

Dani grabbed her cell phone and turned it off. There was nothing Alex could say to her that she wanted to hear.

An hour and a half later, she was in an oversized dressing room with Bailey and laughing so hard she was afraid she was going to pee her pants.

"Stop!" she insisted, as Bailey danced like a chicken in a seriously ugly, yellow tulle gown. "Stop, I swear, I'm too old. I'll collapse or something."

"But it's so fluffy," Bailey said, actually doing a fair imitation of the horrible salesclerk "helping" them. "And the yellow is so perfect for my hair."

Dani blinked away tears and sank onto the floor. "I give," she said. "This place is awful. We'll go to another store where they have pretty dresses."

"But I want to be a chicken," Bailey insisted, her eyes twinkling with humor.

"Sure you do. Oh, man, what was that woman thinking?"

She'd brought in four dresses, each worse

than the one before. One had been marked down three times and Dani wasn't surprised. Who would buy it?

They'd been to other stores in the mall and nothing like this had happened. Was the salesclerk reacting to the fact that Bailey had Down's syndrome? Dani didn't want to think so, but she had a bad feeling that might be the problem.

She reminded herself that people like that were stupid and had their own problems. Dani wasn't going to sweat it. She would simply get Bailey out of here and they would go somewhere else.

Once Bailey was dressed and the awful gown was on the hanger, Dani led her out of the store.

"So, I'm thinking we need some fuel to help with our search," Dani said. "How about a snack?"

"Pretzels?" Bailey asked hopefully.

"Pretzels it is."

They went to the Auntie Anne's stand and each got a pretzel with a drink, then sat on a bench and ate. Dani listened to Bailey talk about her school.

"I like reading better than math," Bailey told her. "Sometimes Alex comes over and helps me with my math. You know I'm in special classes, but I'm doing really well."

"I'll bet you are. You study hard."

"I do." Bailey smiled and tucked a long, red curl behind her ear. "I'm glad you're my sister. Mom explained about how we're sisters now."

"I'm glad, too," Dani said. "I have three brothers, which means they're part of your family, too, right? Or are they. I can't keep it straight."

"I can't, either."

Bailey snuggled close and leaned her head on Dani's shoulder. "You're nice. Fiona was never nice." She looked at Dani and covered her mouth. "I shouldn't say that."

"It's okay. I won't tell anyone you did."

"Good." Bailey rested her head on her shoulder again. "She said mean stuff to me. Not when Alex was around. Sometimes she scared me. But I didn't want to say anything."

What a bitch, Dani thought, furious with the other woman. What on earth could Alex have seen in her? To think he knew she cheated on him and he went back to her.

Dani's stomach twisted at the thought. She wanted to tell herself to give him the benefit of the doubt — that there was a perfectly good explanation — but she couldn't. Not when Katherine had confirmed her worst fears. Once again her life was a nightmare.

Well, not all of it, she thought as she stroked Bailey's head. Having a new sister was nice. Today was nice. That was how she was going to get through the pain — one moment at a time.

They finished their pretzels and went into another store. Bailey found a pretty pale green dress that fit her perfectly. She turned back and forth in front of the mirror.

"I love it."

"You look like a princess."

"Really?" Bailey beamed.

"Uh-huh."

Dani studied her. The dress was perfect — youthful without being childlike. The neckline was conservative, the bodice fitted, the skirt all floaty, and it twirled when Bailey spun.

"It's a perfect party dress," Dani said. "Are you wearing your hair up?"

"I think so. Mom said she knew how to pin it up and everything."

They paid for the dress, bought a pair of matching shoes and made their way back to the car. It was later than Dani expected, and already dark. She held the packages in one hand and Bailey with the other as she led the way to her car.

Suddenly three teenage boys stepped right

in front of her.

"Well, what have we got here?" one of the boys asked. He was the tallest of the three, dressed in jeans, an oversize T-shirt with an open flannel shirt on top. He stared at Dani. "I know you."

"You don't," she said and started to move around them.

Only they stepped in front of her, blocking her way.

She stiffened, not sure what to do next. What did they want? They looked like regular suburban kids. Were they going to steal her purse? Hijack the car?

The kid on the left frowned. "You're right. I've seen her picture."

"She's the chick in the paper. The one sleeping with her brother." The guy on the left snickered. "You know. The daughter of that guy running for president."

"Senator Canfield," Bailey said. "He's my dad. Now leave us alone."

The boys hooted. "Look, J.P., the retard has balls. You got balls, honey? Can you understand me?"

Concern for Bailey overwhelmed Dani's fear. She started moving toward the car.

"I'm not retarded," Bailey said clearly, her head held high. "There's nothing wrong with me."

"You look like there's something wrong with you." The guy on the left grabbed Dani's arm. "Hey! Where do you think you're going?"

She jerked free. "To my car."

"I don't think so. We're not done here."

"Leave her alone," Bailey said fiercely. "We're not afraid of you."

Dani wanted to disagree. She was plenty afraid. Now that the boys were closer, she saw their eyes were dilated. Great — they were high on something. So she wasn't dealing with rational attackers. Not that any attacker was good.

She pushed the panic button on her key fob. Nothing happened. She must be too far from her car. If she could just get them closer, the loud noise might scare the kids away.

She pushed forward a few steps. The boys continued to crowd around. J.P. pushed between her and Bailey.

"People like you shouldn't be allowed to live," he said, his face inches from Bailey's. "They should drown you at birth, like deformed kittens."

"You're nothing but a butthead," Bailey yelled and pushed him.

Dani turned to get between them, but the other two teens grabbed her arms. She twisted and squirmed but couldn't break free.

J.P. pushed back, his hands coming down on Bailey's chest.

"Whoa, lookee here. The retard's got some curves on her." He reached for his belt. "Let's have a little fun with her. I'll go first." He smiled at Bailey. "I'll bet you're still a virgin, aren't you? You're going to like what I do to you."

Dani lost it. In that moment, it was as if she were possessed by a rage and need to protect she'd never experienced before.

"Get the fuck away from her," she screamed.

She pulled free of her captors and started swinging her packages as if they were weapons. She shrieked as she cracked one of the kids in the head with the shoe box and kicked out at the second. J.P. swung toward her. His arm came up and before she could get out of the way, his right fist crashed into her face.

Pain exploded. The impact of the blow sent her spinning into a support pole where she hit her head hard. There was a bright light, a blurring of sound, then what looked like a car racing toward them.

"Help," Dani said weakly as she collapsed

to the cement floor. "We need . . ."

The world went black.

CHAPTER SEVENTEEN

Dani woke up to find herself propped up against a pole in the parking garage. She knew exactly where she was and what had happened.

"Bailey," she yelled.

The strange man holding a flashlight in front of her eyes smiled at her. "It's okay," he said. "Bailey's good. Nothing happened to her. You're the one who got hit. You're gonna have a black eye."

"Great," Dani said, still looking for the teenager. Her face hurt, as did her head, but none of that mattered.

There were a dozen or so people milling around. Several EMT workers, police officers and a few shoppers being kept at a distance. Dani continued to search the crowd until she saw Katherine and a young woman she didn't recognize holding Bailey.

"She looks okay," Dani breathed in relief.

"She's fine. Tough. Her mom said she was

standing over you like a lioness, prepared to take on all those kids."

"The boys got away, didn't they?" Dani asked, wanting them punished for what they'd tried to do to Bailey.

"They'll be caught. We have good descriptions. Bailey was paying attention."

Katherine looked up and caught Dani's gaze. She said something to Bailey and the other woman, then hurried over.

"How is she?" she asked. "She hit her head."

"Yes, ma'am. She looks good. We're going to transport her to the hospital to run a few tests, probably keep her overnight. But she's doing well right now. You want to sit with her a minute?"

"Yes. Of course."

Despite her pale wool slacks, Katherine sank onto the cement and took one of Dani's hands in hers.

"My God," she breathed, as tears filled her eyes. "How can I ever thank you?"

Dani sniffed. "Don't thank me. It's all my fault. Those damn boys recognized me from the paper. They started taunting me, then they noticed Bailey. They went after her. If they'd hurt her . . ."

Katherine reached out and wiped away tears Dani hadn't even felt fall. "If they'd hurt her, there would be no place on this earth for them to hide. Alex would hunt them down and kill them, then I'd dig up their bodies and do it all over again."

She spoke so fiercely that Dani believed every word.

"It's not your fault," Katherine continued. "Please don't think that."

"But they —"

"Were assholes." She smiled slightly. "Don't let the press know I can talk like that, but I can, if necessary. Little bastards."

"She was so calm," Dani said. "I was terrified, but Bailey stood up to them. You would have been so proud of her."

"I am, and of you. You defended her."

Dani touched her swollen cheek. "I didn't do a very good job."

"You were amazing." Katherine squeezed her hand. "I can never thank you enough."

"Don't thank me. I swear, I feel so horrible about what happened. I was so scared for her."

"You care about her."

Dani nodded, then wished she hadn't as her head began to ache. "She's my sister."

More tears filled Katherine's eyes. "I have been so horrible. I didn't . . ." She swallowed. "There's no excuse for what I did."

Dani frowned. "I just hit my head and

blacked out, which probably explains why I have no idea what you're talking about."

"Did you see a car, just before you hit your head?"

She caught herself before she nodded again and said, "Yes."

"It was me. Julie and I had plans for this afternoon. I made her come to the mall so I could spy on you."

"What?" Dani knew she had brain damage for sure. Katherine couldn't have just said "spy."

"I was so hurt and bitter and stupid. I wanted to be the one to take her dress shopping." She covered her eyes with her free hand. "I'm so ashamed. I love her so much and I wanted that memory. In that moment, I saw you as the personification of everything wrong in my life. I lashed out."

"You followed us?" Dani said, not sure she was keeping up. "I would never hurt her."

"I know. I know. I'm so sorry. I was stupid and jealous and ridiculous. I just hurt. It was never about you — not really. I should have said something. I should have asked to come along." Katherine lowered her hand. "I'm sorry."

Dani stared at her. "Katherine, I would have loved to have you along. I admire you so much. There have been times . . ." She drew in a breath. "I've often wished you were my parent, not Mark."

New tears fell down Katherine's face. "Oh, don't. I'm not who you think at all."

"You saved us. I saw the car speeding toward us. You made those guys run away."

"I saw you defending my child with your life," Katherine said. "I can never repay you for that. Especially because of what I did before." She paused and looked away for a few seconds. "When you asked me about Fiona and Alex . . . If it was possible for them to still be together? I lied. I was hurt and I wanted to lash out, so I did. They're not together, Dani. They haven't been since he left her."

Dani pulled her hand free and pushed herself into a more upright position. She rubbed the side of her head, then winced when she touched the swelling in her face.

Facts and information swirled inside her fuzzy brain. They danced and came together like mismatched puzzle pieces. Nothing made sense except for the fact that once again, she'd hurt Katherine. And . . .

Wait a minute? Alex wasn't with Fiona? That was too much for her to take in. She went for the easier topic.

"I'm sorry I made things worse for you,"

Dani whispered. "I keep doing that."

Katherine made a sound that was part laugh, part sob. "Is that all you got from my confession? I was horrible. A disgusting human being. I lied."

"You reacted. I understand that."

"Oh, God. You're going to be sweet and understanding. Can't you please be angry with me? You could slap me. We could roll in a catfight like they did in those 1980s soaps."

"My head hurts too much."

Katherine leaned in and hugged her. "Dani, please forgive me."

"I do."

"It can't be that easy."

"Maybe it is."

"But I lied about Alex."

"I don't understand what happened with him," she admitted. "Fiona was so convincing and then when I accused him, he barely defended himself. It was almost like it was all true."

"Or he was shocked you'd think that and disappointed you wouldn't trust him. Alex is a proud man, Dani. Honor is everything to him. He's worth fighting for."

"He could have told me the truth," she said, wishing her head would stop hurting.

"Didn't he?"

"Maybe." She couldn't seem to remember anymore.

"I want to offer to help, but I think I've gotten involved a little too much lately." She touched Dani's arm.

Alex wasn't with Fiona. Was that possible? So why hadn't he tried to convince her? Why had he just walked away? Okay, so he hadn't cheated, but obviously he wasn't willing to fight for what they had. Better that it was over now.

Only she didn't feel better. She felt a whole lot worse.

"I've never been in an ambulance before," Bailey said from her place next to Dani. "I'm glad they didn't put on the siren. It would be really loud."

Dani was glad, too. The noise would probably finish her off.

"Are you okay?" Bailey asked. "You're real pale and your eye is all swollen. I can't believe you were in a fight."

"Me, either. My brothers are never going to stop teasing me about it."

"They'll be glad you're okay. I'm glad, too."

Dani reached out and grabbed Bailey's hand. "You were so brave. The EMT guy told me how you stood over me and kept those boys away."

"I wasn't going to let them hurt either of us."

Dani smiled at her. "I'm proud to have you as my sister."

Bailey beamed, then rested her head on Dani's chest. "Me, too. I love you, Dani."

Dani's throat tightened. "I love you, too." She stroked Bailey's hair. "You're not going to let this ruin anything, are you? I mean about the dress and the dance."

Bailey straightened. "I'm still going to the dance. I have a pretty dress and Mom is going to put my hair up. She said I could borrow some earrings, too. Do you think I'll be as pretty as her?"

Dani thought about Katherine's confession at feeling left out of her daughter's life. She wished the other woman were here to hear what Bailey was saying.

"I think you should ask her to make you as pretty as her. I think she'd like that."

Bailey nodded. "Mom's the best."

"I agree."

"There are too many visitors," the nurse said sternly. "There is a limit to the number of people in a room at any one time."

Reid walked over to the fifty-something woman and smiled. "But she's our family.

We'll be real quiet and if the fire marshal shows up, we'll hide under the bed. How's that?"

Dani watched Reid Buchanan work his magic. The nurse glared at him for about two more seconds, then relaxed.

"All right, but you *do* have to be quiet. If my boss finds out . . ."

"Never," Reid promised.

"Amazing," Dani breathed.

"I agree," Lori said as she casually checked Dani's pulse. "He's the master. I just stand back and watch." Lori spoke with the confidence of a woman who was well loved. She released Dani's wrist. "You'll live."

"Was there a doubt?"

"No, but I wanted to be sure for myself."

Lori moved next to Reid — a bit of a trick in the crowded hospital room. The whole family was there, including Gloria, along with Katherine and several of her children. Only Mark, Alex and the three youngest Canfields were missing.

"Hi, I'm Julie."

Dani glanced at the beautiful, petite young woman who had moved next to the bed. She had long, wavy dark hair and skin the color of coffee.

Dani smiled. "Second oldest, you're in college. Do I have that right?"

"You do. I'm sorry we haven't met before. I've been hearing good things about you. It was fun reading about my brother's sex life in the newspaper. I'm going to be able to hold that over him for the rest of his life."

Dani winced. "I like your attitude. I need a little of that myself. I still want to crawl under a rock when I think about it."

"You can't let the bastards get you down. I don't." Julie pointed at Gloria. "Is that your grandmother?"

"Yes."

"She's a tough old bird. I've read about her. She built an empire from nothing. I'm doing a paper on powerful women for one of my classes. You think she'd let me interview her?"

"I think she'd be flattered."

"Cool. Nice to meet you. I hope you feel better."

Julie made her way to where Gloria was talking with Katherine.

Dani rested her head on her pillow. Walker came over and kissed her forehead.

"I talked to one of the cops. They've caught all three kids. They'll be charged. One of the advantages of having a senator in the family."

"Good thing, otherwise you'd have to kill them."

He stared at her. "I wouldn't have killed them."

She knew her brother. "You would have gotten damn close."

"You're my sister."

She was getting a lot of that lately. A lot of connection, a lot of caring. Katherine was hovering, probably in an attempt to make up for lying about Fiona. When they were next alone Dani was going to tell her she meant what she said — she understood and forgave. She was more upset with Alex's reaction. Why hadn't he pushed back harder? Why had he let her go so easily?

Three hours later she still didn't have the answers to her questions, but at least she could wonder in silence. The nurses had finally shoved everyone out so Dani could rest. She'd just closed her eyes, prepared to finally go to sleep, when she heard someone walk into the room.

She opened her eyes and saw Alex standing by her bed.

The only light came from the hallway, so his face was in shadow. She couldn't tell what he was thinking but she was glad he was here. More than glad. It had to mean something, right? He hadn't just stayed away.

She was spineless where he was concerned, she thought. Spineless and weak and desperately in love.

"That's a hell of a black eye," he said as he lightly touched her cheekbone.

"You should see the other guy."

He didn't smile. Instead he bent down and gathered her in his arms. He was strong and warm and the second he embraced her she felt totally safe.

"God damn sonofabitch," he said, his voice muffled by her shoulder.

She clung to him. "I'm taking that as a statement against those guys and not a comment on my lack of makeup."

He released her, then dragged a chair over to her bed. When he'd sat down, he took both her hands in his.

"I couldn't believe it when I heard," he told her. "I want to ask if you're okay. Stupid question. How could you be?"

"I'm fine," she said. "A little shaken, but okay. Assuming I don't fall into a coma or have a seizure or whatever else they expect when they keep you overnight for observation, I'm out of here in the morning." She pulled one hand free and touched her face. "I'll have a great story."

"You had to be scared."

"More than I've ever been in my life. But

mostly for Bailey. I was terrified they were really going to rape her."

"You knocked 'em around. There are bruises."

"You've seen them?"

"I've been off intimidating them and their parents. Those teens have a history of making trouble. Nothing this bad, but they've always gotten off with light sentences. Not this time."

"Is Bailey okay?"

He smiled. "She's being treated like the heroine she is. She says she wasn't that scared. That she knew you'd take care of her. Then when they hurt you, she wanted payback." He squeezed her fingers. "She even confessed that she used bad language, but she was given a free pass this one time."

Dani chuckled. "I believe the phrase was 'butthead.' She's such a sweetheart. I can't believe how cruel those kids were to her. The things they said."

"There's no law against being stupid."

"Speaking of which," she said, staring at the blanket on her lap. "I believe I'm falling into that category." She forced herself to look at him. "I guess Fiona sucked me in."

He stared into her eyes. "I haven't slept with her. I'm not interested in her. I won't go so far as to say I hate her because that

371

implies a level of energy I don't have where she's concerned. She's nothing to me, Dani. I want you to know that."

"I do. Really. I should have thought it through. I should have asked instead of yelling."

"No. I'm to blame for that. Your accusation caught me off guard. My pride got in the way. I thought you should have believed in me. Later I realized that given your past and how short a time we've known each other, believing what looked like real proof made sense."

"Yeah?" Did this mean he wasn't going to let her get away?

"Yeah." He leaned in and kissed her.

"It's just she knew stuff about the house. Like the fireplace being on a remote."

"She'd seen the place. She was pissed I'd left her so when she found out I was interested in that house, she bid against me. The irony is that because of the divorce settlement, she was bidding against me with my own money."

Dani sighed. "I never thought of her seeing it any way but with you. I'm sorry."

"Don't be. I should have handled things differently. The pregnancy thing threw me. I was trying to figure out who she could have been seeing. After the fact I thought maybe

372

you would have seen that distraction as guilt or surprise."

"Kind of."

He kissed her again. His mouth was warm and promising. She wanted to keep kissing him, but considering their location and how much her head hurt, it was probably not a good idea.

"I don't want her," he said. "I want you."

"Good answer."

"Are we okay?"

She nodded, then touched her head. "I have to stop doing that."

"What about the poll numbers?" he asked. "They were bothering you before."

"I don't know. You're the expert at this — not me. Do we ignore them and hope they go away?"

"You can't run your life based on the campaign."

Which sounded great, she thought. But was it reality? Mark was her father. What did she owe him?

"I don't want to ruin anything," she admitted. "I don't want to be the reason he doesn't become president."

"You'd walk away from me?" Alex asked.

She studied him, trying to figure out what he was thinking. "Are you saying you wouldn't? That if Mark asked you not to see me, you'd tell him to go to hell?" She placed her fingers on his mouth. "Be honest. He's your father. You value loyalty above everything else. This is his dream. Do either of us have the right to destroy that?"

"There will be other scandals."

But right now she was the scandal du jour.

"We don't have to deal with this tonight," Alex told her. "Get some rest. I'll be by to take you home in the morning."

"I look forward to it."

He kissed her and left.

She shifted on the bed, trying to get comfortable. Her head still pounded and that would make it difficult to sleep, although she was plenty tired. Maybe she should —

Someone knocked on her door. She looked up and saw Mark standing in the shadows.

"You're still awake," he said.

"I am."

"Good. Good." He walked into the room and smiled down at her. "How are you feeling? That's quite a black eye."

"I know. I looked in the mirror earlier and frightened myself."

"You'll heal."

He was alone for once. No entourage, no family or staff. Just the man. He seemed less grand by himself, she thought. Still handsome and very much a stranger. Would he always be? Was that just who he was? Someone she couldn't get close to?

He settled into the chair Alex had just left.

"Do you need anything?" he asked. "They're treating you well here?"

"They're great and I'm doing fine. I'll go home in the morning."

"Good. Excellent." He patted her arm. "You made the news. You and Bailey are heroes. That's what's important. We're expecting this to play favorably with the voters. Show them my family has character. The numbers will be back up, especially now that we can leak that you and Alex aren't dating anymore. Interesting about you and Alex. Not a pair I would have put together. But it's over now. All's well."

All was not well. She and Alex were very much a couple. At least they were trying to be. The road of their relationship was rocky, to say the least.

She looked at the man who was her father. She knew in her heart he wasn't the fantasy she'd hoped for. But he was a good man who had plans. Big plans. He wanted to be president. She'd only ever wanted to run Buchanan's. Who was she to stand in the way of his future?

CHAPTER EIGHTEEN

Alex showed up at his parents' house early in the morning. Katherine was still in her robe, making coffee in the kitchen, when he walked in. She looked up and froze. Her mouth twisted, her eyes widened, but she didn't speak.

He'd been more angry with her than he'd ever been in his life. He'd known that not talking to her was punishment because she hated to be disconnected from her children in any way. He'd wanted her to suffer.

But then he'd remembered who she was. That she'd found him, a half-wild boy who had screamed most of the night as he relived the nightmare of his birth mother's murder. He remembered how she'd patiently taught him how to read, how to add and subtract, how to take a shower, to function in normal society. She'd been the one to assume he would catch up in school and go to college. He still remembered the amazement of overhearing her talking with one of her friends.

"Alex is brilliant. I can already tell. He's going to do something special with his life. I wonder which college he'll go to."

He'd been ten at the time, still struggling to fit in. Her casual words had inspired him. She'd worked a miracle in him. He owed her everything.

But even if he didn't, he would still have come to see her this morning — because he loved her. He would always love her. Everyone was allowed to screw up — it made her human.

He held open his arms.

She rushed into them and he pulled her close. She was so small, he thought absently. He always saw her as such a powerful woman, but she was almost frail. On the outside — on the inside, she was a powerhouse.

"I'm sorry," she began.

"No," he told her. "You've apologized. I didn't come here to get you to say it again. I came to say I appreciate that you regret your actions and that we're okay."

She raised her head and looked at him. "Oh, Alex, I love you so much."

"I love you, too."

"I can't believe you've forgiven me."

"I'm an amazing guy. You're lucky to have me in your life."

She smiled, then started to laugh. "I guess I am." She stepped back. "I was making coffee. Want some?"

"Sure." He settled on one of the stools. "I need to talk to you about a couple of things."

"I didn't think you were here for my cooking."

"You make a mean cinnamon roll."

"If only. I do a fabulous job opening the package and putting the prepared rolls onto a pan. Later, I'm almost artistic with the little container of icing."

"Still, I like them."

"That's why I make them."

She would always go out of her way to do something special for each of her children. She was honest to a fault, never searching for the spotlight. She pushed everyone else ahead of herself. Family was her world. A family he was about to rip apart.

"I'm resigning from the campaign," he said.

Her breath caught. "Alex, no."

"I have to. I'm not the right person to help him."

"But it means so much to have you involved."

He knew he was offering her an impossible choice — siding with the father or the son. Ultimately she would pick Mark because he was her husband, but it would devastate her to choose.

"I haven't made this decision lightly," he told her. "He's important to me, too. I want to do the right thing, but I can't ignore the feeling in my gut. I'm not political. I don't like it and I don't do it well."

She folded her arms across her chest and looked at him. "I know," she whispered. "I know you were only there because he asked you. Because he wanted it to be a family affair."

"I'll still campaign, if it comes to that. I'll show my support in other ways."

"He's going to be disappointed."

"He'll get over it." Alex had a feeling Mark's biggest concern would be how it looked to the voters, which probably wasn't fair.

"This can't have been easy for you," she said, showing the understanding that always came so natural to her. "You would have seen staying as your duty."

He shrugged. "This way is better. Ultimately for both of us, although I'm not sure he'll see it that way."

She nodded. "He'll understand with time.

When are you telling him?"

"The end of the week."

Even as he said the words, he felt guilty, as if he was doing the wrong thing. Everything he'd been taught, everything he owed Mark and Katherine, told him he should stay. Just suck it up and deal. But he couldn't. She'd also taught him to be his own person.

"I'm sorry," he told her. "It's just one more thing, after the hell you dealt with yesterday."

She wrinkled her nose. "Not me. Dani and Bailey are the ones who really suffered. I'm so glad no one was seriously injured. If those boys had hurt either one of them . . ."

There was a fierceness in her voice, an anger and a strength. He liked that she was protective of both of them. "They would have had to answer to us."

She flipped on the coffeemaker, then leaned against the counter. "Are those boys going to be charged?"

"They're going to be convicted. I'll make sure of it. How's Bailey?"

Katherine relaxed. "Mostly empowered. She seems very clear that the boys were bad and what they were doing was wrong. Dani protecting her made her feel special and her being able to save Dani makes her feel tough and capable."

"Good."

"I know she's your favorite."

He shifted on the stool. "I love all my brothers and sisters equally."

"Oh, please. You have a soft spot for Bailey. You always have."

"Maybe."

"I'm glad. Dani really cares about her, too. Dani's very special. I like her."

There was something in the way she said the words, as if testing the waters.

"She hasn't been easy for you," he said. "Not because of anything she's done but because of who she is."

"Agreed."

"Is it okay?"

Katherine stared at the coffeemaker. "Okay is such a weasel word. What does it really mean? Do I like what's happened? Do I enjoy people talking, speculating? Of course not. Do I blame Dani? Not when I'm myself. Do I wish she'd never shown up?" She looked at him. "Never."

"I love her."

He hadn't meant to say the words. He'd barely recognized the truth of it himself. But last night, after he'd left her in the hospital, he'd realized how much he would have been destroyed if she'd been critically hurt. He hadn't been looking, but he'd found her all the same.

"I sort of figured that out," his mother said with a smile.

"How?"

"There's something about your eyes when you talk about her. A light. I don't know. It's subtle, but I saw it."

Hated it, he thought. She had hated it, then accepted it and now she would embrace it. Because of who she was.

"It's serious," he told her.

"I figured that, too."

"I want to marry her."

He waited for her to react — to collapse or fall into tears. He thought she might get angry or beg him to change his mind.

Instead she poured them each a cup of coffee, handed him his, then said, "Let me be clear. This time I expect grandchildren. Lots of them."

She smiled.

He might have known, he thought as he put his arm around her. She always took the high road. No matter what.

"Damn, you're good," he said.

"I know. I'm a constant surprise. It's part of my charm."

Katherine closed her eyes and knew that finding a way to welcome Dani as Alex's wife would be easier today than it would have been yesterday. Dani had more than proved herself and was exactly who Katherine would have wanted for her son.

She refused to think about the gossip or potential scandal. That would happen and she would deal with it because she was good at dealing.

"When are you going to propose?" she asked.

"Tomorrow night. I'll plan a romantic dinner. I'm picking her up at the hospital this morning. She probably still hurts from what those bastards did to her, so I'm giving her time."

She sighed. "I raised you right. You're a good man, Alex. She's lucky to have you."

"That's what I'm going to tell her."

"I'll want details. I'm seeing her tomorrow at the charity luncheon. It will be hard to keep quiet. But I will."

He stared into her eyes. "Thank you. For everything."

All she'd ever done was love him, the way she loved all her children. She'd made mistakes, but she kept trying to do the right thing. Just as *her* mother had taught her.

Alex marrying Dani would bind the two families together. Make them both stronger.

"Don't think that's enough to get you out

of the whole grandchildren thing," she said with a laugh. "I mean it. I'm tired of waiting."

He chuckled. "Not to worry. I'll get right on that."

The charity luncheon in support of breast cancer was held in a downtown hotel. Dani hovered in a bathroom stall and knew that eventually she was going to have to leave the tiny space and go face the room. And she would. Just as soon as she was sure she wasn't going to throw up.

Her stomach kept flipping and spinning and trying to escape. Her chest was tight and her legs trembled. She was past nervous. She was in that fight-or-flight state. Even with the black eye, she was more than willing to fight anyone rather than speak in public.

"I'm fine," she whispered to herself as she tried to breathe. "I'll get through this. It's only six minutes. Five if I talk fast. I can do it for five minutes."

She didn't actually convince herself, but maybe if she kept up the cheerful talk, she would start to feel better. The speech was fine. It was charming and heartfelt. The Canfield speech writers had even given her a funny new opening that mentioned her black eye. Mostly because all the concealer in the world couldn't hide the bruise.

She clenched her hands together and sucked in another breath, then heard several women walk into the bathroom.

Dani told herself it was time to leave, so she wasn't hogging a stall for no good reason, when she heard their conversation.

"Oh my God! I can't believe Katherine went through with this," one of the women said. "I can't decide if she's a saint or just an idiot."

"She looks tired," another said. "I'm sure it's the stress. Mark's child. Can you believe it? She's actually going to be seen in public with her. I wouldn't do it."

"Your husband isn't running for president. A woman will put up with a lot to get that kind of life. She sure has. People are talking about her everywhere. It has to be killing her."

The speaker sounded as if she was thrilled at the thought of Katherine's pain.

"Do you suppose she told him she couldn't have children before or after they got married?" another woman asked.

"I don't know," the first one said. "Either way, he's got to be disappointed. That group she's put together. There's something wrong with all of them. It's horrible. Not that we can say that, of course. We all have to pretend she's just so wonderful."

Dani's temper exploded. She stepped out of the stall and faced the three well-dressed women.

"Pretending isn't required," she told them. "Katherine is an extraordinary woman. Something none of you can relate to, I'm sure."

They stared at her. Dani calmly walked over to the sink, washed her hands, dried them and left. She was still shaking when she entered the main ballroom.

Damn those women and their petty comments. Dani didn't know who they were, but she hoped Katherine didn't consider any of them close friends. They were like snakes in couture. The only bright side was one of them had obviously had an unfortunate eye lift.

She looked around for Katherine, but instead found herself cornered by two reporters.

"Just a minute of your time," the woman said. "Please."

Dani tried to inch away. "This is a private event. Unless you bought a ticket, you have to leave."

They both held up tickets. Dani stifled a groan.

"Did you stage the attack yesterday to help your father's campaign?" the man asked.

"Is it true you and Alex Canfield aren't seeing each other because of the falling poll numbers. Did you give up love for the campaign?"

Dani pushed her way past them and headed for the front of the room. She found Katherine speaking with the event coordinator.

"Standing room only," Katherine told her as they stepped into a quiet corner. "We've sold out, thanks to you."

"You mean thanks to the fact that everyone is hoping for juicy gossip to tell their friends," Dani said bitterly.

Katherine's gaze sharpened. "What happened?"

There was no way Dani was going to mention what she'd overheard in the bathroom. "Some members of the press bought tickets and they tried to talk to me. Honestly, I don't know how you stand this, being in the public eye. I hate it. I'm not good at it and it's not how I want to live my life."

"There are compensations," the other woman told her.

Dani was tempted to ask what they were. It wasn't about money and power. Katherine came from a wealthy family. She was a private person; she couldn't actually like being so exposed all the time, could she?

Then Dani remembered watching Katherine with Mark and had her answer. The compensation was that Katherine got to be with the man she loved and make him happy. This was all about Mark.

Thinking about her father brought her back to where she'd been the previous night at the hospital. Where she'd realized that her father's dreams could impact history and that she was in danger of destroying that. Just by showing up, she'd shoved the campaign off course.

"Dani?" Katherine asked. "What's wrong?"

"I've screwed everything up," Dani said, trying to stay calm despite the feelings welling inside of her. "Those boys would never have attacked Bailey if it hadn't been for me. They recognized me. That's how it all started."

"That's their fault, not yours."

Logic. It wasn't helping. "Bailey could have been seriously hurt. They were going to rape her, Katherine. It would have been because they recognized me. Sure, I wouldn't have committed the crime, but how could I have lived with myself after-ward?"

"Nothing happened. You're both safe."

"For how long?" Dani asked. "Who's next? Who else will I ruin in some way? What about you? Don't you hate what I represent? Don't you hate people talking?"

"People will always talk," Katherine told her. "We can't stop that."

"You always say the right thing."

"Not always. Very recently I said the wrong thing."

Dani dismissed the reference to their conversation about Fiona with a flick of her hand. "That's not important. I mean about the big stuff. You'll deal with me because you have to. You'll smile and pretend it's okay when every time you look at me, I'll break your heart."

Katherine smiled. "Okay, you're being a little dramatic here. You're not breaking my heart."

"They hurt you with what they say, what they speculate about. It can't be easy."

"Dani, stop it. You're taking way too much credit."

"I don't think so. I need to go."

"You're giving a speech in five minutes."

That almost made her smile. "After. Later. I'm leaving Seattle."

Katherine stared at her. "You're *not* running away."

"It solves everyone's problems."

"Shouldn't we be the ones to decide if we want your help in solving the problem?"

"None of you are going to ask me to leave. You wouldn't." Mark might, she amended, but what was the point in saying that?

Leaving was the only thing that made sense, Dani thought. With her out of the way, life could return to normal. She would go somewhere big. L.A., or maybe New York. There were thousands of restaurants there. She could easily find a job.

"You're not by nature a quitter," Katherine said quietly. "Why now?"

"It helps the most number of people."

"What about helping yourself? What about what you want?"

"That doesn't matter."

"What about Alex?"

Dani didn't have an answer for that. "He'll understand."

Something shifted in Katherine's eyes. "I don't think he'll understand at all."

Dani didn't want to face anyone, deal with the fights and arguments that were sure to follow her telling them her plans. She just wanted to be gone.

Except for Alex, she thought wistfully. She wanted to be with him, in his arms, talking and touching and being together. She wanted so much with him, from him. She wanted to give him everything she was.

She checked her watch and saw he was due to come by in a few minutes. They were supposed to go out to dinner — somewhere nice, he'd promised.

She would like that, she thought wistfully. A quiet dinner with the man she loved. Spending the night with him. But to what end? Wouldn't being with him now make it harder to leave later?

She sank onto the bed in the room she'd been using at Gloria's house. She didn't want to go — not deep down inside. She wanted to stay because this was her world. This was where she belonged. But at what price? How could she be happy with herself if that happiness came at the price of destroying all those around her?

She stood and walked into the bathroom. She'd washed off the makeup she'd carefully applied for the luncheon. The dark bruise under her eye was in sharp contrast to her pale skin. She looked lost and beat-up — which fit exactly how she felt.

She hated this. Hated feeling torn. Hated the sense of there being no good solution to her problem. Hated being controlled by circumstances and other people.

All she'd wanted was to find out where she belonged, to find her family. She'd found them, all right, and because of that, everything was a mess. It was time to start fixing that.

She went downstairs to wait for Alex. She didn't want to think about telling him she was leaving. It was all too sad. So instead she walked through the empty rooms, marveling at the fact that Gloria wasn't here — she was out. With friends. Friends she'd made at the local senior center.

The image of her grandmother scrapbooking with other old ladies made her smile, yet it was happening. Maybe not the scrapbooking, but the hanging out and meeting people. It had been Lori's idea and Gloria had listened.

Dani walked into the living room and stared out at the view of the city. Lori had been good for her grandmother and for Reid. She'd brought the family together. Elissa had healed Walker's heart and given him something to live for. Cal had always been in love with Penny, he'd just been too stubborn to recognize it for what it was.

The doorbell rang. Dani hurried to let in Alex. As he stepped across the threshold, she took in the sight of him. The strong shoulders, the shape of his jaw, that mouth that could always reduce her to a sexual puddle.

She loved him. After more evil frogs than any woman deserved, she'd found a prince. A prince she was going to be leaving.

"Hi," he said, then bent down and kissed her on the mouth.

She leaned into him, kissing him back, letting her body say what she wouldn't let herself speak. That she loved him. That she would always love him and no matter how far away she had to go, she would never forget him.

"Hi, yourself," she whispered as he straightened.

"I picked a very special place for dinner," he told her. "Soft lights. Very romantic. You probably want to brace yourself. You know how being with me makes you weak in the knees."

She smiled because he was funny and charming and always knew the right thing to say.

"It's a curse," she said. "You handle it with grace."

"I know. I use my power for good." He cupped her face and lightly touched the bruise under her eye. "Seeing that makes me want to go beat the shit out of those three boys."

"But you won't."

He hesitated just long enough to let her know that doing the right thing wasn't his first choice. "I won't," he agreed. He glanced at his watch. "You about ready?"

She took his hand and led him into the living room. When they were settled on the large sofa facing the window, she turned toward him.

"I'm not really hungry," she said. "I thought we could skip dinner. There are a couple of things I need to —"

"We can't skip dinner," Alex said, his face tight in an expression she couldn't read. "Dinner is important. I talked to the chef. There's going to be a special dessert. You don't want to miss this. It will be great."

"Alex, I'm serious."

"We have to go to dinner."

"I can't. I . . ."

He frowned. "Are you sick? Do you need to go back to the hospital?"

"No. I . . . I'm leaving."

"What?"

"I'm leaving Seattle. I've already given notice at Bella Roma and I haven't started at Buchanan's, so the timing is good. I need to do this. Go somewhere different. A place where I'm just a stranger. I want my life back. I want to live in my own house and not have the press bother me. I want to stop hurting the people I care about."

He stood and stared down at her. "What the hell are you talking about? You can't leave Seattle."

"I have to. It's for the best."

"It's running away."

She was disappointed. She'd thought he would at least understand. Although it was gratifying that he was so upset. Maybe her feelings weren't all one-sided.

"Sometimes a strategic retreat is the best thing for everyone," she said as she stood and faced him. "Please don't be angry with me."

"Why the hell not? You didn't even discuss this with me. You announce you're leaving and that's it? What happens now? You walk away?"

She nodded slowly, then sucked in a breath as her head began to pound. "Everyone's problems are solved. Katherine won't be hurt anymore. I know what I've done to her and I feel sick about it. Bailey's safe. It will help the campaign."

He glared at her. "Fuck the campaign. You think the press is going to forget you because you move away? They'll run with the story. As for Bailey, you don't know what would have happened. Those kids were wrong and they'll be punished, but you have no control over their actions or any way to predict them." He moved toward her. "You're giving up. I never thought you were a quitter."

Okay, she'd been understanding for long enough. "I'm doing the best thing for the greater good."

"You're not willing to fight for what you want."

"I'm not willing to hurt people I care about. You should be grateful. You love Katherine and you know how much having me around has devastated her."

"Katherine is stronger than you think. What about the father you were so desperate to find? What about finishing what you started?"

"Mark doesn't need me. He needs to be president. He needs you at his side, working for that goal. Not fighting the press about me."

Alex drew in a breath. "I'm not with the campaign anymore. I haven't told Mark, but I'm leaving."

Dani stared at him. "You can't. He needs you."

"He has a very skilled staff who will take

care of business. It's not my world. I can't be like him."

Obviously an announcement hadn't been made or Dani would have heard about it. When the press found out, it was going to be ugly.

"All the more reason for me to leave," she breathed. "That will disconnect us in the mind of the press."

"And that's what matters, right?" he asked, sounding bitter. "Good to know which side you fall on. You got political real fast. You really are your father's daughter."

The unfair accusation hurt nearly as much as her head. "That's not fair. Do you think this is easy for me? I love my new family. I don't want to leave them and I sure as hell don't want to leave my old family, either. I'm making a hard choice for the greater good."

"It looks pretty easy from here."

"Then you're not looking hard enough." She wanted to grab him and shake him. She hadn't wanted them to fight. She thought he would be sad she was leaving. Not angry. So much for fantasies, she thought grimly.

He walked to the window and stared out at the view. Finally he looked back at her. "And us?"

"I don't know how to make it work," she

admitted. "It's too high a price. Even with you leaving the campaign."

"So we're a casualty of war? It's over?"

No, she screamed inside. She didn't want it to be over. "I care about you."

"I feel very special."

"Don't," she said and sank back on the sofa. "Don't get cold and sarcastic."

"How should I act? I thought I mattered to you. I thought this relationship was significant. I thought you were the one I was supposed to be with." He walked back to her. "You're not the only one with a lousy track record when it comes to relationships. First I fall for a woman who lies about who she is and cheats on me, then I fall for one not strong enough to fight for what matters."

Fall for one? As in . . . She looked up at him. "Alex?"

"Are you going to tell Bailey you're moving on or do you want me to? She thinks you're friends, so this will come as a shock. But then she's always led with her feelings. That girl has the heart of a lion. I admire that about her. I thought you had that in common. Guess I was wrong."

Tears filled Dani's eyes. Her vision blurred. She blinked to clear it and when she could see again, Alex was gone.

Just like that. He'd heard what she'd had to say and then he'd left.

She covered her face with her hands and gave in to the tears. She didn't want to go. That's what was killing her in all this. She didn't want to go, but she didn't see another way to stay out of trouble.

CHAPTER NINETEEN

"Katherine! I didn't expect to see you today." Mark stood and walked around his desk at campaign headquarters. "Is everything all right? Is Bailey . . ."

"She's fine," Katherine said as her husband kissed her on the cheek.

He always looked so happy to see her, one more thing she loved about him.

He wrapped his arms around her waist and drew her against him. "I've been busy lately," he said as he ran his hands up and down her back. "Working here, flying back to D.C. I've missed you."

His light touch was enough to ignite every nerve ending in her body.

"I've missed you, too," she told him. "But we knew it would be like this if you ran for president."

"The price of glory."

He bent down and kissed her again. The contact was tender, yet sexual and she melted against him.

Only Mark, she thought as she gave herself over to sensation. Only ever Mark. She loved him more than she'd thought possible. Her guilty secret was that she loved him more than she loved her children. But that didn't make her blind to his flaws.

She drew in a breath and pulled back. "We need to talk," she said.

He put his hand on her rear and squeezed. "Can we talk naked?"

She laughed. "At any moment, five of your staff members could burst through that door. Do you really want them to see you doing it with your wife?"

"Why not?" But he straightened as he spoke. Then he took her hand and put it on his erection. "What do I tell this big guy?"

"That I'll see him tonight."

"Fair enough." He led her to the sofa by the wall. "So what do you want to talk about?"

She stared at the man she loved, taking in the familiar features. She still remembered the first time they'd met — how she'd literally seen him across a crowded room and had known that nothing would ever be the same again.

"What would have happened if Marsha hadn't broken things off?" she asked, jumping right into the uncomfortable conversation. "When I came back to find you, would you have left her for me? You would have had to make a choice."

She thought he might get angry. Instead he angled toward her and stroked her hair.

"Don't do this," he said quietly. "There's no answer, Katherine. You know that. It's a situation that never occurred and it doesn't matter what I say. You'll believe what you want to believe."

He was right, of course. He knew her well. "She gave you the one thing I never could."

"You're talking about a child. But you did give me children. You gave me eight of them. Selfishly, what's more important to me is that you gave me myself. I'm the man I am today because of you. That might not be saying much, but I know I'm a better person for having loved you all these years. You are the best part of me, Katherine. You always have been. You see me through eyes blinded by love and most of the time I want to live up to your impossible expectations."

His words reached out and hugged her heart. She felt both exposed and gratified. "Really?"

"Yes. There's no choice, there was never a choice. Life happened and now look at what I have. Would I choose Marsha? I can't regret Dani, but I wouldn't trade her for one of our children. Who would I have to give up? Julie? Alex? Oliver? Whose smile would I not see? Bailey's? Sasha's? They're my children, too. I can't live without any of them. Or you. You have always been the heart of me, Katherine. I love you."

Mark was good with words, but this time she believed him. Believed them. They washed over her, healing old wounds, making her certain that loving him had been the right thing to do.

"You are the light of my life and I would be lost without you," he said, then he kissed her.

She kissed him back, putting all of her passion into that moment of lips and tongue and breath.

He chuckled. "Okay, now you're making trouble on purpose."

"A little." She stroked his face. "I have to. You're going to be very angry with me in a minute."

"Why?"

"Because of what I'm going to say. What I'm going to ask you."

His humor faded. "You never ask me for anything."

"I know." It had been a point of pride with her. Sometimes a stupid point of pride, but there it was. She drew in a breath. "Alex wants to leave the campaign. He's not a political animal. He doesn't want to disappoint you, but he can't do it anymore."

Mark leaned back and swore under his breath. "I need him. He's good at what he does."

"Dani's leaving Seattle. She feels responsible for what happened to Bailey and for the declining poll numbers. All she wanted was to find her family. She thinks she's made a mess of everything and the easiest way to fix things is for her to go away."

He looked at her, his blue eyes dark with questions. "What do you think?"

She took his hands in hers. "That you are the only man I will ever love. That I would change the tide for you, if that's what you wanted. I would die for you, Mark. You know that. But you can't do this anymore. The price is too high. It's time to let the dream go."

Color drained from his face. He seemed to shrink a little, hunching down as if crushed by disappointment. It physically hurt her to say those words and she would have given anything to call them back, but she couldn't. There were too many other lives at stake. She might be willing to die for her husband, but she wouldn't continue to hurt those she loved for him.

She braced herself for the argument, the rage, the accusations. She knew how much he wanted the chance to make history. He stunned her by straightening, then squeezing her fingers and saying, "If that's what you think is best."

"What?"

He smiled. "I trust you, Katherine. I've always trusted you. You wouldn't have asked me on a whim. You know what this means to me and what I'll be giving up. What was that line from that *Star Trek* movie I like so much? The needs of many? I'll have them write up an announcement today and get it out to the press. It will be the usual statement about spending more time with my family. Ironically, it will be true."

That was it? No protesting? No yelling? No anything? "Just like that?"

He kissed her. "Just like that, Katherine. I love you. Someday you're going to have to start believing that."

She sucked in a breath, then threw herself into his arms. Tears burned in her eyes. "Thank you."

"No, don't thank me. You're the amazing one in this relationship. I'm just along for the ride." He ran his hands up and down her back again. "What if I told you the door has a lock?"

She'd always carried a weight inside — the heavy burden of being the one who loved, rather than the one who was loved. For the first time ever, that weight cracked and fell away. She felt light, happier, filled with possibilities.

"I'd tell you to use it and get naked."

Alex sat at a table in the Downtown Sports Bar. He'd been there a few times but it had been nothing more than a place to meet friends. Now he knew it to be part of the Buchanan empire, a place that mattered to Dani and therefore mattered to him.

A busty, blond waitress came over. "Hey, darlin'. What can I get you?"

He barely glanced at her. "A beer. Whatever you have on tap."

"Sure thing." She leaned over, giving him a view of her low-cut T-shirt and her impressive, barely contained breasts. "Anything else? My shift ends in about a half hour. We could go somewhere and talk."

He looked at her face. She was pretty enough, seemed friendly and there was no doubt as to what she was offering. He couldn't have been less interested.

"No, thanks."

"If you're sure?"

"I am."

She straightened and gave someone behind her a thumbs-up. "He meant it. He wasn't interested. Swear to God, I don't think he could pick me out of a lineup. Dani's a lucky girl."

"Appreciate it, Heather," Reid Buchanan said as he walked up to the table and gave Alex a rueful smile. "Hey, she's my sister. I was just checking."

Alex wanted to hit him. Just once, with enough force to break his nose. Not that he would. While he resented being tested, he knew that he would do exactly the same thing for one of his sisters.

"No problem," Alex said. "I'm not worried about passing any test you have. I love Dani. I want to marry her."

Reid sat down. "That's putting it on the table. So why did you ask me to come meet you? You want permission or something?"

Alex shook his head. "Not permission. Just a little help. I'm planning an intervention."

"What? Why?"

"Dani thinks she has to leave Seattle. It's complicated and a lot of it is about the senator's run for president. She doesn't like being in the press, doesn't like that she upset my mother. So she's going to run away. Or so she thinks."

"I don't know anything about this."

"I doubt she's told very many people." He pulled a small, velvet box out of his jacket pocket and put it on the table.

Reid picked it up, opened it and studied the ring. "It's so sudden," he said. "We barely know each other."

"I work fast."

Reid grinned. "I thought I'd make you squirm."

"It would take a lot more than that. I'm going to ask Dani to marry me and I'm not taking no for an answer."

Reid's gaze narrowed. "It's not your decision to make."

"She loves me. She wants to stay in Seattle. But she's hell-bent on sacrificing herself for the good of the family. The whole family. Your side and mine."

"So why tell me all this?"

For the first time since Reid showed up, Alex felt uncomfortable. "I don't know how to approach her. I tried the romantic dinner route and that was a total failure. She's going to be leaving in the next couple of days so I don't have much time. I figured a frontal assault might work. You, me, the rest of the family. Together we can convince her to stay, I'll propose, she'll say yes and we'll live happily ever after."

"You have it all planned out. What if Dani doesn't want to marry you?"

Alex didn't want to think about that. He didn't want to think about how dark and cold his world would be without her light.

"No one could love her more than I do," he said at last. "If she says no, I'll keep trying. She's everything to me."

"Why should I believe you?"

"Because from what I hear, you know what it's like to want to sell your soul to be with the one woman who matters."

Reid nodded slowly. "Good answer."

Katherine rode the elevator to Fiona's high-rise condo. She only had a few minutes, which was fine. She didn't have all that much to say.

Fiona wasn't expecting company so she wasn't her normally perfectly groomed self. Her hair was loose and a little stringy, her sweatshirt had a stain on the front and her jeans hung open, exposing a growing belly.

"Katherine!" Fiona touched her hair, then pulled her sweatshirt down over her stomach. "What are you doing here?"

"Something I should have done a long time ago."

"Oh. All right." Fiona sounded wary.

"Please come in."

"I don't think so. What I have to say will come more easily in the doorway." She smiled coldly. "You're good, I'll give you that. You played the mourning, lost ex-wife so well that I bought in to the whole story. You had me doubting Alex, which is too stupid for words. I know the kind of person he is and now I know the kind of person you are."

Fiona shifted uneasily. "I don't know what he's been telling you —"

"Very little," Katherine told her. "That's part of the problem. If he'd told me the truth from the beginning, I would never have trusted you. But he didn't want to speak ill of you, which is a testament to the kind of man he is."

Katherine took a step closer. "I know what happened. I know you cheated, I know you lied and tried to get between him and Dani. I know you've been using me to get to Alex, all in the hopes of being the daughter-in-law of the president. I hate to destroy anyone's dreams, but that isn't going to happen. Alex will never go back to you, I will never trust you again and for the record, Mark is no longer running for president. Stay away from me and my family. If I ever see you trying to ingratiate yourself with someone I know, I'll tell that person everything that has happened."

She glanced down at Fiona's stomach. "I suggest you get the real father of your baby to marry you."

"Are you kidding? He's a nobody. Damn him. This should have been Alex's baby. He was supposed to stay married to me."

Katherine wondered how she could have been so wrong about Fiona. She was usually a good judge of character, but apparently everyone had an off day.

"Stay away from Alex. Stay away from me. Go somewhere else, Fiona. Trust me, it would be for the best."

Katherine turned to leave. Fiona followed her into the hallway.

"You can't do this," she cried. "We were friends. That has to mean something."

Katherine glanced back at her. "We were never friends. You played to win and you lost. Deal with the consequences. They're relatively minor. If you're smart, you'll appreciate that and disappear. If you try to cross me, you will be very sorry. I promise you that."

"You don't frighten me."

Katherine smiled slowly. "Don't I? Are you sure?"

Fiona took a step back. "Bitch. Stupid old

cow. I hate you."

"Really? I don't have the energy to even think about you."

"This is a mistake," Gloria said as Dani pulled out more clothes and put them on the bed. "You can't run away. I forbid it."

Dani tried to smile. "Then what? I'll be grounded."

"If that's what it takes."

"I'm doing the right thing and deep in your heart you know I'm right. There's no other solution."

"There's always another solution. You can't leave now."

"I don't want to," Dani admitted, wishing they could talk about something else. It was hard enough to think about leaving without facing her grandmother. "I can't keep hurting the people I love."

"You're not hurting your Buchanan family. So what if you hurt them?"

"That's warm and loving."

"Katherine and Mark have eight children of their own. They'll hardly notice you. You're the only granddaughter I have."

Dani didn't know if she should laugh or burst into tears. "You do have a way with words."

"Am I wrong?"

She sank onto the bed. Gloria sat next to her.

"Don't go," her grandmother said. "I'm old. What if I get sick and die and you never see me again?"

"Don't you dare play the death card. That's not fair."

"I don't care about being fair. I want you to stay. Dani, you have to stay. We just found each other."

It hurt so much, Dani thought as she fought against the pain. It hurt to breathe. She didn't want to leave — not now when she'd found everything she'd ever wanted. She was supposed to be starting her dream job, learning about her new family while being with her old family, being in love with a great guy. It should have been perfect. If only . . .

"I know," Dani said, staring into Gloria's eyes and seeing the pain there. "I'm sorry."

"Don't be sorry. Stay. We'll work it out. I didn't raise you to be a quitter."

"I'm not quitting. I'm doing what's best. Can't you see those things are bigger than us?"

"They might be bigger than you, but they're not bigger than me."

Dani managed another smile. "You are determined, aren't you?"

"I fight for what's mine. You could learn from that. What about that boy you're seeing? Alex?"

"I don't know. We had a big fight."

"So that's it? One fight and it's over?"

"I can't make him love me."

"How do you know he doesn't? Did you ask? Did you tell him you love him?"

Had she? "Not exactly." And Alex *had* said he'd fallen for her. Which meant what?

"Not exactly?" Gloria stood and glared at her. "Dammit all to hell, Dani, you're really screwing this up."

Dani opened her mouth, then closed it. "You're swearing. I'm shocked."

"Get over it. This is important. This is your life. This is for real. Why do you feel that everyone else comes first? Why do their dreams matter more than your own?"

"Because she's afraid."

Dani rose and turned toward the speaker. It was Alex. He stood in the doorway to her bedroom.

Her heart instantly started dancing in her chest. The rest of her body sighed in appreciation, as if every cell had always been waiting for him.

She ignored the biological betrayal and raised her chin. "I'm not afraid."

"Sure you are. You've been fighting your

whole life and time and time again you got slapped down. All those years fighting Gloria." He glanced at the older woman. "No offense."

"I'll decide if I'm offended when I see where this is going."

Alex turned back to Dani. "You gave everything you had to Hugh and he dumped on you. Ryan was worse because he planned it. Gary was . . ." He shrugged. "I don't know what Gary was."

"Biblical humor," Dani murmured, not sure what she thought of Alex's words.

"You've been burned so many times, you're afraid to get near the fire. So when you and I got together, you were terrified. Maybe not consciously, but somewhere deep inside. Then you found out you were hurting Katherine, which you hated. You respect her and didn't want to make things harder. You were totally out of your comfort zone. Throw in a political campaign and the attack on Bailey and you reached your breaking point. It makes sense."

"Thanks for the recap," she murmured, knowing he might be right. "Now what are you doing here?"

He stepped into her bedroom. "Fighting for you. I'm making sure you don't do something you'll regret for the rest of your life."

"Which would be?"

"Walking away from me."

"You've never lacked confidence."

"Not really. But I've never been as sure of something as I am of knowing we belong together. You can't leave, Dani. This is where you belong."

If only, she thought again, wishing it were possible. She loved him, needed him, wanted him. Only him. Being with Alex had taught her to understand Katherine's devotion to Mark. "There are complications."

"Not as many as you think," Katherine said as she and Mark walked into the bedroom, followed by Dani's brothers.

Dani found herself backed into a corner — literally. "What's going on?"

"We're holding an intervention," Alex told her. "It was my idea. You can thank me later."

"I don't understand."

"We're not letting you go," Cal said, then grinned. "I don't mean that in a scary stalker way."

"Good to know," she murmured.

"You belong here," Walker said. "With all of us. Maybe with that guy." He jerked his head toward Alex. "He seems okay."

416

"I like him," Reid said. "He's got good taste."

"But what about how much I've hurt you?" Dani looked at Katherine, then at Mark. "I'm hurting the campaign."

Mark, as handsome and smooth as ever, put his arm around his wife's shoulders. "I'm pulling out of the race. This isn't a good time. My press office is issuing a statement —" he checked his watch "— right about now."

Dani felt the need to sit down. Everything was happening too fast. "But you want to be president. It's your dream."

"Some things cost too much." He looked at Alex. "I got a little carried away before. With the charges. We'll talk later?"

"Okay. Yeah." Alex turned back to Dani. "You're running out of excuses."

Dani's mind went into a free fall. If Mark wasn't running for president, then the press wouldn't care about her, or anyone in the family. If there weren't any watchful eyes around, then life could be normal.

Alex reached into his jacket pocket and pulled out a velvet box. Dani's body froze.

Her first thought was that he was going to propose. Her second was that proposing probably meant that he loved her, which made her want to do the happy dance. Her third was how much he was putting on the line by doing this in front of both their families.

Her last thought was that she couldn't wait to say yes.

"Oh, dear," Katherine said, putting a hand on Alex's arm. "I should have gotten to you sooner. I have something to tell you."

He looked at her. "Mom, this isn't the time."

"I know, but I have to say it. I'll talk fast." She reached into her pocket and pulled out a diamond ring. "If you'd prefer the one you bought, I'll completely understand. But in case you want something different . . ." She handed him the ring. "This belonged to my grandmother. I don't know why I didn't think of it before, with Fi—" She cleared her throat. "Anyway, I saw it this morning and hoped . . ."

Alex stared at the ring. Dani knew exactly what he was thinking. That the ring should stay in the family and until that moment, he'd never been totally one of them. She recognized the emotions chasing across his face because she'd felt them herself when she'd been with her brothers. That sense of belonging and not belonging.

Was that the connection she had with Alex? That they shared a basic knowledge of what it was like to be on the outside? That they were both looking for a place to belong?

She moved toward him. "I want to be the one," she told him, not caring who else was in the room. "I want to be the only one. I want to be that safe place where you can go no matter what."

"You're stealing my speech."

"You had a speech?"

"I was going to tell you I loved you more than I've ever loved anyone. That you're the only one I want to be with. That I belong when I'm with you."

Belong. There was that word again. Those on the inside would never know how much it meant to feel it.

"I love you, Dani," he continued.

"Move back," Gloria whispered. "Everyone move back and give the boy room to kneel. You were going to kneel, weren't you?"

Alex grinned. "Is it always going to be like this?"

Dani glanced around at the people who loved her, then looked at the one man who would always make things right. "I have a feeling we're not getting away from that."

"Is that okay?"

"It's the best."

EPILOGUE

The summer evening was warm, with a perfectly clear sky. It was after seven and the sun was hours from setting. After all, this was Seattle and the city was known for endless summer nights.

Over three hundred people sat in white chairs on a lush, green lawn. The scent of roses and jasmine filled the air. On the left, a small orchestra played softly as the groom's grandmother was seated.

"Arthur seems nice," Reid said as he walked Gloria down the aisle.

"Don't be smart with me," Gloria snapped, a little embarrassed to be her age and dating. She'd been seeing Arthur for three months now and had brought him to the wedding.

"I'm not. Just don't ever tell us if you're having sex. It would be too weird."

"I had to read about your sexual abilities

in the paper. I think a little payback is in order."

Reid grinned at her. "Okay, but I won't like it."

"I can live with that."

They reached her seat and he handed her into the care of Arthur, a local entrepreneur who was eight years younger than Gloria. Then Reid bent down and kissed her cheek.

"You look hot."

Gloria swatted his arm, but smiled.

Dani stood inside the Canfield's family room and stared out through the blinds.

"I'm thinking Elissa is going to be disappointed by the twinkle lights. It's too bright out. They're not showing up at all."

"They will later," Lori said as she adjusted the front of her frothy pink bridesmaid gown. "Do I look fat? I can't believe I'm asking that, but do I?"

Dani smiled at her sister-in-law. Despite Lori and Reid's plans to wait and marry after Walker and Elissa's big event, an unexpected pregnancy had sent them to Las Vegas a month ago. They'd married quietly and were now preparing to move in with Gloria. As the newlyweds weren't strapped for cash, the only reason could be they liked living with the old bird. Lori was a brave woman, Dani thought with a smile.

"You look beautiful," Dani told her. "The style of the dress totally hides any hint of a bump."

"Did you see the canapés?" Penny asked as she stalked into the room. "I'm not sure the salmon is fresh enough. Do you think it's fresh?"

Cal moved next to his wife and kissed her. "Deep breath," he said. "Let it go. You look beautiful."

"I was frightened the first time I saw these dresses," Penny admitted. "But now I like them."

Katherine stepped into the room. "Are we ready? It's nearly time."

Dani watched her future mother-in-law and marveled at her ability to pull off something as complicated as a Buchanan wedding.

Alex came up behind Dani and kissed the back of her neck. "Taking notes for our wedding?"

"Most of the planning is done," she reminded him. They had a fall event scheduled. Something much smaller than this. Mostly family, which was a party in and of itself. Penny would be catering — Dani wasn't as brave as Elissa. Better to put her friend and sister-in-law to work than risk the complaining.

"Twinkle lights?" he asked in a low voice.

"Absolutely. I love them. I'm thinking we'll only have your sisters in the wedding party. Much less fighting on the dress front. You should have heard the four of us at the bridal shop."

She smiled as she spoke, remembering the afternoon of arguing, chocolate and champagne. In the end, they'd all been tipsy and hadn't remembered what they'd agreed to. When the fluffy pink dresses had arrived, they'd been shocked.

"Have I told you how much I love you?" Alex asked.

Dani smiled at him. "I think you mentioned it one time. It's hard to remember."

He kissed her. "I love you. For always."

"Good. Because I'm holding you to that."

"A challenge? I like a good challenge."

"Then you're going to enjoy me."

Katherine raised her hands. "All right. Form your couples. Get ready. When the music changes . . . and now."

She opened the French doors leading to the patio. The orchestra switched to a romantic song. Cal and Penny stepped out first. They moved arm in arm up the petal-covered path between the chairs to where Walker waited for Elissa.

Lori and Reid went next. Dani glanced

back at the bride and smiled, then slipped her arm through Alex's. Katherine signaled them to pause before they started down the aisle.

She leaned close. "Don't tell anyone," she whispered. "But you're my favorite couple."

"Mine, too," Alex told her, before leading Dani out into the sunlight.

ABOUT THE AUTHOR

Susan Mallery is the *USA TODAY* bestselling author of over seventy romances. Her combination of humor, emotion and just-plain-sexy has made her a reader favorite. Susan makes her home in the Seattle area where she lives with her husband, the world's cutest dog and two aging cats who are unamused by the presence of the world's cutest dog. Visit her Web site at www.Susan Mallery.com.